Unraveled

OTHER BOOKS AND AUDIO BOOKS

BY JULIE DAINES

A Blind Eye

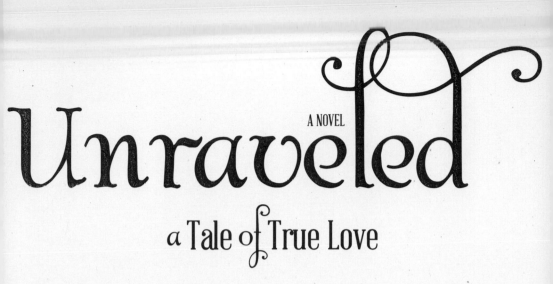

A NOVEL

Unraveled

a Tale of True Love

JULIE DAINES

Covenant Communications, Inc.

Cover image *Silver Shoes SCM29893* © Sandra Cunningham / Trevillion Images

Cover design copyright © 2014 by Covenant Communications, Inc.

Published by Covenant Communications, Inc.
American Fork, Utah

Printed in the United States of America
First Printing: February 2014

20 19 18 17 16 15 14   10 9 8 7 6 5 4 3 2 1

ISBN 978-1-62108-627-7

To the Bronwens of the world, everywhere.

The most beautiful things in life are found only in the heart.

Acknowledgments

THIS BOOK HAS BEEN A long time coming. It's needed a lot of research, tons of nurturing, and even a trip to Wales. I owe an enormous debt of gratitude to everyone who helped along the way—except maybe the grumpy marine biologist I e-mailed about coastal animals in Wales. He was no help at all.

First off, I have to thank my amazing writers group. They come through for me every time: Taffy, Yamile, Scott, and Jaime. The next drink (of bottled water) is on me. A big hug to all of my beta readers who take time out of their busy schedules to plow through some very rough drafts. I especially want to thank Michelle Ratto, Tiffany Dominguez, and Brooke Emery.

Thanks a million to the whole team at Covenant for helping make this book the best it can be and especially my editor, Samantha Millburn, for keeping my writing on the straight and narrow.

On behalf of Bronwen, myself, and women everywhere, I have to thank my parents. In this day of unbelievable pressure to look and be a certain way, I'm grateful to have been raised in a home in which I was taught where to find the worth of a soul.

And most of all, I thank my husband, who exemplifies daily the true meaning of unconditional love.

Chapter One

Even black hens lay white chickens.

BRONWEN PLACED THE TIP OF her crutch on the jagged rocks. She planted her feet and steadied herself before gazing across the chasm that separated her from the rest of the village. If her mother saw her perched this close to the ravine, she would scold her. Her father, had he lived, would be beside her.

Tomorrow she turned sixteen. For most girls, that meant old enough to marry. For her, well, who would want a crippled wife?

A gust of wind whipped her dress and pushed her closer to the edge. Bronwen leaned on her crutch, bracing herself with the wooden limb.

"Come away, child!" her mother called, her hands cupped around her mouth. "You'll fall to your death. There's a storm moving in, and the geese are out."

"I'm coming," she said, though her mother could not have heard her over the moaning of the wind.

Evening swifts darted and soared across the sky, their scythe-like wings silhouetted by the low-hanging sun. They circled the heavens, impervious to the troubles of the world below. How would it feel to be so free?

The swifts always returned this time of year—a sign that the first day of summer approached. And the festival of Calan Mai. Another year of watching while other girls danced around the bonfires. There would be no dancing for her. Not now or ever.

Bronwen stepped back, casting one last glance at the cottages across the ravine. She loathed going down into the village, where eyes never met hers and hushed voices spoke of weakness and frailty. She bore their looks with as much dignity as she could muster, but they all spoke the same thing: worthless. This year she would stay home.

If her mother would allow it.

Bronwen and her mother were all that remained of the great Hardd family, and as such, they would be expected to attend the celebrations.

Bronwen prodded the waddling ends of the geese with a birch twig until they crowded into the fold. The overfattened birds were the only creatures that moved slower than she did. Their clipped wings kept them earthbound and home. Nevermind the swifts. Bronwen wouldn't ever be more than a goose.

She turned her crutch in the direction of the house and crossed the threshold just as the rain poured down. With her free hand, she closed and bolted the door, then hobbled over to join her mother at the fireplace, propping her crutch against the wall and sinking into a chair.

Her mother darned a stocking, tilting the wool toward the light from the hearth. There used to be more chairs gathered around the fire. Her father, brother, and sister. They had died when she was eight of the same sickness that had left her own legs bent and bowed.

"It's a terrible night," Bronwen said, tightening her shawl and bending toward the warmth of the burning logs.

"Aye," her mother replied, crossing herself. "There'll be plenty of faerie folk looking for shelter. Pray Saint Morwyn none come here. Villains and mischief makers, all of them."

"Hush, Mother! They'll hear you." How could she be so careless? The faerie folk were always listening. They knew when someone spoke ill of them. Then they would come, and heaven help the calamity left in their wake.

A faint breeze, like the breath of a whispering fiend, tickled the hairs on the back of her neck. Had the faerie folk heard her mother's slander? They wouldn't come so soon. Bronwen glanced around the room, searching the dark corners.

A shutter burst open with a bang, blown by the howling wind. Bronwen screamed and jolted, lifting several inches off her chair. Her mother's mending flew into the air, and she clutched at her breast.

They stared at each other for a moment, panting for breath, then burst into laughter.

"By Saint Calon!" Her mother knew the names of all the saints and exactly which ones to ask for help in every situation. She invoked Saint Calon, patron saint of the body, to calm her racing heart.

The wind blew the rushes across the floor, churning the dust of dried herbs into the air, the scent of heather and yarrow wafting about the room.

Bronwen reached for her crutch and went to window. She peered out into the darkness.

A lantern, flickering between the trees, bobbed its way through the fog and down the mountain path.

Bronwen slammed the shutter closed and secured the latch, then turned and stared at her mother.

"You're pale as a ghost! What is it?" Her mother had just settled back into her mending, but she set it down and rose. "What did you see?"

Bronwen opened her mouth to speak but closed it again and shook her head. It couldn't be, could it? "I thought I saw a light. Coming down Mynydd Moel." On such a night as this, nothing but danger would be out on that mountain.

Her mother unfastened the window and peeked out. The wind whipped the ends of her wimple about her face. Bronwen peered over her mother's arm into the night. A cry, like a woman suffering great sorrow, floated across the mist and trickled down her spine.

Her mother secured the shutter and leaned her head on it. "A Gwyllion."

Bronwen backed away from the window. "Is she coming this way?"

"Aye." Her mother crossed herself again, no doubt offering a silent prayer to Saint Morwyn, protector from the faerie folk, and to Saint Craidd, keeper of the hearth and home. Then she went to work, ordering Bronwen to ready the house for the visit of a faerie witch.

"Quickly. Take the knives and hide them. The faerie folk do not take kindly to the presence of a metal blade."

"I know," Bronwen said, tucking the bundle of silver into the bottom of the firewood crate.

"If she knocks on our door, we must invite her in," her mother continued.

"Yes."

"To refuse hospitality is to beg for trouble."

"I know," Bronwen said, stirring up the flames.

"And be kind. She must not sense our fear."

"I know." Had they not taught her these rules since the day of her birth?

"And give her the good chair by—"

"Mother. I know."

Her mother shrugged and put a kettle on the fire. "No harm in being sure."

A knock at the door, strong and insistent, brought Bronwen up with a start. She smoothed her skirts and placed her hand on the latch but couldn't bring herself to lift the bar.

"Go on, child," her mother said. "We must."

Bronwen took a deep breath and opened the door. She slapped her hand over her mouth to keep from screaming. That must have been just as offensive, but it was the best she could do. She'd never seen such a creature before.

A Grey Maiden. Whoever named her must have been blind—or at least half blind. For a maiden she was not. A hag. With stringy grey hair and ashen skin draping her gaunt face. A grey, woolen cloak hung over hunched shoulders. Her frail body seemed to float in a tide of grey mist seeping from her robes.

She spoke, and her voice sounded like an axe on a whetstone. "Will you give shelter to a poor wanderer?"

Bronwen cast her mother one last look before stepping aside and motioning for the Gwyllion to enter. "Please, be at home." Bronwen dipped into an awkward curtsy on her stiffened legs.

The hag entered, studying Bronwen as she closed the door against the night. The Gwyllion's shrewd grey eyes focused on the crutch hooked under Bronwen's arm. Witch or no witch, Bronwen wanted to trip her for staring.

"Will you sit and rest by the fire?" Bronwen's mother said in the sweetest voice Bronwen had ever heard her use. "We have tea or warm pottage?"

"Tea," the witch said, watching Bronwen shuffle toward the hearth.

Bronwen leaned on her crutch and poured hot water over the leaves. One of the Gwyllion's hollow grey eyes was set higher than the other, and the same misty fog that oozed from her robes swirled inside them.

The three of them sat close to the hearth in silence. Bronwen considered the horror stories she'd heard involving encounters with the faerie folk. Accounts of babies stolen from their cradles, replaced by changelings. Food poisoned by angry elves when they'd been insulted—whole families dying in agony.

And countless tales of the Gwyllion. A weary traveler sees her twinkling lantern and follows. Never able to close the distance, the forlorn traveler is led farther and farther off the path, lured to his doom by the hope of finding rest. The Gwyllion's raking cry is the last sound they hear as they fall from a cliff or sink into a bog. It is said that when a person hears the cry of the Gwyllion, they have assuredly lost their way.

Only rarely did a faerie witch pay a visit to someone's home. So why did the Gwyllion come here? The slip of her mother's tongue could hardly warrant such revenge. Bronwen kept a watchful eye on the intruder. There'd be no poisoning here tonight, not if Bronwen could help it.

When the hag's teacup emptied, Bronwen filled it again with steaming water.

The wind moaned and whistled through the chimney. How long did the faerie witch plan to stay? Bronwen hoped she would leave before morning. If not, it would mean sleeping in her mother's bed and listening all night to her snoring.

"What is your name, girl?" the Gwyllion asked in her grating voice.

Bronwen silently consulted her mother. Should she give the stranger her name?

Her mother nodded.

"Bronwen," she answered. Then, to prove to the Grey Maiden that she was the kindliest of kind, she threw in a dazzling smile warm as the crackling fire.

"And tomorrow you will be sixteen," the witch said. Her haggard face transformed into something Bronwen could only guess was a grin.

"That's right," her mother said with an edge to her words. "How d'you know?"

The Gwyllion waved a gnarled hand, dismissing the question. "I am tired," she said. "I will rest now. Prepare my room."

That meant Bronwen's room. It was the only chamber, aside from her mother's, fit for company. Bronwen would get no sleep, expecting an untimely demise at any moment. She rose from her chair and took up her crutch. The Gwyllion's eyes widened, creating new furrows of wrinkles on her lopsided forehead. She glanced from Bronwen to her mother, then back to Bronwen. A look Bronwen recognized. The look that questioned her ability to carry out such a task.

Bronwen made her way up the stairs, bracing her shoulder against the wall and using the crutch to drag her lameness behind her. Over the years, she'd learned to manage the climb quite well. With her right foot so much stronger than her left, she could almost stand alone on it.

The gaze of the faerie witch burned into her back as she went. It was bad enough to bear the pitying stares of others, but coming from the hag, the humiliation doubled.

Bronwen knelt at the fireplace in her room, stirring and blowing the embers to bring the fire back to life. She laid a few twigs across the flames. Perhaps she should not leave the faerie witch a fire, lest she use it to burn them in their beds. But no fire would be an insult. To offend the Gwyllion would bring certain trouble, while a fire brought only the possibility of trouble. She added a peat log to the flames.

At the sound of rustling cloth behind her, Bronwen turned.

The Gwyllion stood watching her.

Bronwen placed a hand on the wooden mantel and pulled herself up.

"Anything else?" Bronwen asked, trying hard to sound civil. The hag had been in their house for a while now, saying little while observing Bronwen's every move with her crooked, misty eyes.

Fear, it seemed, lasted only so long before running dry. If the faerie witch was going to curse them, why didn't she get on with it? Keeping them waiting was bad manners, like hovering on someone's threshold and never entering in.

The Gwyllion spoke in her raspy voice. "I know what it is you want."

Bronwen took a step back. Was she going to be struck down instantly because of her foolish, wishful thinking? She didn't mean it, about wanting the Gwyllion to get on with the cursing. Not really.

"You watch the swifts from your place on the ground."

Bronwen's eyes flashed toward the window, in the direction of the cliffs. She had thought herself alone out there.

"You yearn for what you can never have." The Gwyllion's hunched and frail body remained motionless, yet all the while, mist curled out from under her robes.

"I . . . don't know what you mean."

The hag must have been at the ravine, watching her. She was not like any Gwyllion Bronwen had heard of from the stories. Grey Maidens were creatures of night. They didn't wander about in daylight hours. Bronwen backed up so far the heat of the fire stung her legs. She shifted to the side, shuffling her crutch and edging toward the door.

Before she could leave, the Gwyllion spoke again. Nothing more than a whisper, yet her words filled the room. "Who would want a crippled wife?"

Bronwen's head snapped up. She had never said those words out loud. Not to anyone. Not even her mother. She already knew the answer. It was why she wept sometimes at night. Why she hated the boys in the village who looked at her, then looked away. If she was whole, they would be vying for her favor even though they were all below her station.

She answered the Gwyllion's question. "No one."

"And yet you dream," the faerie witch said. "The stars do not shine on dreamers. They shine on those who see the truth."

Her dreams meant nothing; Bronwen already knew that. She didn't need the Gwyllion in order to see the truth: that her legs made her repulsive to any man. That she would live her life alone. That she would die alone. The stars had not shone on her for eight long years. Not since the sickness had swept through her family.

Perhaps this had been the faerie witch's plan all along, to make Bronwen more miserable than she already was.

Bronwen looked down at the floor—solid wood. So why did she feel as though she was sinking into a bog? She turned and left the room.

* * *

Bronwen lay on her back, eyes glazed as she stared at the rafters and listened to her mother's snores and the scuffling of mice in the walls. Dawn crept up the hillside and in through the shutter slats. She hadn't slept at all, not with the rumbling of her bed companion in her ears and the fear of their guest in her heart.

A merry birthday to me, she thought, knowing it would be a day just like every other. That is, it would be after the Gwyllion left. She dreaded seeing the hag again this morning. Her words the night before still prickled Bronwen's insides like a pin-pillow with the needles stuck pointy side out. Creatures of the night, she reminded herself. If Bronwen had any luck at all, the faerie witch would be gone.

Her mother stirred beside her, then quietly rose from the bed. Always up with the sun. Bronwen slammed her eyes shut, pretending to sleep, not yet ready to face the world.

They could both sleep late if her mother would be willing to spend for a few servants. They had money enough from the tenants, but Bronwen's mother wouldn't waste a farthing of it on a housemaid. *What do we need a servant for?* her mother said. *There's only the two of us to keep.* She was probably right. Bronwen and her mother carried on just fine, but the house and yard could use some upkeep. For the widow and daughter of a noble, they lived a simple life.

Before the sickness came, the manor had teemed with bodies. Cooks, chamberlains, a bailiff, even some men at arms, though the most they were called upon to kill was an occasional stag for supper. After the death of Bronwen's father, one by one, her mother let them all go.

Bronwen had been most disappointed to lose Rhys, the dark-haired lad who had worked the stock and stables. He lived in the loft for two years. To Bronwen in particular, he had shown kindness, even carrying her out of her bed so she could see the sky and the mountains. He had also made her a doll that she still had tucked away. It had helped her through the pain.

Bronwen listened to her mother creaking down the wooden stairs, the thud of logs being rolled into the hearth, the clicking of flint on steel. The wind must have put last night's fire completely out. No sound came from her own bedroom down the hall, nor did she hear her mother speak, so perhaps the faerie witch was gone.

She mustered the will to get up, putting her crutch under her arm and stepping out of her mother's room.

The door to her bedroom stood open. She poked her head in and found the chamber empty. The blankets lay arranged exactly how she had left them the night before—except for a bundle of grey cloth lying in the center of her bed.

Bronwen went to the top of the stairs and called down, careful to use a tone full of delight. "Mother, is our lovely guest down there?"

"No, thank Saint Morwyn!"

Bronwen grinned. She was tempted to offer her own prayer of thanks that they'd made it through the night unharmed by the Gwyllion. Unharmed in body, at least, if not soul. The Gwyllion's words still rubbed raw around Bronwen's heart.

"She was gone when I awoke," her mother called. "Now make haste. The gate's blown open, and the pigs are into the garden."

Bronwen shook her head. A day just like every other.

She lifted the dark bundle off her bed, thinking to toss it in the fire. Something hard and stiff bulged inside. She dropped it. What evil gift had the faerie witch left behind?

Bronwen cautiously pulled back the folds of cloth.

Inside lay a pair of ordinary brown shoes.

Chapter Two

To sing before breakfast is to weep before supper.

THE MOMENT BRONWEN HELD THE shoes, she knew they were anything but ordinary. They pulsed and thrummed in her hands, calling to her. Not out loud but in such a way that sent warm chills up her arms.

She dropped them on her bed and stepped back. Keep away from anything to do with faerie folk; that was the primary rule. Any object was capable of carrying a curse. Just last year, a boy found an enchanted top that spun without ceasing. He couldn't take his eyes off it. He stared until his mind became addled. Now he wandered the village, never able to walk a straight path or speak a proper sentence.

She took another step back, then moved closer again.

She went to the bed and lifted the shoes. What would happen if she put the shoes of the faerie witch on her feet? Something awful, no doubt. Although what could be worse than what she already suffered?

It didn't matter.

She wanted them on.

She sat on the bed and slipped off her own worn shoes. They fell to the floor with a soft thud. Bronwen slid her twisted feet into the faerie shoes, all the while hearing warning bells ringing in her head.

She could not resist. Like air to drowning lungs, she needed them on. She looped the strap across her foot and latched it over the toggle. First her right foot. Then her left. The instant she latched the second shoe, she gasped for breath. Her legs burned as though they'd burst into flames.

This was a mistake. She reached for the shoes. *Get them off. Stop the fire. Get them off!*

She stopped.

Her misshapen legs stretched and straightened, burning and scorching as they did. Her left foot—long, bent, and bowed—swelled out. Her thin, weak ankles grew round and sturdy. She crawled to the chamber pot and retched, sensing a vague gratitude that the Gwyllion had left it empty.

She rolled onto her side and moaned. A cloud of black smoke fell over her eyes, and just before darkness could take her, the throbbing ceased.

She lay still for a moment, steadying her breath, then wiped the sweat from her brow and examined her feet.

Her legs extended straight and true.

She was healed.

She stood slowly, carefully testing the strength of her new limbs. She gave a little bounce, then smiled. It was easy. She lifted her knees up and down, walking in place. She glanced at her crutch lying on the floor and, in one swift movement, bounded onto her bed. Ignoring the groaning mattress ropes, she leapt and jumped till her breath ran out. She collapsed onto the blankets, arms and legs splayed, and laughed.

This was a true miracle. Not like the time the cat fell down the well and survived, mewing all day until they finally found him. Not even like the time she found a gold coin buried in the grass near the church steps—one whole crown, enough to feed the house for a month.

No. This was an actual and honest miracle. The kind that changed a life forever. Something so far beyond even the wildest of dreams that it could never have been imagined.

She ran—ran!—to her mother's room and raised her skirts, studying the shoes in the tarnished mirror. They appeared sturdy and well made, with a clasp of mottled bronze. None would consider them pretty—weathered brown with no special trimmings, the toe unfashionably stubby. Yet to her, they were the most beautiful things in all the world and heaven above.

Her dress was too short. With her legs tall and straight, it barely hung to her ankles. She opened her arms wide, ready to embrace all this miracle would bring. Marriage? Perhaps. Dancing? Without question. Last night the world was dark and grim. This morning, she welcomed a new world.

Bronwen rushed down the stairs to show her mother.

She found her in the kitchen putting soft mounds of unbaked bread into the hearth. The smell of leavening barm and warm dough filled the room.

"Mother, look!" she cried.

"Just a moment, child. I'm setting the bread to bake." Her mother arranged the first loaf in the oven and then reached for the second. This was taking too long.

"Mother, you must see!"

"What is it, girl? I've work to do, and so do you, birthday or no." Her mother's face, red from the heat, rose from the hearth to look at her, a lump of dough cradled in her hands. "Well?"

Bronwen curtsied, then twirled a circle, dancing lightly on strong, perfect legs.

The dough landed with a smack on the stone floor, splatting flat as an oatcake. Bronwen laughed out loud while her mother's eyes became saucers and her mouth gaped wide. "By all the saints in heaven! How is this possible?"

"They're from the Grey Maiden." She lowered her voice to a whisper. "The Gwyllion."

"Hush, child! Do not speak the name," her mother cautioned, crossing herself. She leaned down, grunting as she bent, and examined the shoes. "A miracle of this kind can come only from the blessed saints above."

"It was the faerie," Bronwen said. "I found them wrapped in her grey cloak. She left them on my bed." Bronwen did not mention the Gwyllion's cryptic message from the night before, nor the way the witch had known her thoughts.

"'Tis a gift from the saints, and I'll not hear a word against it."

Her mother would never admit—at least out loud—the Gwyllion's involvement. It was probably best that way. No one must ever find out Bronwen had been healed by a faerie witch, or they would strip the shoes from her feet and burn them. Bronwen herself scarcely believed that something so wonderful had come from a Grey Maiden.

It's not as though faerie witches were known for miracles of goodness. Maybe a higher power was involved after all. Bronwen seriously doubted that, but if her mother wanted to believe it, who was she to say differently?

* * *

It took Bronwen's mother less than half the day to scoop the coins from the coffer, march down into their village of Glynbach, return with yards of fine silk cloth, and begin work on two new gowns and an overdress of exquisite blue for Bronwen.

Bronwen spent that time testing her new legs, skipping to the well and dancing around the ancient holly tree—the tree her mother forbade her father to cut down because holly was a powerful charm against faerie folk. Much good it did them last night.

When evening came, she sat by the fire and helped her mother with the sewing. "Mother, are you sure we can spare the money?" Bronwen asked, running her fingers over the fabric and trying to decide whether to wear the pear-green or the dove-grey gown first. Both would set off the blue overdress wonderfully.

"'Course we can spare the money," her mother said, barely glancing up from her work. "We've not come so low as that. Besides, it's your birthday. And you are made whole." Her mother halted midstitch. She gazed at nothing for a moment, then nodded her head as though she'd just come to an important decision. "You must journey to the shrine of Saint Cenydd—to offer gratitude. Such a gift as this should not go unthanked."

Saint Cenydd was born crippled. In disgust, his parents abandoned him, placing their infant in a basket and casting him into the sea. He survived, fed by the gulls, until the waves carried him across the channel and washed him ashore. He became a holy man and was later healed by Saint Dafydd, the patron saint of Cymru, her country. Bronwen had heard this story many times and always resented Saint Dafydd for healing Cenydd but not her.

Her mother paused in her sewing and looked at Bronwen. "And you are of age. A woman now. You must present yourself to the king."

Bronwen had never considered such an option. Of course, she dreamed about it all the time. What girl hadn't? But nothing could have persuaded her to waddle on her crutch up to the king and queen. It would have been a disgrace. The king would not welcome a lame girl in his hall when the law wouldn't even allow a crippled man to inherit his father's lands.

With the shoes, no one would ever know she had been crippled. Bronwen closed her eyes and pictured herself in the silken gown, curtsying before the king.

"Now, it wouldn't be proper to have you traveling alone," her mother continued. "I shall accompany you to the crossroads. From there, we'll find a group heading to the city. You can travel with them."

It meant she would be in the city during the festival of Calan Mai. It was said that in Sedd Brenhinol—the King's Seat—they had a bonfire as big as a house.

In the summer of her seventh birthday, she had watched her cousin Iola dance around a bonfire at her wedding. Young men from the village held out their hands while Iola weaved her way hand over hand between them, her soft white dress floating along behind, glowing in the light of the fire. Bronwen thought she looked like an angel. At last, Iola had come to rest in front of her handsome groom, presenting him a crown of white hawthorn blossoms.

Bronwen lowered her sewing onto her lap. She pictured herself gliding around the flames, her long russet hair gleaming in the light of the bonfires. Her dress billowing with her graceful moves. And a man waiting for her. Tall and handsome. Faceless except for his adoring eyes.

"Child, you're no help at all," her mother said.

Bronwen tugged her thoughts back to the present, running her hands across the cool silk cloth.

"Off to bed, and take your castles in the sky with you."

Bronwen folded her work into a basket and rose, placing a kiss on her mother's soft cheek. She grinned as she effortlessly climbed the stairs. No crutch needed. *If the Gwyllion could see me now.*

In her chamber, she slipped off her dress and sat on the edge of her bed. She reached to remove the shoes, then paused. She hadn't thought this far ahead. Would her legs stay straight? Healed was healed, was it not?

Not even the Gwyllion would be so cruel as to give her such a wondrous gift only to take it away.

With a deep breath, she pulled off the shoes.

Chapter Three

If you don't know the way, walk slowly.

BRONWEN'S CRY ECHOED THROUGH THE house.

With horror, she watched her legs shrivel like plums left in the sun. The shriveling hurt less than the straightening—at least on the part of her legs. Her heart bore the brunt of that one.

Of course, the Gwyllion would be that cruel.

Bronwen's mother appeared at the entrance to her room, breathing hard, hands out, steadying herself on the doorframe. Bronwen lay on her bed, her twisted legs drawn up, the empty shoes cast on the floor beside her. She smoothed the blanket out to cover her legs.

She always kept her misshapen feet hidden. Even her own mother rarely saw the way her thin skin stretched tightly over her stunted and weakened legs.

"Oh, dear," her mother said, sitting on the bed and stroking Bronwen's cheek. "We didn't think about that, now did we?" She pulled Bronwen up and closed her arms around her.

Bronwen rested her head against her mother's rough brown dress. "It's not fair," she cried.

"No, indeed." Her mother loosened the pins holding Bronwen's hair and combed her fingers through it, letting it fall softly down her daughter's back.

"It was all for nothing."

"Perhaps." Bronwen's mother leaned over and retrieved one of the shoes. "And perhaps not. Maybe you have to wear them for it to work."

Bronwen lifted the other shoe from the floor and looked at her mother. There was no reason for the magic to not work again once the shoes were back on. She should have realized this from the start.

Her mother nodded. "Try it. And pray Saint Cenydd it works."

Bronwen put them on, and just as before, when she fastened the final clasp, her legs grew straight and strong. Bronwen gripped her mother's arm as the pain took over. She groaned and rolled to her knees beside the bed. Just as before, her stomach twisted and churned, refusing to keep its contents. She collapsed on the hard, wooden floor.

"Bronwen?" her mother called from far away.

She took a moaning breath. "I'm here."

"I know you're here, child. Are you all right?" Her mother knelt over her.

Bronwen tried to sit up, but the pain held on, longer this time than the first. "I'm fine. It just hurts when they grow." She waited a moment for her insides to settle, then checked her feet. Her legs were whole again.

"Well, look at you now. Good as new!" her mother said, her voice not quite as steady as before. "Did it hurt like that this morning?"

"Yes." She nodded. Not quite that bad, but maybe she was just tired.

It made sense. When she wore the shoes, she was healed. When she took them off, she was the same old Bronwen. But what would folks say if they saw her whole one day and crippled the next? She couldn't wear the shoes forever. Not day and night for the rest of her life. Eventually, they'd wear out.

Bronwen tried to guess how long she had. A year, maybe two before the shoes fell apart. And that was only if she didn't wear them every day.

She could do many things in the time she had. She longed to climb the mountain peaks to look for snow lilies. They bloomed only at the start of summer and only on the high, jagged cliffs. She hadn't been able to go that far since her sickness. Before he left, Rhys, the stable boy, brought her a lily. Away from its natural home, it withered and died before the end of the day.

"I will go to the shrine of Saint Cynedd," Bronwen said. "But perhaps it's better if I don't present myself to the king. I am nothing, really. And when the shoes come off, well . . ." She shrugged, wondering why she needed to explain something so obvious. "It wouldn't be right for me to go before the king. Not for a cripple."

Her mother stood and settled her steady eyes upon her daughter. "Hear me now. You are as fine and pretty a girl as ever there was. Nothing can change that. D'you suppose the saints've healed you so you can traipse around this old house and get nowhere with your life?" She glowered at

Bronwen until Bronwen shook her head, more to satisfy her mother than to indicate her own feelings.

Her mother gave Bronwen's shoulders a good, solid squeeze. "Right, then. Now get to bed." She glanced at Bronwen's feet. "And sleep with the shoes on."

* * *

Several days later, they loaded their bundles onto Ferlen, the old palfrey horse useful only for packing belongings and tilling a few furrows in the garden each spring. Bronwen wrapped her crutch in a strip of sackcloth and tucked it into the load. She couldn't bring herself to leave it behind. If something happened to the shoes, without her crutch, she would be helpless.

Her mother placed crosses made of straw on every threshold and windowsill to protect the home from evil spirits while they were away, then bolted the doors. After a quick prayer to Saint Craidd to guard the home and another to Saint Seiriol for a safe journey, Bronwen and her mother turned their backs on their house at the base of Mynydd Moel.

Bronwen had no idea what to expect from the world beyond her home; she only knew that such an opportunity would never come again. For the first time in her life, she would see the royal city—and the ocean. How she longed to glimpse the great waters of the sea. If that was all she got from the gift of the Gwyllion, even that would be enough. She stroked Ferlen's neck as she led him down the path, humming.

Rather than take the road through her village of Glynbach, they skirted the base of the mountain and used the path to the north, along the river. Her mother thought it sensible to avoid inquisitive neighbors. Bronwen could not have agreed more. A quiet departure away from the eyes of the village seemed easiest and best.

Bronwen and her mother traveled two days, stopping overnight at a farmhouse for an evening meal and a bed. As they went, the landscape settled from ragged mountains into soft, green woodlands and fields. The river gradually widened, swelling into lakes and ponds at intervals along the way, always flowing west to the sea.

On the evening of the second day, they reached the crossroads where several small paths joined together, then set out in unison as a larger, well-traveled road. An old inn stood in the clearing with a wooden plaque dangling over the door, creaking as it swung in the breeze. Bronwen studied the picture on the sign. From what was left of the faded paint, she just made out the image of a dagger.

Bronwen's mother pointed at the crest. "The Inn of the Silver Knife," she said as she steered Ferlen toward the stable yard. "Surely we will be protected from any kind of faerie in this place. Better than that farmhouse last night." Her mother leaned close and whispered, "I barely slept a wink for worry of what mischief the woodland folk might be up to."

"Did you see something?" Bronwen asked. Even though they'd traveled many miles since the farmhouse, she couldn't help peering into the depths of the surrounding forest. She doubted very much that another encounter with faerie folk would result in such a happy outcome as the one with the Gwyllion.

"No, thank Saint Morwyn."

The stench of the stockyard hit them the moment they rounded the side of the house. Several horses wandered aimlessly through the muck, and an enormous pig lay in a stall, swarmed by countless piglets. A young boy tumbled down from a pile of straw. He took Ferlen's rope and led him into the enclosure as light rain began to fall. Bronwen and her mother scurried into the inn.

Near as Bronwen could tell, the building must have started out as a one- or two-room home. Then, when more space was needed, someone greatly lacking in carpentry skills had added rooms on with no thought to logic or form.

They followed the innkeeper's wife down a narrow hall that bent in the middle—not enough to be a real corner but not straight either—and into a small, windowless room.

"So many people traveling to the city for Calan Mai," their host said. "I'm afraid this is all I've got left."

Bronwen's mother opened her mouth to say something, but Bronwen spoke first. "It'll be fine." And before the woman had closed the door, Bronwen threw herself onto the bed and closed her eyes. She'd never walked so far in all her life.

The bed wouldn't stop shaking.

"Bron. Wake up, child." Her mother jostled her shoulder. "Bronwen!"

Bronwen cracked her eyes. "Why is the room moving?"

"Get up, or we'll miss supper." Her mother jostled harder.

"What?" Bronwen yawned and wiped her face. "Did I fall asleep?"

Her mother let out an exasperated sigh. "You've been asleep since we got here, and now it's dark outside and supper's set." She tugged on Bronwen's arm. "Come along."

Bronwen stood and shook the wrinkles from her skirts. She twisted her stray strands of hair back into her braid, then she appraised her mother. "Here," she said, reaching out and straightening her mother's wimple.

"Oh, leave it. I'm sure it's good enough for here."

Bronwen followed her mother out of the room and down the narrow corridor. Rain pounded on the thin roof, and Bronwen worried it might blow off. At the bend, they nearly collided with a young man coming from the other direction. The width of the hall did not allow for two-way travel.

Bronwen and her mother pressed themselves against the wall while the youth, dripping wet and smelling of damp wool, edged past. His tall, lanky frame looked like it had grown faster than the rest of his body could keep up with.

"Evening," he said.

Bronwen's mother gasped, then pried her foot out from under his heavy boot.

"Oh, sorry about that, my lady." He made an apologetic bow, and his head smacked into Bronwen's.

"Ow!" Bronwen rubbed her forehead, her eyes watering from the sting.

"Forgive me. I'm so sorry, um . . . It's a bit tight through here." He glanced back and forth between Bronwen and her mother. "I'll just . . . be off, then." He hurried down the hall and into the end room, leaving a trail of wet footprints behind.

"Not too light on his feet, is he?" Her mother snorted.

They entered the common room, where half a dozen tables lined the walls. Most looked like they'd been built by the same craftsman who'd worked on the inn—so rickety they'd be better suited for firewood. A loud murmur of voices and the scent of warm bread filled the air.

"There's people I want you to meet," her mother said.

Chapter Four

Never trust overmuch to a new friend or an old enemy.

BRONWEN'S MOTHER STEERED HER TOWARD a table already occupied by a woman and a girl who looked to be Bronwen's same age—the only other women in the room besides her mother and herself. The girl was dressed in a gown of blue brocaded silk far too extravagant for such a place as this. Most guests were dressed like Bronwen, in dark, woolen traveling clothes.

The woman stood, and Bronwen's mother said, "This here's Elen."

"May God prosper you," Bronwen said with a curtsy. She used the formal greeting reserved for those of higher status and waited for Elen to answer with the customary response.

"God's welcome," Elen said, bobbing her head and jingling a set of ornate earrings so heavy Bronwen worried they'd rip through her ears. Elen had figured out a way to tuck the chinstrap of her wimple back just enough to display her fancy jewelry.

Bronwen's mother gestured at the girl beside Elen. "And her daughter Gwenna."

Gwenna examined Bronwen with a curious look, then she smiled. "Hello."

Bronwen returned the greeting and sat where her mother indicated, across the table from Gwenna. The young lad from the stable yard, straw still mussing his hair, served them each a steaming bowl of rabbit and barley stew, some crusty brown bread, and a mug of watered-down cider.

The moment Bronwen took a mouthful of stew, Gwenna asked, "Did you sleep well?"

Bronwen sucked in a quick breath to cool her tongue from the burning soup. Not wishing to spew food at her new acquaintance, she only nodded.

She glanced at her mother chatting with Elen, spoon in one hand and a wedge of bread in the other, as though they'd been friends for years rather than the lesser part of an evening.

Gwenna spoke again. "While you were resting, your mother told us you are going to Sedd Brenhinol for presentation."

Bronwen chewed swiftly and swallowed, leaving a trail of fire down her throat. She tried to douse the flames with a sip of her drink before answering Gwenna. "Yes, we—"

"Me too." Gwenna scooted forward on her wooden stool. "I dread meeting the king's son, Urien. Don't you? I've heard he's terribly handsome. If we do chance to meet him, I'm sure I shall faint dead away. I can't wait. I haven't slept for a month, I'm so excited. I've never been to the city before. Have you? My father and brother go every year. They say it's beautiful but too crowded by half. I always asked to come with them, but Father said no. He doesn't dare leave Mother home alone with all the little ones. I have seven—you know—little brothers and sisters. And Mother doesn't get on well with any of them. What are you going to wear?"

Bronwen's spoon was stuck somewhere between the bowl and her mouth while brownish drips of stew fell to the table. She blinked, dazed by Gwenna's quick succession of words. It'd just been Bronwen and her mother for so long, she was uncertain what to say. "Well, I have a—"

"At first I thought of wearing this, but can you imagine? It will never do. Only the best is suitable for court. And this gown looks well enough but not for the queen. She's very fastidious. Or so I've heard. Fortunately, I brought another, much finer than this. Completely new. It's gold to match my hair."

Bronwen looked at Gwenna's hair. It was tan colored at best and, really, closer to light brown than any shade of yellow. She considered what this might imply about the goldness of the gown. "I'm sure it's lovely," she blurted out, pleased to have finished her sentence.

"But look at this." Gwenna stretched her leg out around the side of the table and pulled up her hem. "Have you ever seen shoes this grand? Elen, my mother, had them made special." With great solemnity, she added, "The sole is cordovan leather."

It was, indeed, very fine. Made of a dark indigo, with silver stitches swirling all around and a long, elegantly pointed toe. It made Bronwen's faerie shoes look like something a field-hand would wear. She shouldn't be seen in court wearing peasant shoes, yet she had no choice. It was either the faerie shoes or her crutch. Bronwen set down her spoon, her appetite gone.

"Aren't they something? Let me see yours." Gwenna peered under the table.

Slowly, Bronwen inched up the folds of her skirts, exposing her shoe as little as possible.

Gwenna seemed astonished, and then she laughed. "Oh, I see. You haven't yet changed from your traveling clothes. I thought maybe you didn't have . . . But now I see you're just being practical."

Bronwen nodded. "Yes. Practical."

Gwenna leaned in closer and whispered, "Elen told me not change either. She said the wet would ruin everything. But I told her we're not having supper in the stables. It's just down the hall." She burst into a fit of giggles, and Bronwen grinned despite her worries.

She liked Gwenna's ready smile and open manner. Bronwen had never been one to chatter on much, so she didn't mind that Gwenna's words tumbled out like a waterfall. It made conversation easy.

Even with her not-gold hair, Gwenna had pretty features. Her eyes were unusual, blue on the outside with an inner circle of brown around the middle. They lit up when she smiled. A small congregation of freckles bridged her nose, and she had good color, pale but with a rosy glow in her cheeks. Fawn? Bronwen mused, returning again to the color of Gwenna's hair.

"I made Gwil change too," Gwenna continued after her giggles died away. "He was soaked from tending to the horses. Who wants to eat with a boy who smells like a barn?"

"Gwil?"

Gwenna leaned in and rolled her eyes. "My brother." She pointed to the other end of the table.

Bronwen had been so caught up in her conversation with Gwenna that she hadn't noticed Gwil's arrival. He was the young man from the tight corridor. She rubbed the sore spot on her forehead. He'd exchanged his wet tunic for one of dark-blue linen, and the softer fabric revealed he did have some muscles under his leanness. He sat forward, spooning stew into his mouth while his free hand clutched his drink.

He looked up from his meal and blushed a soft pink.

"Hello," Bronwen said, then added, "again." She probably shouldn't have referred to the incident in the hallway, but she couldn't resist.

He stood and reached out his hand. Unfortunately, it was the hand that had been steadying his cup. It tipped, and amber liquid spread out onto the table.

With lightning reflexes that could only have been learned through years of practice, Elen righted the cup before half the drink had been lost.

"Sit down, Gwil," his mother snapped, "before you overturn the whole table."

He sat immediately. The pink flush in his cheeks flared into burning, bright red. He had Gwenna's same blue-brown eyes and freckles. His hair was darker than Gwenna's, which had to bring Gwenna great satisfaction, taking her one step closer to gold.

Elen summoned the straw-haired lad from the kitchen to mop up the spill. Gwil did not raise his eyes from the table.

Poor Gwil. "So you are taking your mother and sister to court?" Bronwen asked.

He looked up. "I—"

"He is," Gwenna broke in. Gwil's mouth clamped shut. "Well, that, and he thinks of joining the King's Men. But can you imagine? Gwil, with a sword in his hand? He'll kill them all before the fighting begins."

Bronwen tried to picture Gwil wielding a sword in battle, and it did seem as though it might give the foe some advantage.

"Leave him be," Elen said, which only served to bring a new rush of color to Gwil's face.

Gwenna groaned and rose from the table. "I can't eat any more of this awful meal. What some people cook is not fit for the pigs!"

Bronwen peeked into Gwenna's bowl and found that every drop had been sopped up with the dark bread and devoured. But Bronwen had never seen her take a bite.

"Gwil is making us leave before first light. He wants to arrive early to watch the swordplay. As if that will help." Gwenna took Bronwen's hand and smiled at her. "Our mothers have plotted that you will travel with us. So I will see you in the morning, and by the time we reach Sedd Brenhinol, we shall be the best of friends." She gave Bronwen's fingers an affectionate squeeze and left the room.

Elen said her good nights to Bronwen and her mother and followed Gwenna out the door.

Bronwen leaned back in her chair and let out a long breath as though she'd just been swept up in a whirlwind and suddenly set free. She'd never met anyone like Gwenna—so confident. So full of words.

Back home, Bronwen hadn't mingled much with girls her own age. Her crippled legs kept her apart. And now, here she was making friends. Another unexpected miracle from the Gwyllion's shoes.

"Are you going to eat that?" Gwil asked, pointing at Bronwen's bowl of stew.

"What?" Bronwen looked down at her food. "Oh. No." She pushed the food across the table to him. "I'm afraid it's gone cold."

"It's fine," he said, ladling it in as though it might vanish at any moment.

Bronwen's mother rose from the table. "Gwil," she said with a nod and turned to leave.

"It was nice to meet you," Bronwen said, extending her hand and giving him a second chance at a proper introduction—or third if she counted the hallway.

He stood, slowly this time, took her hand with a sheepish grin, and gave a little bow.

Someone whistled at them from across the room. Gwil's cheeks flushed, and he took a quick step away. He bumped into his stool, and it toppled to the floor.

Bronwen laughed the whole way back to her room.

* * *

It was still dark when Bronwen's mother woke her. "It's time."

Bronwen's heart skipped a beat. She'd never been away from home before, away from her mother. The farthest she'd gone since her illness was when the stable boy had taken her out on Ferlen, leading the horse along the mountain trails.

Last night, Gwenna had worried Bronwen with all her talk about fancy shoes and plain traveling clothes. She pictured herself curtsying to the king. If he should see her shoes, he might discover she was lame.

Her mother had been presented many years ago to the king before this one. "What's it like?" Bronwen asked, gathering her belongings and tucking them into her bags. She hadn't brought much—her new gowns, naturally, and the best of her older kirtles and overdresses that she'd lowered the hems of until they dragged on the floor.

"What's what like, dear?"

"Going before the king."

"Oh." Her mother's face lit up. "It's a fine thing. To go into the great hall dressed in your finest and kneel before the king and queen. You state your name and your father's name, then you kiss the ring of the queen. It's as simple as that."

For any other girl, that might seem very simple. But for Bronwen, it stirred up even more bits of doubt.

"Mother, are you sure this is a good idea?" she said. "They will know the name of my father and what happened to our family. They will see my shoes and how plain they are and question my impertinence." Her mother opened her mouth to speak, but Bronwen cut her off before she could suggest the unthinkable. "And I'll not hobble in on my crutch like a mangy farmyard cat that's been run over by a cart."

"Good heavens, child! Calm down. All will be well. They will recognize your father's name, but no one will know enough to question your ability to walk. Stop your worrying. The blessings of Saint Cenydd are with you. It will take but a moment. Quick as a fox."

Quick as a fox. That didn't sound too bad. "But why does it even matter if I go?"

Her mother finished fastening her wimple, then placed both her hands on Bronwen's shoulders. "It must be done. We must keep our family's name alive to the king. If our name dies, if they think we cannot manage our holdings, they will take our lands and give them to a new family."

This had never occurred to Bronwen. She thought her mother wanted her to present because it would be fun. A wonderful adventure for her sad little girl. Most daughters of the nobles looked forward to the year they turned sixteen so they could stand before the king and queen. And so had Bronwen . . . until that autumn of sickness.

"You must do it," her mother continued. "As long as I'm alive, by rights, they cannot take our home. If they think we are still strong, perhaps they'll let us stay longer."

By us, her mother meant Bronwen—alone with the house and the lands. A confirmation of the bleak future that lay before her. Alone in the house was better by far than alone on the street; a crippled beggar never lasted long in the world. At least at the manor, she had the income of tenants. She could always hire a serving girl to stay with her.

Her mother's words made sense, but Bronwen would have felt much better about this plan if she didn't have to go on to the city by herself.

"Do you have to go back? Can't you come with me?" Bronwen asked.

"No, my dear. I must go home. Quarter days are approaching," her mother said. "Madog arrives any moment. I must be there."

Madog was the family's steward. He was about eight generations old but refused to die. He'd worked for Bronwen's father and his father before him. Still strong and vigorous, he came every quarter day to collect the rent from the tenants and settle disputes. He always brought Bronwen honeyed plums and stayed for a few weeks. She would be sorry to miss him.

Bronwen's mother placed a heavy coin purse in Bronwen's hand. "Take this. Use it for an inn and for whatever else you need."

There was a knock on the door. Her mother lifted the latch and swung it open.

Gwil gave a quick bow. "You ready?" he asked Bronwen.

She nodded and bent to lift her belongings, hoisting her packs into her arms.

"Let me help with those." Gwil tried to scoop them from Bronwen all at once, the process bringing his face inches from hers. When their eyes met, he paused for a moment. Even in the dark of early morning, Bronwen could see the color rise to his cheeks.

He turned and hurried out the door.

Bronwen's mother smiled at her. "See there. I knew you couldn't be so beautiful for nothing. You've already caught someone's eye."

Bronwen shook her head. "You're forgetting about something." She lifted her last possession to be loaded onto the horse—her crutch. If Gwil knew the truth about her, he would be no different from the boys back home. Look at her, then look away.

* * *

They set off from the Inn of the Silver Knife and headed west as dawn lit the horizon. On the third day, the road turned south and, little by little, filled with fellow travelers, most on foot, like themselves, pulling their beasts of burden behind them, but some on horseback or riding in carts. Rain fell constantly, and the road became a river of mud. They walked along the sides as much as possible to avoid the worst of it.

Despite the weather, Gwenna was cheerful and chatted enthusiastically about every topic imaginable.

Bronwen learned that hers was not the only family with difficulties. A few years ago, the lands belonging to Gwenna's father flooded. It cost him a large sum of money—more than they had—to build a dam, drain the land, and get it back into working condition. By the time the fields could be cultivated, many of his tenants had moved away. Now he struggled to pay the debts and keep his holdings.

It was up to Gwil to find work suitable for a nobleman's son and earn enough money to keep them from losing their lands. This was why he had hopes of being a King's Man—it was an honorable position and brought in a sturdy wage.

"He'll never make it though," Gwenna said, nodding in Gwil's direction.

Bronwen looked up in time to see Gwil's foot sink into a mud-filled rut. They stopped and waited while he tugged his leg, fighting off his mother, who was trying to help him, until his foot slurped out. His shoe did not come with it. Gwil stuck his hand into the muck and fished around, finally pulling out a brown, dripping mass of slop.

He wiped it in the weeds on the side of the road until the general shape of a shoe could be seen, then stuck it on his foot. Bronwen and Gwenna looked at each other and stifled their laughs.

"We're almost there. Only a few miles more to go," Gwil said.

As he spoke, they crested a hill. Elen swept her hand out in a broad motion over the landscape below. "Now look here and see what a sight."

Bronwen's breath caught as the city of Sedd Brenhinol came into view. A tall castle of honey-colored stone stood edged on two sides by water, while a teeming mass of thatched-roof buildings surrounded the castle walls. A few threads of houses and inns stretched out along the roads that fed into the city gates.

Never could she have imagined so many structures, so many people all in one place. She gulped, trying to swallow the epiphany of her own insignificance. In her village, there were perhaps thirty families scattered about the base of the mountain.

"There must be more than a hundred people down there," she said.

Gwenna chuckled. "More than a thousand, I should think."

Bronwen tugged on Ferlen's rope, and they started moving again, following the road that would feed them into the mouth of Sedd Brenhinol.

"They say there's a city much grander than this to the east, across the mountains." Gwenna jerked her head eastward. "Llundain. I once heard an ironmonger tell of it. He said in that place lived more than twenty thousand! But I don't see how that's possible. How could they all be fed?"

Away in the distance, across a thin ribbon of sea, the green vastness of an island stretched as far as the eye could see. The Isle of Ynys Môn. Bronwen would have to cross the tidal river and all of Ynys Môn to a smaller islet to reach the shrine of Saint Cenydd.

She'd never seen the sea before. After her rugged mountains, it seemed so calm and gentle—just a rippling plain of blue.

"Wait till you dip your feet in it," Gwil said. "There's nothing like it. Cold yet soothing, salty but fresh, sandy and soft."

It sounded heavenly. *I will do it somehow*, she vowed.

They joined a slow-moving line of travelers and descended into the city in silence until they reached the heavy wooden gate.

A soldier wearing a stiff leather jerkin stopped them. "State your business," he said, scarcely lifting his eyes from a parchment in his hands. A long sword hung from his belt and clanked against the stones behind him when he shifted his weight.

"Have you no eyes?" Elen said.

The man's head jerked up, and he scowled at her.

"I'm bringing these girls for Calan Mai and for presentation."

The man gave the girls an exaggerated appraisal. His eyes lingered on Bronwen, and he leaned back on his heels, looking her up and down. He waggled his eyebrows. "She'll do very fine."

Elen harrumphed, and the soldier urged them on. Bronwen glanced over her shoulder, out past the gate to where lines of people were crowding to get through. When she saw the gatekeeper still watching her, she swung her head forward and smiled.

The city buzzed with the clink of shod horses on cobblestones and the shouts of vendors vying for customers. The stench of animal waste and sewage stung her nose. Occasionally, pleasant aromas of baking sweetmeats or spicy mead wafted over from the public houses, giving her welcome relief.

Ragged children with wet noses ran wildly through the streets, and elegant ladies in robes of linen or silk passed by. Bronwen dared not stare at them long for fear of being trod on by the masses of people flocking the streets. No one seemed aware of her existence. If she'd been on her crutch, dragging herself along, every eye would have followed her, some with pity and some repulsed. Before now, she had never been able to enjoy the anonymity of fitting in.

Gwil led them to the inn where he always stayed when he came to the city with his father, a modest place in a quiet—and clean—part of town.

Bronwen read the name above the door: Fib and Flounder Inn. How her mother would have fretted. A lying fish, she would have said. Nothing in that to keep the faeries at bay.

Gwil unloaded the horses, then disappeared to watch the tournaments. Despite Gwil's efforts to get them here early, they had missed evening meal.

Bronwen ate from a tray of bread and cheese set on a small table in the corner of her room—the only other piece of furniture besides the bed and a chest.

She tried to scrub the clotted mud from her faerie shoes. She'd not taken them off since the first day she got them. She wanted to remove them tonight to rest her feet and clean them, but it would be too risky. Gwenna could come bursting in at any moment. Elen and Gwenna had offered to share a room with her, but Bronwen had refused. They would have liked a third person to share the cost, but if they saw her crippled legs . . . Gwenna and her mother knew nothing of her lameness. Bronwen hoped to keep it that way.

She finished her meal, then fell back on the bed and closed her eyes. She had three days to prepare herself before standing in front of the king. She would never sleep tonight. Not with so much before her.

The rhythm of the city crept in through her shuttered window. Carts on the cobblestone roads. Shouts from the tops of houses to people below. Dogs barking and growling, fighting for the refuse tossed into the streets.

She pictured the quiet mountains of home, black and rugged, rising up to meet a peaceful sky. Her breathing deepened, and she was almost there when Gwenna flew into her room.

She ran to Bronwen's bedside in a fit and said, "They've made a change of plans. Presentations are set for tomorrow! I have to get ready." In a swish of green and blue, Gwenna was gone.

Bronwen sat up in bed. "Tomorrow?"

Chapter Five

If every fool wore a crown, we should all be kings.

"Oh! I'm sure there'll be none so fair as my Gwenna."

Bronwen had just reached the bottom of the Fib and Flounder's staircase when she heard these words from Elen. Poor Gwenna—she must be mortified for her mother to say that in front of so many people.

As Bronwen rounded the corner toward the common room, Gwenna ran up to meet her. No sign at all of mortification.

"Oh, you do look lovely," Gwenna said, pecking Bronwen's cheek with a kiss.

Bronwen had settled on the dove-grey gown and the blue overdress. Her silk clothing was simple and unembellished, but she liked the way it fell softly over her body and made a swishing sound when she walked. A belt of silver rings that had belonged to her father's mother circled her hips, clasping in the front with a long chain hanging down. She'd woven a matching strand of silver beads through her hair.

"A little pale though." Gwenna reached up with both hands and pinched Bronwen's cheeks.

"Ouch. Stop," Bronwen said, pushing Gwenna's arms away. Bronwen had spent half the morning trying to make her faerie shoes look shiny and new. No matter how hard she brushed them, they still looked plain and ordinary.

"What do you think?" Gwenna asked, spinning around in a circle.

Gwenna's gown was indeed gold—a beautiful, warm shade of gold with a brocade of darker stitching covering the entire garment. Her hair fell in long, aimless curls down her back. Set against the dress, it looked a dull, mousy brown. Bronwen's fingers itched to weave it into something orderly.

"Very pretty," Bronwen said.

"Thank you. Is this not a beautiful gown? You can tell now why the other would never do." Gwenna hooked her arm in Bronwen's and towed her into the eating hall. "I was up all night getting ready. I made Elen wash my hair twice so it would shine like silk today. Of course, we didn't know until we arrived that presentations would be so soon. Lucky for us, Gwil made us come early, and I set all my things out to let them air. And look how perfectly it matches my shoes." Gwenna exhibited her ornate foot coverings again.

"Perfect." Not wanting to dwell on the subject of shoes, Bronwen stepped aside to greet Gwil, who'd not taken his eyes off her since she approached their table. Elen, who was already gathering her things to leave, gave Bronwen a little nod.

"We'd best be off," Elen said.

"What about Bronwen's breakfast?" Gwil asked.

Bronwen grabbed a piece of bread from the table. "This is fine. I'm really not hungry."

The streets were even more crowded than they'd been the night before. Progress toward the castle was slow, especially because Gwenna was very particular about where to place her precious shoes. Bronwen hid a grin more than once, knowing full well that the value of Gwenna's cordovan leather didn't come close to that of Bronwen's faerie shoes, plain though they were.

Elen spent the time reviewing with her daughter the correct manner to present oneself to the king and queen: down on one knee, state your name and your father's, kiss the ring. Surely Bronwen could manage that and still keep her feet hidden. She had to. It was her only chance to see the king. "Quick as a fox," her mother had said. But by the time they had reached the castle, her breathing was coming hard and her palms were sweaty.

A stout woman with no visible neck, just a great round head set upon broad shoulders, and looking like a potato in her dress of brown wool directed Elen to the mother's room on the other side of the keep. Then she escorted Bronwen and Gwenna into a chamber filled wall to wall with girls. Gwil took one look inside and fled.

Bronwen rose on her toes. Every face glowed with anticipation. The room smelled heavily of rose water and lavender, as every young lady there had most likely washed with one or the other, or in Gwenna's case, both. Most of them would be married before the year's end. By next Calan Mai, they'd be mothers of their own.

Gwenna was telling Bronwen something about the king's son, but Bronwen found it hard to attend.

The round servant sent a dark-haired girl through a rear door. After a minute or two, there was a knock on the door, and another girl went through. The woman seemed to be choosing at random whom to send in, and the crowd around her thickened as each girl hoped to be the next.

Bronwen wrung her hands and wiped them on her dress. She looked down and tugged her skirts lower until they brushed the floor. The number of girls in the room depleted slowly as, one by one, they were ushered through the door.

"Did you hear what I said?" Gwenna asked.

Bronwen looked at her and nodded once, then shook her head. "Not really. No."

"The servant over there," Gwenna pointed to the potato woman, "said the queen is—"

The woman motioned at Bronwen, summoning her to enter. Bronwen's heart squeezed painfully in her chest. She pulled down her gown one last time and glanced at Gwenna.

"You're next," the servant said, and with a large, firm hand on Bronwen's back, she pressed her through the door.

Bronwen stumbled into the great hall, blinking at the brightness. Two walls, the front and back, had high windows cut into the thick stone. Streams of sunlight shone through, illuminating the motes of dust circling the ceiling. No fire burned in the massive hearth, and she shivered as the cold from the floor seeped in through her shoes and up her legs.

Under the windows at the far end, on a raised dais, sat two people in high-backed, ornately carved chairs. In one, an older man reclined, wearing a gilded crown and a cloak edged with ermine: King Brenin. He stared off vacantly, out through the glazing opposite his throne, his eyelids half closed. Behind him stood two guards, who seemed about as near to sleep as the king.

In the other chair, where Bronwen imagined the queen should be, sat the most handsome young man she'd ever seen. His hair was the color of gold. Not Gwenna gold but true gold, bright and shimmering with a halo of light from the windows behind him. He wore a smaller crown, and Bronwen assumed him to be Lord Urien, the king's son. He was turned sideways in his chair, speaking to a dark-haired soldier bending down beside him.

When Bronwen stepped to the center of the room, Urien cast her an indifferent glance. He opened his mouth to speak to the soldier again but instead turned and faced her, a look of sudden interest on his face.

Bronwen curtsied almost to the floor, making sure her dress stayed long and low. She rose and stood frozen in place, listening to her pounding heart. Where was the queen? She was to kiss the ring of the queen. No queen was present. Should she approach the dais anyway?

"Have you a name?" the king said in a tired voice.

Right, name first. She swallowed and wiped her sweaty hands on the back of her gown. This was her one moment, and she was muddling it.

"You may approach," the king's son said.

She curtsied again and crossed the stone floor until she stood near the edge of the step. "My name is Bronwen—"

Did she know the soldier conversing with the king's son? He looked familiar, like Rhys, the stable boy, the one who had worked for her family during her illness. Same dark eyes and dark hair. But that was years ago, when she was young. She couldn't be sure.

Their eyes met, and his head dipped. Was that a nod of acknowledgment? The last time she saw him, her legs were twisted and bent. She couldn't let him recognize her, or her secret would be out.

"Just Bronwen?" Lord Urien asked with a trace of amusement. "No family name?"

Bronwen's eyes snapped back to the king's son. "No. I mean, yes." She scrambled to untangle her thoughts. "That is to say, no, not just Bronwen. And yes, I do have a family name." She forced a smile at Urien and wondered why they kept the room so hot.

Urien laughed outright. "And will you tell it?"

She couldn't. If the man was Rhys and she told them her family name was Hardd, he would know her for certain. Her fingers brushed the silver belt around her waist. She made an instant decision.

"Mawr." It was her grandmother's name. "My name is Bronwen Mawr." She rubbed at her neck as she said it and dared a glance at the soldier.

The dark-haired man's brows lifted in surprise. "You're from Glynbach, yes?"

"No," she practically yelled. It was Rhys! He had recognized her. How else would he know her village? But then, did he not remember that she was crippled? He must because he narrowed his eyes and glanced down toward her feet. As long as she kept her deformity hidden, he couldn't know for sure. There had been an edge of uncertainty in his voice. She tugged her skirts lower and, after a steadying breath, added in a cheerful voice, "I'm from a small village to the north. Coed." She scratched at her ear, and a bead of sweat trickled down her back.

"Ah, the forest country," the king said, startling Bronwen. In her fluster, she'd forgotten about him. "I don't recall a family by that name." He grunted and shrugged his shoulders. "Age is no friend to memory," he said, tapping a bony finger on his silver temple.

"My father died years ago," she said. That at least was truth.

This was not going well at all. What had happened to "it will take but a moment?" Quick as a fox. She turned her head, searching for the door.

"As you can see," Lord Urien said with a wide—and, she had to admit, very attractive—grin, "my mother, the queen, is not in attendance. Therefore, in lieu, you may kiss my ring." He stepped down from the dais and stood before Bronwen, holding out his hand and displaying a gold band set with a giant blue sapphire that perfectly matched his eyes.

"Thank you." She curtsied again, wishing to be free of this room before she fainted from lack of air.

She hesitantly took Urien's hand and bent over the ring. But before she could kiss it, his fingers closed on hers, and he lifted her hand. Leaning over, he raised it to his mouth and softly kissed the back of it.

She looked up. He smiled at her, holding her gaze until over his shoulder she saw Rhys rolling his eyes.

"Thank you," she repeated, not sure what else to say. Urien still held her hand—with a grip that felt almost intimate. If all her blood had not already pooled in her feet, she would have blushed scarlet.

Lord Urien chuckled and pointed her toward a door on the side wall. "You may go."

Without a word, and with great effort to avoid Rhys's gaze, she turned and left.

When the door closed behind her, she sagged against the wall, letting out a long, moaning breath. Her head sank into her hands. What had she done? She'd lied to the king. The king! Twice.

And the king's son had kissed her. Was that the custom? Her mother had never mentioned it. But her mother had not had an absent queen or Lord Urien. Had he done that to all the girls? It couldn't have been just her.

She certainly didn't deserve it; she'd not accomplished one thing according to instruction. There was nothing for it now. She'd done it and, with any luck, would never see a single one of them again.

Especially Rhys. Under normal circumstances, she would have been glad of the reunion. But circumstances now were far from normal. She couldn't have a conversation with Rhys about any part of her life, especially in front of the king and Lord Urien—she wore enchanted shoes from a faerie witch to hide her crippled legs, and she'd just lied to them about who she was and where she was from.

She lowered her face into her hands. *By all the saints, what have I done?*

She wanted nothing more than to get out of this castle. She pushed off the cold wall and looked around, finding herself in a hallway lined with doors. At the far end, one stood open, and the merry chatter of girls and mothers drifted out.

"A moment, Bronwen," a voice from behind said.

She spun around and came face-to-face with Rhys.

Chapter Six

A work ill done must be done twice.

"Yes?" Bronwen straightened herself up. She couldn't allow even a glimpse of recognition to show through. Already, she worried he would take her out back and examine her legs. Rhys had never been one to tolerate deceit of any kind. As long as she was in the city, he could never know. If the truth got back to the king . . .

He stood far too close. She took a step back. In the dim hallway, his eyes were solid black. "The king's son sends a message."

"What now?" She hadn't meant to sound so vexed.

He gave her a reproachful look, but Bronwen offered no apology. Her stamina for decorum had been depleted in the throne room, and at this moment, Rhys was the one person she most wished to avoid. She inched her way down the hall, toward the sound of laughter and deliverance.

"Urien requests that you dine with him at the king's table tomorrow for the feast of Calan Mai."

"Me?" She'd blundered her way through the presentation, acting more like a fool than a girl who dined with royalty. She touched the back of her hand, where Urien had kissed it. "Why me?"

Rhys stared at her for a moment, clearly questioning her intelligence. "Well," he said, "I suppose he liked what he saw."

Her mouth fell open. "But I'm—" She nearly forgot herself. She looked down at her gown so Rhys couldn't read her face, but she bent too far, and the tip of a brown shoe poked out. She quickly straightened, tugging her dress low.

The door to the great hall opened, and Gwenna walked out wearing a huge grin. When she noticed Rhys and Bronwen, her steps slowed, and her eyes grew wide. Bronwen shook her head an infinitesimal amount, hoping Gwenna would get her silent message and keep walking.

Rhys, it seemed, cared little for subtlety. He raised his arm and pointed to the open room down the hall. Gwenna obeyed, her curiosity scalding Bronwen the entire way.

When Gwenna passed through the door—her head and gaping eyes the last to disappear—Rhys asked, "Well?"

She had to give an answer. It was a great favor to be asked to dinner by the king's son. Lord Urien had been kind to her, even when she had performed the presentation so ill. But she could not accept, especially with Rhys hanging about. It would take only one misstep for Rhys to know the truth. Rhys had said Urien found her pleasing, but Urien didn't know she was a cripple and unworthy to accompany the king's son. She had to refuse.

"It would be my honor," she said in a miserable voice. How could she say no to the king's son? She wanted to go more than anything. She'd keep her feet hidden and avoid Rhys at all costs.

Rhys gave her a nod. "Someone will call for you. Where are you lodging?"

"At the Fib and Flounder." She took a step toward the doorway at the end of the hall, anxious to be gone. "It's down the main road and then—"

"I know it," he said. She attempted another retreat, and he grasped her arm. Not tightly, just enough to detain her. "You did not tell the king your father's name."

She didn't need reminding of that. Neither was she about to confide it to Rhys. "The king did not ask."

Bronwen curtsied, then turned and escaped into the room where Gwenna waited.

Gwenna hovered one inch inside the door, peeking through the crack in the frame. Before Bronwen could catch her breath, Gwenna seized her hands and asked, "What was that about?"

Bronwen's legs wobbled, and her head spun like she'd just climbed a mountain of stone steps. What was she thinking? She couldn't go to the feast with Lord Urien. This wasn't supposed to happen. It was to be but a moment, no sticky questions, no extra attention.

"Do you know who that man is?" Gwenna asked, apparently deciding this question was of greater importance than the first.

Bronwen nodded and then said mournfully, "Rhys."

Gwenna huffed, and for once, Bronwen decided Gwenna had shown too little reaction. Had Gwenna known the whole truth, she would have behaved like a proper friend and fainted, thus granting Bronwen justification for her churning insides.

But Gwenna did not know, so she said in a patient voice, "He's the captain of the guard. Lord Urien's most important man."

Lovely. That meant Rhys would attend the feast with Urien as well. Captain of the guard was quite an accomplishment. Good for Rhys. But just now, Bronwen couldn't help wishing there was a war far away that he needed to fight. Bandits in the woods he should see to? She shook her head. This would never work out. She pondered the punishment for lying to the king's son. "I'm dead," she said.

Gwenna's eyes widened. "Why? What did he say?"

Before she could answer, Elen found them. "Well? How'd it go?"

Awful. Humiliating. Handsome. Wonderful. She settled for, "Fine." She turned to Gwenna, "And you?"

Gwenna would not be distracted. She pointed at Bronwen. "The captain of the guard spoke to her privately in the corridor. I saw them."

"Hush," Bronwen said. Two more girls came through the door. The king's son must be going through them quickly now. "Something did happen. But here is not the place. Let's leave, and then I'll tell." Once Gwenna found out about the feast, she would likely burst. Best to avoid a scene inside the castle.

Gwenna hurried them out the door. They made their way toward the practice yards, hoping to see how Gwil's attempts at swordsmanship were coming along.

"Well?" Gwenna said when they'd left the scent of lavender water and the rustle of silk gowns behind.

Free of the castle and the immediate threat of discovery, the wonder of it all settled on Bronwen. She straightened up as she said, "Lord Urien, the king's son—"

"Yes, yes. We know who he is," Gwenna said and then got an elbow in the ribs from her mother.

"Has asked me to dine with him at the feast tomorrow night," Bronwen finished.

The two ladies stared at her, stunned looks in their eyes. Gwenna's lips moved, but no words came out—something Bronwen had never witnessed since she'd first met her.

"And"—Bronwen paused for effect—"he kissed my hand." She held it out for examination, and there was a unified intake of breath. Apparently, he hadn't kissed anyone else's. At least, not Gwenna's.

Bronwen turned to Gwenna, who had not yet spoken a word. Bronwen thought Gwenna would be happy for her, but not all girls looked on with a smile while another got attention—especially from the king's son.

When Gwenna at last emerged from her stupor, she screamed, hugging Bronwen while at the same time jumping up and down. Bronwen's head bobbled back and forth. It took a little longer than Bronwen had anticipated, but this was the reaction she didn't want seen by the other girls in the waiting chamber.

Elen's were the eyes that narrowed. Like any mother, she would have wanted the honor for her own daughter.

"This is perfect." Gwenna licked her lips like an eager puppy waiting for a bone. "You'll be in with the royal family, and you can introduce me to all the handsome men. Starting with Rhys."

Oh, yes. Perfect, Bronwen thought.

"And if you marry Lord Urien, I can be your lady in waiting."

For the briefest of moments, Bronwen saw herself seated on the dais beside the handsome Lord Urien. No. One dinner invitation did not a queen make. She'd run too far ahead of herself. Gwenna's outlandish predictions had affected her. She shook her head; such an eventuality could never be. "Gwenna, please."

"I said *if*." Gwenna slipped her arm through Bronwen's, and they set off again, following the sound of clanging swords and jeering men. Elen had other plans involving more fine cloth and trinkets and fewer sweaty and grunting men. She took her leave and walked with some of the other mothers to the market square.

"If you marry him, it won't take long," Gwenna said. "You'll be queen in no time. My father told me the king's mind is slipping. He rarely does anything now to rule the kingdom. Urien practically runs things by himself, even though he's only one and twenty. And when the old man finally dies—may he rest in peace—well, someone new will be the queen."

Bronwen listened to Gwenna's summary of life in the castle until they reached the lists. If the presentation room had been crowded with girls, the practice yards were equally packed with men. Bronwen and Gwenna were vastly outnumbered, and Gwenna was already salivating.

They leaned against the low fence rail and searched for Gwil. A few other girls had also made their way here. They stood out like sparkling gems against the sea of leather and thick, dark wool.

Inside the enclosure, men slashed and hacked at each other with long, gleaming swords in a rhythmic dance. Those not practicing loitered along the perimeter, hounding and heckling the fighters.

Gwil caught Bronwen's eye and made his way toward them, skirting the swinging metal blades. "Ho, there. And how are the king and queen?" he asked, thumping a patch of dust off his tunic. Bronwen coughed and fanned the air.

"Lord Urien invited Bronwen to feast with him tomorrow night," Gwenna blurted out.

Gwil stared at Bronwen for a moment, then nodded with a smile. "Well played."

Bronwen curtsied to him. "You're too kind."

Gwenna snorted. "How's it going here? Did you kill anyone yet?"

Gwil's cheeks flushed, and he looked away.

"Gwil? What did you do?" Gwenna asked.

Gwil pointed to the far corner of the listing yard. A man sat on a three-legged stool, holding a blood-soaked cloth to his head. "It's not as bad as it looks. Head wounds are heavy bleeders."

"At least you beat him though, right?" Bronwen asked, trying to offer some encouragement.

The color in Gwil's cheeks deepened. "Well, I wasn't actually fighting him. We were practicing on the dummies, and he must have walked by too close."

"Anywhere in the country is too close when *you* have a sword in your hand," Gwenna said.

Poor Gwil. He'd never make it into the King's Men at this rate.

A hush fell over the yard. Bronwen turned her head to follow the gaze of the crowd. Lord Urien and Rhys approached. The eyes of the king's son fell on Bronwen.

Chapter Seven

Don't rest your eyes beyond what is your own.

LORD URIEN GREETED VARIOUS PEOPLE as he made his way toward Bronwen. Rhys followed on his heels, eyeing the spectators, wary of trouble.

When Urien finally reached her, Bronwen curtsied. *Do it right this time*, she told herself. *Don't be a fool again.*

"May God prosper you." Bronwen recited the required greeting used for those of higher status. The rules stated that she must speak her part first and then wait for the king's son to say God's welcome. That was the proper response—if he felt so inclined.

She waited with lowered eyes, still bent in her curtsy. Urien was silent. What was taking him so long? She felt Gwil stir impatiently. Perhaps Urien didn't want to speak with her after all. Maybe he had already changed his mind. Even then, how could he disregard her very proper greeting—the only one she'd actually managed to give him? Maybe Rhys had told him something.

She peeked up and saw Lord Urien grinning. Apparently, Rhys thought the joke had gone on long enough because he cleared his throat a little too loudly.

"God's welcome," Lord Urien said at last.

Once again, Rhys rolled his eyes.

Who knew that the heir to the throne was so full of jests? Whatever she had expected of the royal family, it wasn't this. Nor did she ever imagine that she would be speaking to the king's son personally twice in one day.

The men in the listing yard started their maneuvers again, reclaiming the crowd's attention.

"Are you good with a sword?" Urien asked Bronwen.

"Me? N-no, my lord. At least, I don't think so." Bronwen couldn't recall ever holding a sword in her life. Was he teasing again? Why did he always fluster her?

His smile broadened, and his blue eyes burned bright like the sky beyond. "Perhaps another time. I see you are not dressed for sparring today." He eyed her up and down, clearly taking in more than simply her attire.

Bronwen tugged her gown lower. She cast about for something to say but came up empty.

"Are you here alone?" Urien asked, eyeing Gwenna and Gwil. The teasing had left his voice, and he spoke to her in an open, friendly way.

She should've introduced her companions before now. She had forgotten them. "These are my friends." Bronwen made a quick introduction of Gwenna beside her and Gwil on the other side of the rail.

"Your Highness," Gwenna said, curtsying low. "I'm so very pleased to see you again. I enjoyed very much meeting you earlier today. And His Holiness, your father."

Holiness?

Urien and Rhys exchanged amused looks.

Gwenna seemed to have no problem talking to royalty. Without pausing for breath, she prattled on. "It's such a pleasure to be here for the festival of Calan Mai. You have a wonderful city. So many people and cows and things. I've never been here before. My brother, Gwil, comes every year with my father. I told my father he should bring me too sometimes. It's not fair that Gwil can come and not me. But he—my father, not Gwil—says business in the city is for the men, and I can come when I'm sixteen, old enough to present. We met Bronwen at the Inn of the Silver Knife and came on together. So here I am."

"Here you are," Lord Urien said. Before Gwenna could start up again, he turned to Gwil. "I see you are the swordsman."

Gwil gave a quick bow. "Yes, sir. I—"

"He wants to be a King's Man," Gwenna announced. Bronwen wished she hadn't scoffed as she said it.

"Does he, indeed?" Urien said. He gave Rhys a nod, then spoke to Gwil. "Let's see what you've got."

Rhys eyed Urien with a look that clearly said, *You cannot be serious.* The king's son simply smiled. Rhys leapt the fence in one quick, agile bound. The men in the listing yard backed away, giving the arena to the captain of the guard.

For once, Gwil's face did not turn red. It drained completely of color, pale as a milking cow's udder.

Rhys drew his sword from its scabbard with the sound of steel scraping on leather. Gwil gulped and selected a weapon from the few swords leaning against the rails. He stepped to the center of the yard. Gwil held his blade out in front of him, the tip shaking slightly as he faced Rhys. Every eye focused on the two men.

Rhys whooshed his sword around in a fancy pattern, showing off his skills. He looked almost bored.

Bronwen considered Gwil's chances. He would probably be killed.

Or he would kill. Gwil's efforts would never break Rhys's defense. It was the group of onlookers she worried about. What if he sliced open the king's son?

She laid a hand on Urien's arm. "My lord, I don't think this is such a good idea."

Urien looked at her hand. She pulled it away. Rule number one: you didn't touch royalty. As if that weren't enough, she had implied that Urien's command to see Rhys and Gwil spar was a mistake. Rule number two: you didn't second-guess royalty, leastways not to their face. "Your pardon, sir. I meant no disrespect."

Urien didn't seem bothered. He merely laughed. "You needn't worry about my man. He's unbeatable. Why else do you suppose I put up with his gloomy disposition?"

"Sir, it's not for your man that I worry," she said.

Rhys circled Gwil, then stood in front of him. "Come on, then; make your move," Rhys called.

Gwil took a swing at Rhys, but his stroke went wide, disrupting his balance. He stumbled as he tried to right himself. Rhys was perfectly safe.

The scuffling of feet—mostly Gwil's feet—in the dirt was the only sound. Gwil swirled his blade and lunged at Rhys over and over again. A few of Gwil's strikes came close enough to clang against Rhys's sword. Most fell wide, and Rhys had no need to defend at all. Gwenna covered her eyes.

When Gwil swooped his sword around for another set of stabs, Lord Urien grabbed Bronwen and leapt out of the way.

"Perhaps you're right," he said to Bronwen.

Gwil seemed not to have noticed Lord Urien's evasive maneuver.

"Enough," Urien said, and the action ceased.

Gwil used his forearm to wipe the sweat from his brow. Unfortunately, it was the arm that held his sword, and a pair of squire boys dove for cover.

Rhys spat into the dirt, returned his weapon to its sheath, and joined Urien at the fence. He wasn't even breathing hard.

Lord Urien said to Bronwen, "A King's Man?"

"Yes, sir. It is his greatest desire." Bronwen tried to keep the hopelessness out of her voice. After this display of Gwil's pitiful talents, he didn't have a chance.

Urien moved closer and whispered so only she could hear. "Would that please you?"

"Sir?"

Urien offered no clarification. Instead, he turned to Rhys and instructed him to set Gwil up with livery and a weapon.

Gwil looked stunned.

Lord Urien shook Gwil's hand. "Congratulations. The King's Men are honored to have you as one of our own." Then he smiled and bowed at Bronwen. "My lady, I look forward to seeing you tomorrow night."

Lord Urien and Rhys departed in the direction of the castle, Rhys shaking his head as they walked away.

Every face in the crowd stared at her. Gwil staggered a bit, then leaned against the fence. Bronwen looked at Gwenna.

"My lady?" Gwenna's voice filled with awe.

Bronwen shrugged. "Can you believe that?"

Gwenna shook her head. "Can you believe Gwil almost killed the king's son? And still, he admitted him?"

As a matter of fact, the whole incident had Bronwen baffled. It seemed that Lord Urien had received Gwil into the King's Men simply to make Bronwen happy. But that couldn't be true. She was no one of any importance.

Gwil put a foot on the fence rail and scrambled over. He went straight to Bronwen and hugged her so tightly she rose off the ground. When Gwenna smacked him on the back, he released her.

Gwil took Bronwen's hand and kissed it. "My lady," he said in a voice that mimicked Urien's. "I don't know what you did, but I thank you for it."

Bronwen had done nothing. She'd stood there like an oaf, criticizing Urien's orders. If she was to continue an acquaintance with Lord Urien— which she most certainly could not—she needed to pull herself together. No more bumbling over greetings or staring like a frightened fawn every time he spoke to her.

At least it all worked out for Gwil. She offered a silent prayer to Saint Cadoc, giver of wisdom. *Please let Urien know what he is doing by arming Gwil.*

They hurried back to the inn to tell Elen the news.

* * *

Early the next morning, an errand boy came to the Fib and Flounder, bringing Gwil his new livery: a deep red tunic with the emblem of a heavily tusked boar embroidered on the chest.

If Gwil got hurt trying to protect the king's son, it would be Bronwen's fault, though she was unsure what she'd done to bring it about, nor what she could have done to prevent it. Not that she wanted to prevent it. Gwil was the happiest man on earth.

Lord Urien must know what he was doing. After all, he was of royal birth. His golden hair and eyes of summer blue. Tall and strong. That he should favor her, an unknown girl from the mountains—

The forest. She mustn't forget that to the king's family, she was from Coed, in the north, and that her surname was Mawr, not Hardd.

If only she had not been so muddled when she'd chosen her false name. Mawr meant great. Bronwen the Great? Hardly. Wasn't there a name that meant Bronwen the Weak and Useless? Without her enchanted shoes, that's exactly what she was. If she ever took them off, she would return to being the girl whose legs were twisted and bent. Lord Urien wouldn't dream of kissing the hand of that.

If she had any sense, she would leave. Run home and fall into her mother's arms. But how could she say no to the king's son? She would much rather fall into his arms.

Stop! There was no point dreaming about what would never happen. Could never happen. Best to keep that in mind before her dreams carried her away. It was just one dinner, after all.

Bronwen and Gwenna spent the morning meandering through the streets while the city scurried about preparing for the festival. Men stacked wood into large piles for the bonfires. Women cooked and baked. The squawking of chickens and geese being carried by their feet to the chopping block sounded from every direction. Young girls set off into the forest, returning with armfuls of hawthorn blossoms and meadowsweet.

Bronwen slipped her pear-green kirtle on over her chemise, tugging it down to conceal her shoes. Then she layered the blue overdress on top and wrapped her grandmother's silver belt around her waist. It was the only belt she had fit for feasting with the king's son.

She plaited her chestnut hair into a pattern of fish bones and crosses, leaving some strands hanging long to soften her neck. She had no mirror at the inn, so she could only hope she looked presentable. Except her shoes. But they would have to do.

She checked the weather through the window of her room. The cloudless sky showed no signs of rain. Not that she wanted rain, but rain would bring mud, giving her reason enough to wear plain shoes.

There was a quick knock at her door before Gwenna burst in.

"How do I look?" Gwenna spun around fast so her dress swirled up, exposing her beautiful cordovan shoes. She wore a kirtle of pale lavender with a silver overdress. The fabric was not as elaborate as her gold brocade from yesterday, but the color suited Gwenna better, giving her mousy hair a hint of luster.

"It's lovely," Bronwen said.

"I think it becomes me. Mother says the silver silk was imported from Persia, wherever that is. She made it specially for this dress. I don't think it matches my shoes as well, but no one can match every gown to their shoes." She examined her prized slippers for a moment, then said, "You look well. Let me see your shoes."

Bronwen lifted the hem of her dress a hair's width from the floor. It was enough.

"You can't wear your traveling shoes to dine with the king's son. It's unthinkable." Gwenna marched over and rummaged through Bronwen's chest of clothes. When she came up empty-handed, she asked, "Where are your good shoes? You wore them yesterday, didn't you?"

Gwenna never noticed that Bronwen had indeed not worn her better shoes to present herself to the king. Bronwen tugged on a lock of loose hair and cleared her throat. "I only have these. My others must have . . . fallen out of my trunk along the way."

Gwenna looked down at the plain shoes and cringed, appalled, it seemed, by the thought of Bronwen wearing such ordinary footwear before the king. Then she held up her hands. "Wait here." Gwenna disappeared through Bronwen's door, returning a few minutes later holding a pair of green slippers with fashionably pointy toes.

"These are my mother's old shoes. She doesn't mind if you wear them."

They were beautiful. But out of the question. "You are very kind, but I fear they don't match." It was the best excuse Bronwen could come up with.

Gwenna laughed out loud. "Nonsense! Green and green. They are a perfect match. Sit on the bed. I'll help you put them on."

Bronwen backed away. She had to stop Gwenna before she pinned her to the floor and forced the shoes on. "What about the rain? I don't want to ruin your mother's shoes in the mud." She knew her excuse was pitiful the moment she said it.

"There's not a cloud in the sky." Gwenna scowled at her. "Why won't you wear them?"

Bronwen closed her eyes. If Gwenna knew about her crippled limbs, she would be disgusted. It would cost Bronwen her only friend. She could never tell Gwenna the truth about her legs.

At least, not the whole truth but perhaps something closer to the truth. "I have . . . unusual feet. All the shoemakers say they are extremely difficult to fit. Without my own shoes, I can barely walk." She smiled at that one. It was ingenious. "I'll just make do with these until I can get proper replacements. How's Gwil doing?"

It worked. Gwenna shrugged her shoulders and launched into an oratory on Gwil's excitement to be in the King's Men, how ridiculous he looked in such a fancy tunic, and how every soldier in the army was at risk of losing life and limb.

As if on cue, Gwil knocked on the open door and stepped into the room. Bronwen thought he looked rather handsome in the king's livery. He stared at her for an uncomfortable length of time.

Gwenna sighed with exasperation. "Gwil, you are witless. What makes you think she would notice you when the king's son is courting her hand?" Gwenna grabbed her mother's shoes and marched out of the room while Gwil's face burned bright as ever.

Bronwen felt Gwil's pain all the way down to her toes.

Bronwen took his hand. "Don't listen to Gwenna. You look very fine, and no girl will be able to help taking notice of you." She laid a quick kiss on his cheek.

Gwil nodded, seeming pleased. "I came up to tell you that Lord Urien's man is here to take you to the feast."

She looped her hand through the crook of Gwil's arm and let him lead her down the stairs into the common room.

She should have known. Why didn't she see this coming? The man sent to bring her to the feast leaned against the wall, arms folded, wearing perhaps the most smug expression she had ever seen.

Rhys.

Chapter Eight

A wise wolf hides his fangs.

RHYS SHOOK HANDS WITH GWIL, congratulating him again for his fine accomplishment of becoming a King's Man. If he was still irritated at Urien for his erratic decision, he masked it well. But perhaps not as well as he supposed. When he shifted his attention to Bronwen, she had the distinct impression he blamed her for the Gwil situation.

Rhys opened the door to the Fib and Flounder and ushered Bronwen out. This would be a long and tedious walk to the castle with—what word had Urien used?—her gloomy escort. She hoped they could walk in peace. And by peace, she meant silence.

Rhys had different plans. He turned his black eyes on her. "Bronwen Mawr," he said. "Do you know who I am?"

They had passed only two houses, and already this felt like some sort of test. Did Rhys doubt Bronwen was the girl she said she was? She never knew for certain whether or not he recognized her. He seemed to at first, during the presentation, but she hoped the lies and her lack of crippled legs had changed his mind. It had been so many years, and Bronwen had been just a girl.

Rhys had never spoken much about his family or where he came from. As far as Bronwen remembered, he strayed into Glynbach one day, alone and looking for work. Her father hired him when no one else would. Was that what he wanted to hear? A recognition of their past together?

He could never know. If Urien learned the truth, Gwil might be stripped of his title as a King's Man. His family needed that income. Perhaps Bronwen and her mother would be forced to forfeit their land. This was a secret she had to keep. She pulled her skirts low and took small strides in order to prevent her feet from showing.

"You are Lord Urien's captain of the guard," she said at last and because it was common knowledge.

Rhys watched her face carefully. She kept her gaze forward and down. She felt like a traitor. Bronwen and her mother would never have made it through that awful year without Rhys. She should be throwing her arms around him and thanking him. Instead, she bristled with resentment—angry at herself for lying, angry at Rhys for being the one person who could expose her.

Besides, it was not as though he was going out of his way now to be overly kind to her. His temperament had always tended toward serious and brusque until you got to know him. But the two times she'd spoken with him here in the city, he'd bordered on surly and gruff. If that was how he wanted things, then so be it. Especially if it kept him at a distance, away from the truth.

"Yes." He nodded. "I am the captain of the guard. The guard protects the king. And the king's son." After a few more steps, he asked, "What do you think I protect him from?"

He obviously wanted to make a point. Why didn't he skip to it instead of putting her through all these questions? If he knew who she was, she wished he would come out and say it instead of acting like a cat toying with a mouse before he devoured it.

"Invaders from Éire?" she said.

Rhys stopped walking and turned to face her. "From anything that might hurt him. You're hiding something. I know it."

This was what she had dreaded. He did suspect her of being herself. It would have been a relief to admit her deceit and be free. But now Gwil was involved. And the king's son awaited her for dinner. Rhys had made it clear he would safeguard Lord Urien against anything, including liars and cripples in disguise. If he found out now, he'd go straight to Urien.

"I don't know what you mean," she said.

She couldn't tell him the truth. She couldn't give herself away. Nor could she meet his eyes. She carefully examined the timberwork on the house behind him and the small whisps of smoke puffing from the chimney. A white dove cooed on the roof.

"You are from Coed?" he asked.

"Yes, from the forest lands."

"Then why did you meet your friends at the Inn of the Silver Knife? I know that place well. I used to live near the mountains." He kept a watchful gaze on her.

She shored her courage and met his eyes, keeping her breathing steady even though her ears burned and she longed to scratch her throat. He was testing her.

"It is more than a day's journey backward from Coed to the Inn of the Silver Knife," Rhys said.

She swallowed hard. "I was visiting family." In her heart, she begged him not to ask who. She didn't know any families outside her village, and she couldn't name one from Glynbach without giving herself away. Rhys seemed to have a fair knowledge of lands and people. If she said the wrong name, Rhys would pounce.

"Who?" he asked despite her desperate wishing.

"What do you mean, who?"

"What is the name of the relatives you were visiting?"

"They have a name."

His eyebrows went up.

She was such a straw head. If she wanted him to believe her, she had to lie smoother than that. "Farfog. Their name is Farfog." Farfog? She couldn't think of anything better? That was not a common name.

He stared at her for a few moments longer, then took off walking again.

"You must forgive my questions. You remind me very much of someone I once knew." His sudden formality surprised her. Only moments ago, his black eyes had been boring into her, trying to read her soul. Now he spoke as though they discussed nothing of more consequence than the weather.

"Not at all."

"Her name was Bronwen also," he announced as if this statement was his last and final thrust.

"Is that so?" Her eyes were back on the ground. If he saw her face now, he would know for sure.

"Hmm," he said, and his questions ended as suddenly as they'd begun.

They closed the remaining distance in blessed silence. As they approached the courtyard, evidence of the festival unveiled itself. Bronwen had nearly forgotten why she was walking with Rhys toward the castle. Calan Mai, the first day of summer, and a feast with the king's son.

Mounds of wood for the bonfires dotted the grounds, and tables set out in the open air spread across the bailey.

Torches burned along the castle walls, and lanterns glowed on all the tables. The heavy scent of hawthorn flowers filled the air as garlands of them were strewn everywhere. Girls wore circlets of them as crowns around their heads. Hawthorn blossoms were a powerful defense against the faerie folk. Her mother would have been pleased.

"It's beautiful," she said.

"As are you," was Rhys's reply. He grinned, the first real smile she'd seen from him. "Lord Urien awaits." He motioned to the head table, set at the top of the courtyard nearest the keep.

Rhys delivered Bronwen to the king's son. Urien stood as she approached.

She curtsied. "May God prosper you."

"God's welcome," he said without a moment's hesitation. He crowned her head with one of the hawthorn wreaths.

As Rhys turned to leave, Lord Urien called him back. "A word, Rhys."

They stepped aside a pace, but Bronwen overheard bits of what Urien said.

"There's a beggar outside the gate . . . unsightly, crippled . . . a coin and send him away."

Bronwen pulled her skirts low. This was not a good sign. Calan Mai would be the end of it. Just the feast, and nothing more.

Urien put his hand on her back, guiding her to her seat. "You look very well."

She smiled up at him.

The king emerged from the castle keep, and the crowd fell silent, rising to their feet. He came alone, without Urien's mother, the queen, and took his place in the gilded chair beside Urien. When the king was seated, all others did likewise. Bronwen sat in a high-backed chair on Urien's right. Rhys took a seat farther down the table. He must have sent someone else on the errand of the beggar.

She searched the masses and found Gwil, Gwenna, and Elen seated near the castle's main gates. Gwenna waved at Bronwen, flailing her arms as though stopping a runaway horse. Bronwen waved back with one quick motion.

She could not believe she was here, at the king's table, beside Lord Urien. This would forever be the most remarkable day of her life. She closed her eyes and let the sounds and smells burn into her memory.

Servant upon servant poured out of the kitchen, carrying platters and trenchers of food. Roast grouse, stewed eel, and barley lamb—all accompanied with soft, white bread. She sipped from a cup of spiced elderflower wine while a huge wild boar turned on a spit, its juices sizzling as they dripped into the fire.

While everyone ate, musicians played on their harps and sang songs of heroes and saints long dead. Bronwen let the music lift her and carry her away. One song spoke of the mountains to the east and of the elusive lilies that grew there. She'd heard this song many times around her own hearth. It was one of her mother's favorites. She quietly sang along.

"You know this?" Urien asked.

"Yes, my mother sings it." She smiled at him before she realized her mistake. She sent an involuntary glance toward Rhys, who looked at her through dark slits. "She—my mother—is from the mountains," she added quickly. "Before she married my father and moved to Coed. Um, this laver is delicious."

"Do you think so?" Urien reached over and dipped his crust into the small green mound of boiled seaweed on Bronwen's plate, then popped it into his mouth. "I've never much cared for laver. It tastes a bit like blood. Bloody seawater."

Bronwen grimaced. When put like that, it did sound rather unappetizing. "I've never tasted seawater. I've never seen the sea. At least not up close. I saw it on my way to the city. And I can glimpse it from my window at the inn."

Lord Urien laid his hand on Bronwen's shoulder. "Then I shall take you there tonight, after the feast." His eyes glowed. "It will be my honor to be the first to show you the sea."

They ate and talked of the beauty of the day and the mildness of the weather. The king often took Urien's attention as he spoke quietly to his son. Away from his throne in the great hall, the king looked old and frail. Bronwen wanted to ask about the queen, who still had not made an appearance, but she dared not.

When the sun fell below the castle walls, soldiers plunged the torches into the waiting pyres. The flames caught quickly in the dry wood, and soon a blaze from each bonfire burned bright, casting the whole courtyard into light and warmth. True to its reputation, the bonfire in the center of the courtyard could have easily swallowed a house. The servants pulled the tables back to make room for dancing and merriment around the bonfires.

Lord Urien walked with the king amongst the groups. The king seemed to leave it to Urien to carry out the formalities of the feast, rarely speaking or engaging in any kind of interaction with his subjects, save the occasional nod when someone dared address him directly. Bronwen slipped away and ran to Gwenna.

Gwenna kissed both of Bronwen's cheeks before launching into a lengthy discourse on the exceptional merits of the food. They huddled their heads together, recounting the deliciousness of each dish. Bronwen discovered that Gwenna did not get elderflower wine but instead mead spiced with woodruff.

"Lord Urien looks ever so handsome tonight," Gwenna said.

"Yes," Bronwen agreed.

"You promised to introduce me to Rhys, remember?" Gwenna stood on tiptoe and peered through the crowd.

Bronwen remembered making no such promise. Nor would she have. Gwenna knew nothing of Bronwen's lameness or that Rhys had been part of her childhood. Bronwen had laid an intricate groundwork of deception to keep Rhys from finding out her identity, and all it would take was one word from Gwenna about Bronwen's true name or where she came from to ruin everything. Bronwen tried not to think about all the untruths spinning in her head. It made her stomach knot.

She would do her best to keep Gwenna and Rhys from ever becoming friends.

"I fear Rhys is not as kind as he first appears," Bronwen said. Not a complete falsehood, but close. When she was ill, he had been kinder to her than anyone. But here, as captain, he didn't seem the same. "Rhys cares little for the feelings of others. He treats everyone with disdain and has done nothing but glare at me since I first saw him."

Distress crossed Gwenna's face, and she shook her head.

"He was actually quite rude tonight on our way to the castle, and I pray to Saint Cadoc that I never see Rhys again."

"Bronwen," a deep, curt voice said.

She turned to find Rhys standing right at her elbow. The odious, sneaky man. Had he heard what she'd said to Gwenna? Most likely, judging by his clenched jaw.

"Yes?" she answered innocently, as though she hadn't just spent her last breaths berating him.

Rhys glared at her with the same disbelieving yet impertinent look he'd shown Urien at the lists when Urien had made him spar with Gwil. "Lord Urien is looking for you."

Bronwen nudged Gwenna with her elbow. "See. I told you so."

Gwenna sucked in a horrified breath.

Rhys motioned toward the inner court. "This way, my lady."

Bronwen followed him through the crowd, leaving Gwenna standing alone, gaping. Every moment with Rhys put Bronwen that much closer to being discovered. The less time spent with him, the better.

Lord Urien waited for her by a small side gate in the bailey wall. "There you are. I thought perhaps you'd gone home."

Bronwen smiled. "No, my lord."

"I promised you a look at the sea." He smiled at her and offered her his arm. Bronwen rested her hand in the crook of his elbow, and they passed through the door. He smelled deliciously of clove oil, a sweet yet peppery scent that reminded her of cold winter days by the fire. A perfect contrast to his summer-blue eyes and sunshine-yellow hair.

The path to the ocean wound down a steep hill. Bronwen clutched Urien's arm to keep steady on the rugged slope. Away from the bonfires, the landscape was nothing but dark silhouettes of grassy mounds and plump trees.

"Did you enjoy the feast?" Urien asked.

"Very much. Though I wonder . . ." Again, Bronwen wanted to ask about the queen but decided it might be presuming too much.

"Yes?"

"It's nothing, sir."

"Bronwen. You can ask."

It thrilled her to hear him speak her name so softly and gently. "I didn't see the queen. I wondered if she is unwell."

They stepped out onto a pale, glistening plot of sand.

"Thank you for your concern," Urien said. "She is, as you have guessed, ill." He sounded final in his answer, and Bronwen dared not ask more.

The sea spread out before her. The rhythmic lapping of the water replaced the laughter and music from the festival in the courtyard. In the moonlight, it looked like wave after wave of silver making its unhurried way to the shore. The water stretched out until it merged with the darkness of the sky so the heavens could be distinguished only by the stars.

"It's so peaceful," she said, taking a deep breath of salty air.

"This is Farrow Point. My favorite place is a cove farther down the path. The sand is softer, and when the tide is out, you can walk into the empty sea. But this will have to do for tonight." He picked up a pale, moon-shaped shell and gave it to her. Rough ridges covered one side, and the other was like polished bone. She ran her thumb along the shiny surface. She'd never touched anything so smooth in all her life.

"Amazing," she said.

From what she could make out in the dark, most of the coast was rocks and sea grass, with a few tenacious trees scattered along the way.

Faerie folk would be out in legions tonight. They always were on Calan Mai. It was their favorite time of year for mischief. Countless families would wake on the morrow with their lives upturned by misfortune. Bronwen was glad she had her circlet of hawthorn to ward off any spirits. She crossed herself, offering a silent prayer to Saint Morwyn to keep the faerie folk at bay.

Someone—or something—shrieked in the distance, followed by the angry barking of a dog. The cry sounded remarkably like a Gwyllion. But it couldn't be. They never wandered so far from the mountains. Bronwen's skin prickled with the feeling that someone was watching her. She stepped closer to Urien.

"Calan Mai." He laughed. "The Eve of the Faeries. You're not scared, are you?"

"Of course not," she whispered, searching the darkness beyond for the soft glow of an approaching faerie lamp. A few bonfires burned in distant villages among the hills, but that was all.

"Don't worry, I'll keep you safe." He guided her toward the water and sat her on a large rock. "Come, I want to be the first to see you press the sand through your toes and feel the chill of the saltwater. Take off your shoes."

Before Bronwen could recover from the horror of his suggestion, Lord Urien knelt down and reached for her feet. She jumped from the rock and backed away. Had he seen her shoes? She'd been so caught up, she'd forgotten about her shoes. In the dark, he might not have noticed that they were plain and old. But more importantly, and no matter what, she could not remove them.

"I can't."

"Nonsense. I'll help you." He rose and came toward her. Bronwen backed farther away, stumbling as she scrambled to put some distance between herself and the traitorous water. She should never have come to this city. She should have known better than to think she could dine with the king's son and get away with it. If he saw her crumpled legs, he would despise her.

"Sir, please. I can't." She considered running, bolting for the darkness. An encounter with the faerie folk would be more welcome than Lord Urien tugging her shoes off. She wrung her hands together and spun in a circle, looking for someplace to hide.

Hide? What a ridiculous notion. Urien was right in front of her. She couldn't hide. *Saint Cadoc, help me!*

"Bronwen, be easy." Lord Urien came close and gently gripped her shoulders. "It's all right; we don't have to wade. The ocean can be frightening to those who are not accustomed to it."

Frightening. Yes. A brilliant idea. "Thank you, my lord. I'm terrified. Of the water." Her panic from moments ago surely made that easy for him to believe. She put her distress to her advantage. She sniffed and wiped her eyes. "Ever since my brother drowned."

"Drowned?"

"He and I were splashing in the lake near our village. In the forest. We paddled out on a piece of driftwood, but it became waterlogged and couldn't hold us both. He tried to swim to shore. It was too far. I watched him sink into the water and disappear." She sniffed again, proud of her tragic story.

"How horrible!"

"It was a long time ago, but I've been afraid of the water ever since. Very afraid."

"I'm sorry you've had such an unfortunate experience." He put his hand on her chin and lifted it. "You don't need to worry. You will always be safe with me."

"Thank you," she said, looking into his eyes, which had turned the color of indigo in the moonlight.

"Do you know why I asked you to accompany me to the feast?"

"No, sir." Although she couldn't help recollecting it was Rhys who did the actual asking.

He took both of her hands in his and leaned in close, his breath mingling with the salty breeze that brushed her face. His lips touched her cheek. A soft and lingering kiss. Her heart swooped and soared like the swifts dancing across the sky.

He whispered into her ear. "Because you are perfect."

She fell. Pierced by an arrow at the height of her flight. She was not perfect. She was a crippled girl who couldn't resist a golden-haired king. Or at least his son. This had to stop.

"Sir, I—"

"And no more sir this or my lord that. My name is Urien."

"Yes, sir. I—"

"No. Say it. Urien." His mouth was so close to hers she could feel his warmth on her lips.

She sighed and closed her eyes. "Urien."

He cradled her head in his hands and kissed her.

Bronwen was lost. Hopelessly and irrecoverably lost. The moment his lips touched hers, she forgot about Gwyllions and magic shoes and twisted legs. She forgot about dark-eyed strangers who weren't really strangers. It was just her and Urien alone under the midnight sky. A bonfire ignited inside her, and there was not water enough in the world to put it out.

He took her hand, and they started back to the castle, climbing slowly up the hill. She would conceal her secret for as long as she could, savoring every moment she got to spend with him. And when it was over, well, then it was over. She had no idea where this path might lead, but if she could walk it with Urien—even a short ways—it would be worth it.

Who could say? Perhaps if he came to truly love her, he would overlook her imperfection. Until then, she must keep the shoes on.

"Bronwen, what do you say?"

Bronwen gave him a blank look. She hadn't heard a word he'd spoken. "About what?"

"A hunting trip, for all of us." He laughed and shook his head. "What were you thinking about so intently?"

"Oh. I was thinking about . . . how . . . I want to always remember this night."

"This is a perfect night." He squeezed her hand. "I thought maybe you were thinking about shoes."

"Shoes?" Her footsteps faltered. What did he know about her shoes? What if Rhys really had recognized her and told Urien? Or what if Gwil had let slip that she was from Glynbach? Rhys would have figured it out and informed Urien immediately—to protect him. And yet, if Urien already knew she was crippled and still he'd kissed her . . . maybe there was hope after all.

"I can't help but notice that you're always wearing peasant shoes," he said. "Why is that?"

Bronwen thought she glimpsed a hint of his mischievous smile. But she had no way of knowing for certain what Urien knew. No sense giving up her secret prematurely. She was in so deep now she might as well keep digging.

"My good shoes were stolen. From the inn. On the day we arrived."
She rubbed at her neck. "All I have left are these. My traveling shoes." All
her efforts to keep her feet hidden had failed. He'd noticed anyway.

"I'll have Rhys look into it," he said. They stood outside the bailey
door now. The commotion from the courtyard had grown loud and coarse
in the time they'd been gone, the abundance of mead and ale finally taking
effect. "In the meantime," Lord Urien continued, "I'll send my cordwainer
over tomorrow to have you fitted for new ones."

Unless his shoemaker was a faerie witch with the ability to create
enchanted shoes, it wouldn't help. "These are comfortable and fit me
well. I know they're not much to look at, but I'm quite fond of them.
You needn't trouble yourself, sir."

He shook his head. "I'm not sir, remember?"

She grinned, knowing it must make her look like a besotted puppy.
"Urien."

"It's no trouble at all." He gave her another heart-sputtering kiss, soft
and deadly on her lips, then opened the door and ushered Bronwen into
the courtyard. Out of nowhere, Rhys appeared, slipping in through the
door behind them.

Chapter Nine

Those not ruled by the rudder are ruled by the rocks.

HAD RHYS BEEN FOLLOWING THEM this whole time? Watching them together on the beach? He took his guard duties very seriously. Surely Urien wouldn't want Rhys spying on him at such a private moment. Rhys must have been waiting for them here by the castle door. Yet part of her knew Rhys would never waste his time loitering about when he could just as easily be observing.

And listening. What if he heard her talk about her shoes? He might suspect something.

Urien bowed to Bronwen. "I ride south tomorrow on matters of the kingdom and return the following day. I will order our hunting party for the day after that. I shall see you again then." He squeezed her hand, keeping things more formal now that they were back in the public's eye. "Rhys will take you home." He turned and strode toward the castle doors, then disappeared into the keep.

Bronwen stared after him. Heavens! He was handsome. And kind. And he wanted to see her again, to take her hunting—in three days. It was a long time to wait.

"You ready, then?" Rhys asked.

She dreaded facing him again, with his black eyes that saw everything. The one person who could ruin it all.

She glanced around, looking for Gwenna and Gwil. They were nowhere to be seen. Most of the crowd had left now that the barrels of ale had run dry.

Bronwen knew how to find her way home. She had no intention of making the trip with Rhys a second time in one day.

"Sir," she said in a tight voice, hoping to deter him from any more involvement in her life. "You made it perfectly clear how you feel about me. I assure you the feeling is mutual. I know the way. I prefer to go alone."

Rhys glowered at her—a look he had mastered and most likely used to subdue the hardest of criminals. Then he shrugged and walked away.

Bronwen wove her way through the crowd of people, staying as much as possible in the dying light of the bonfires. A few men called out to her, goading her with comments too slurred to understand. They reeked of filth and debasement. Several soldiers stood watch, keeping an eye on the revelers' various states of inebriation.

She left the courtyard and stepped out into the city. It was late, and the roads were dark and deserted. She saw a few people with their heads tucked in, moving quickly on their way, and several stray carousers whose lack of decorum had probably earned them eviction from the castle yard.

She hurried along, rubbing her arms for warmth, threading her way through the narrow streets. She wished now she had brought a cloak or anything to cover her silk dress that marked her as a target for a cutpurse. She rounded a corner and nearly collided head-on with a large, teetering man.

"Well, look at this. Here's a beauty."

A shorter, much thinner man stepped out from behind him. He had been completely concealed by the larger one's girth.

"You're very right. A beauty, indeed." In the blink of an eye, the thin one grabbed Bronwen's arm. "And walking the streets by herself, poor thing."

"Poor, indeed," the wide one answered. "And none too bright. Out alone on Calan Mai."

"Alone, indeed."

Bronwen struggled to free herself, but the small man's grip was surprisingly strong. "D'you know? I think she's in a hurry."

The beastly one chuckled. "Perhaps she's tired and needs a rest."

"Tired, indeed. You're right again. Let's take her in an' give her a rest."

Bronwen pulled harder. "Let me go." His handhold was like a slipknot—the more she fought it, the tighter it squeezed.

"D'you know?" the giant said. "A good long rest might be just what she needs." He stroked her neck with his rough and filthy hand.

"Leave me alone," she tried to yell, but her mouth was too dry for any volume. "If you hurt me, the king's son will come after you," she choked out. She hoped her threat was true. She struggled harder, but the thin man's wiry arm snaked around her waist and pulled her close.

"The king's son, indeed!" the big one said, fingering a lock of her hair. His breath stank of sour ale, and she craned her neck in search of fresh air.

A voice growled from behind her. "Off you go, boys. Leave her be." It was Rhys, once again appearing from nowhere. His lighthearted words did not match his threatening tone.

The men appraised him with his King's Men tunic and his hand on his long, gleaming sword. The broomstick man released his grip, and Bronwen dove into Rhys, clinging to him.

"D'you know?" Tiny said. "I don't think she needs a rest after all."

"No, indeed."

They turned and faded into the shadows.

It took Bronwen a moment to realize she was standing there with her arms wrapped around Rhys. She pushed him away and straightened her dress. She'd never been more relieved to see anyone in her life, even though she wished to high heaven it was Urien—or even Gwil—who had come to her aid. Anyone but Rhys.

Rhys folded his arms and stood in front of her. "Have you changed your mind about the escort home?"

Once, when Bronwen was young and whole, she'd gotten lost in the mountains. When at last they'd found her, her mother hugged her so tightly she'd cried out in pain. In the next moment, her mother yelled at her, shaking her and scolding her for wandering too far.

Now, with her hands clenching into fists, Bronwen at last understood how short the distance was between terror and anger. Why couldn't she be rid of him? Everywhere she turned, he was there, reminding her with his presence that she was nothing more than a crippled girl.

"Were you following me?" she asked. Because if he was, she wanted to slap him for waiting so long.

"Of course I was following you," Rhys said. "This is the worst night of the year for a lady to be out on the streets alone. Lord Urien asked me to see you home. What do you think would happen to me if he learned you'd been murdered under my watch?"

He'd said enough. He was right. She was a fool. As captain of the guard, Rhys did what Urien commanded. He'd come to her rescue, and look how she'd thanked him. Her father would not be proud.

She peered at him and offered an apologetic smile. "Murdered, indeed."

Rhys laughed out loud. "That's just Rowli and Clovis. They're really quite harmless unless they get their hands on free ale."

Rhys stretched out his arm. Bronwen took it, and they walked the rest of the way to the Fib and Flounder in peace.

* * *

"Lord Urien kissed you?" Gwenna's eyes came dangerously close to popping out.

They sat together on Bronwen's bed, recounting their adventures of the night before at the feast. Gwenna had danced with several soldiers Gwil had met from the guard. She seemed particularly taken by Dai, a young man about Gwil's age with—as Gwenna described—feathery brown hair and stormy blue eyes. They must have danced very close to the bonfire for her to glean that much detail.

At least Gwenna wasn't begging to meet Rhys anymore. Even though Bronwen and Rhys seemed to have formed an unspoken truce last night, she had no desire to take that any further.

Gwenna flopped back on the bed and squealed. "I can't believe I'm friends with the future queen! I'm going to live in the castle. I'll be your lady in waiting. We'll go everywhere together. And when you have a passel of plump, straw-haired babies, I'll help you rock them and tend them and teach them all they need to know about courtly manners and keeping up with the modern world."

"Hush." Bronwen laughed. "You are ahead of yourself."

"That's what you said before. But look at you now, favored by Urien, alone with him by the sea. He loves you."

Bronwen shook her head. Even if that was true—and it most certainly wasn't—it wouldn't be the real Bronwen he was in love with. Just this new Bronwen, a momentary Bronwen who wore the magic shoes. Bronwen Mawr. A person who didn't really exist.

There was a knock at her door.

"Come in," Gwenna called.

Gwil stepped in and bowed low, with great decorum. "My lady."

"Not you as well," Bronwen groaned.

"None can deny that Urien is taken with you," he said. "You're famous. Even the innkeeper is charging double for rooms now. He is sure everyone will pay extra to stay in the same inn as the future queen." He walked over to a stool, but as he swung around to sit, his sword knocked it away. Gwil hit the floor with a thud.

"You are hopeless," Gwenna said. "Besides, I thought Mother told you not to wear your sword indoors."

Gwil ignored her. He righted the stool, brushed himself off, and sat down, continuing as though nothing had happened. "You must speak to the innkeeper's wife," he said to Bronwen. "Tell her if she doubles our rent, you'll move out. We can't afford more."

"I'll be sure to mention it," Bronwen said.

"As it is, I came up to tell you there is a craftsman downstairs waiting to fit you with new shoes. Says Lord Urien sent him."

The cordwainer! Bronwen bolted off the bed. She had forgotten. Under no circumstances could she see him. He'd have her shoes off in an instant, and the whole inn would watch her legs wither and bend. How much would the innkeeper charge then?

She needed Gwil to stall the man while she snuck out the back. There was someplace she wanted to go, and fate told her now was the time.

"Gwil, I can't. I have an errand I must do immediately. Tell the shoemaker I am out, that something important came up."

Gwenna stood up. "Lord Urien is giving you new shoes and you're running away? What is wrong with you?"

Bronwen grabbed her two friends by their sleeves and pushed them toward the door. "It's a wonderful gift, I'm sure. But I just remembered I have . . . an important . . . meeting. With . . . the falconer. In preparation for the hunting trip. Give the cordwainer my truest apologies." She nearly shoved them down the stairs.

Gwenna frowned. "What about our plans to go to market at midday?"

"Don't worry, I'll be back before then." She ran through the hall in the opposite direction and hurried down the second staircase. It was closer to a rickety ladder than an actual staircase, used only by the innkeeper's children and servants to move quickly between levels without disturbing the guests. She would have never been able to manage these stairs on her crutch. She cut through the kitchen and out the back door, leaving the cook and the spit boy looking bewildered.

The streets were busy again, full of people going about their daily business. Bronwen blended in easily. Knowing she wouldn't see Urien today, she wore her woolen kirtle and left her hair simple, plaited in one long rope down her back. She headed toward the castle.

Ever since she stood by the sea the night before with Urien, she'd wanted to return. Saints willing, the shore would be deserted. Urien was away, the queen unwell. Perhaps this morning she might at last set her feet in the salty water as she had promised herself she would.

According to Urien, the king's family owned the coast stretching from the castle southward. It would be unlawful to trespass on the king's private land, but she was willing to risk it in order to be alone and unseen.

Bronwen skirted the castle walls and exited the city through the east gate. The guards posted there paid no attention to her leaving Sedd Brenhinol; they only questioned those coming in. She followed the road for a bit, then turned south and headed toward the water.

Soon, she reached the path she had taken with Urien. She went past the first beach, where she and Urien had kissed. She wanted to find the other place, Urien's favorite, that he'd said was farther down the shore.

The path brought her to a small, sandy cove the length of a stable yard. The coast here took a sharp bend, leaving a little protected stretch of land. Large black rocks pockmarked the beach, and clumps of weathered trees and tall marram grass shielded the whole inlet. It was the perfect spot.

The steeply sloping shoreline, aided by the trees, blocked the view of the cove from every angle. A person would have to step onto the sand to find her here. She would take her shoes off and experience sea for herself.

Bronwen wished now she had brought her crutch. It lay wrapped in sackcloth under her mattress at the inn. She hunted through the wooded border until she found two long, straight sticks she could use as canes. Then she sat down in a clump of grass.

"Saint Cenydd, help me stay hidden." She offered her prayer in a whisper.

It had been weeks since she'd taken the shoes off, even sleeping in them every night. She carefully unlatched and removed the Gwyllion's gift from her feet, watching in disgust as her legs withered like the beaten and twisted trees surrounding the cove. She would pay the price for her folly when she put them back on. But this was her only chance to feel the sea.

Last night, Urien had called her perfect. Gwil had been speechless when he'd seen her dressed for the feast. Even Rhys had complimented her looks. Now she was hideous. She'd forgotten over the last few days, walking in her dreamland with the king's son, how truly repulsive she was.

Forgive me, Saint Cadoc, saint of the wise.

Bronwen laid her shoes in a hollow at the base of a tree. She tucked up her skirts so they wouldn't get wet, and leaning heavily on the sticks, she pulled herself up. Checking one last time to make sure she was utterly alone, she hobbled out onto the soft, golden sand.

With every slow and labored step, her feet sank into the tiny grains. The sand coated her feet in warmth from the sun.

The tide was out, exposing—as Lord Urien had said—a large portion of seabed. She wandered amongst the rocks, finding little pale crabs scuttling sideways along the beach. She made her way to the water's edge. The sand here was hard, wet, and cold. She dug her feet in, enjoying the way it molded to the shape of her feet. She turned and looked behind.

A wavy trail of oddly shaped markings led back to the trees: her footprints—two holes from her stick canes, one stunted half print, and an almost normal impression of her stronger right leg. After she had her shoes back on, she would wipe those out with a branch.

At last, she reached the sea. She watched for a long time as the swells came in, rising with a bold display of strength, then folding in on themselves at the last moment before finally hitting the beach. She stood in the surf, leaning on her canes as each wave buried her feet deeper and deeper into the sand. Gulls flew overhead, calling to each other, and curlews waded along the grassy shore, snatching up crabs.

This was worth it. Whatever pain came after, right then was worth it.

The sun warmed her face while the water chilled her feet. Hers was a life of opposites. Hot or cold. Beautiful or revolting. Loved or despised. Only here, alone in this hidden cove, with one part in the water and one part in the sky, could she feel both at the same time.

She shuffled over to one of the larger rocks. Pushing herself off with her canes, she managed to scramble up to the top. Endless time and the constant scouring of waves had left the surface polished and smooth. She lay back with her arms out wide, welcoming the advent of summer, which she had celebrated last night in the arms of Urien. She closed her eyes and let her breathing relax.

A surge of cold water wet her back. Her eyes flung open.

She had fallen asleep. The warmth of the sun and the rhythmic rushing of the waves had lulled her into peaceful slumber. She looked at the sky. The sun had traveled far; she'd been here for hours. Now the tide was in, bringing with it a turn in the weather. Heavy clouds gathered overhead, and a fierce wind bit at her cheeks and whipped her hair.

Water surrounded her stone. It churned and heaved, lapping up and reaching for her. The stick canes were gone, turned into driftwood and probably floating out to sea.

Despite her imaginative lie to Urien, Bronwen did not know how to swim. Her mother had never let her into the water for fear of Anfang, the demon wolf that lived below the surface, waiting to grab both man and beast.

She crossed herself. *Saint Morwyn, save me from the creatures beneath.*

Perhaps she should wait for the tide to recede—unless the water was still rising. Already, it seemed higher than moments ago, soaking her skirts and weighing her down. If she managed to paddle toward shore just a little, she might touch ground. Even with her crippled legs, she could crawl to dry land.

The water swirled around her, wave after wave crashing against the stone, which sank lower and lower into the swells. She scooted to the edge of the rock and hung her legs over, testing. The surge of the tide almost pulled her off and flung her out to sea.

If she lowered herself into this, she was dead. There need not be an Anfang prowling below the waves; this water had power enough to suck her down to an eternal rest in the angry sea.

Chapter Ten

Never ask a fox to mind the hens.

"Bronwen!" someone called from the shore.

If Lord Urien emerged from the trees, she would throw herself into the water. She would never let him find her like this.

It wasn't Urien who stepped out onto the sand. It was Rhys.

He jogged to the edge of the water, took off his sword belt, boots, tunic, and undershirt and tossed them aside into the grass. He waded into the waves until the water pummeled his chest, then he dove into the surf.

Bronwen tucked her feet up and covered them with her skirts. She held down the cloth to prevent the waves from pushing it up. If she could keep her crooked legs hidden, she might still have a chance. Although she would never be foolish enough to remove her shoes again.

Rhys fought the heavy waves until he reached Bronwen's rock.

"Can you swim?" he called over the roar of the sea.

Bronwen shook her head. "No."

"Give me your hand," he yelled.

She reached out, and Rhys snatched at her, pulling her off the rock and into the salty deep. He twisted her so his arm wrapped around her waist, her back pressed against his body. With remarkable strength, he pushed off the rock and towed her toward the shore. It was a long ways away. They would never make it. Bronwen struggled to keep her head above the waves, choking and gagging on seawater. When Rhys could touch down, he walked, still dragging her along behind him.

They reached dry ground. Rhys set her on the sand. Bronwen pulled her legs up and flung her skirts out over her mangled limbs before he could see them.

Rhys collapsed onto his knees, breathing hard. "You," he said between huffs, "are more trouble than you are worth."

If only he knew how true that was.

Bronwen coughed and gasped. "How did you find me?"

Besides the crippling sickness, this was the closest she'd ever come to death. And now that it was over, the fear settled into her bones. Her folly had nearly cost her her life; she'd been moments from being pulled into the sea and drowned.

Rhys wiped his hair from his face. "Urien postponed his trip to the south until week's end. He sent me to the Fib and Flounder to collect you." He sat back on his heels, his breathing steadying. "You weren't there. Your friends were worried. We've been combing the city looking for you."

Did that include Lord Urien? What if he suddenly showed up here, on the beach? "Is Urien out searching also?" Her eyes darted to the hollow tree that concealed her shoes. She had to get them on before Urien found her. But she could hardly start scooting across the sand with Rhys still there.

"At this moment, he doesn't know you are missing. And I assure you that when I return, I'll have the devil to pay for taking so long. So get your shoes, and let's be off." He stood and dusted the sand that clung to his legs.

"How did you know I was here?" she asked, still astonished at his miraculous appearance.

Rhys slipped his linen undershirt on over his bare chest, then sat down on a grassy mound and started working on his boots. "Well, if you must know, when you seemed to have vanished, I decided to pay a visit to your good friends Rowli and Clovis. I thought maybe they didn't sober up as quickly as they should. Before I reached them, an old hag dressed in grey rags stopped me in the street. She said she'd seen a pretty girl with long, chestnut hair in the forest outside the eastern gate."

"Was it a Gwyllion?" She whispered the word. This hag sounded a lot like the Gwyllion. Impossible. Gwyllions belonged to the mountains, creatures of darkness and night. She wouldn't be wandering through the city in the middle of day. "Did she have grey eyes with swirling mist inside them?"

"A Gwyllion?" He shook his head. "I don't believe in such superstitious nonsense."

He never had. When Bronwen's mother had instructed Rhys to take special care of the goat—because goats were friends with the faerie folk— Rhys had dutifully combed the billy's beard every Saturday night, but it was clear even to young Bronwen that he considered it an absurd waste of time.

Rhys went on. "That's when I realized you'd gone back to the beach."

The way he said it, with a glint in his eye, he knew what had happened last night on the sand—when Urien had kissed her. He probably had been watching, keeping a weather-eye on Lord Urien.

She should not be so hard on Rhys for his sense of duty. Especially since this time it had saved her life. If only it had been Gwil instead.

"When I didn't see you at Farrow Point, I came here, to the cove." He strapped his sword belt around his waist. "It goes without saying that you have an uncanny knack for trouble."

Bronwen hadn't moved from the spot where he'd dropped her. Her legs were curled up under her skirts, her shoes still trapped on the far side of the cove. She had to get rid of Rhys quickly if she wanted any chance of getting out of this situation undiscovered.

"Thank you for saving me. Again." she said. "But I don't want Urien to worry. You should go ahead and tell him I'm on my way."

Rhys spun around and stared at her. Nothing got past this captain of the guard. "Where are your shoes?"

"Um, I left them by a tree. Over there." She pointed, expecting him to go retrieve them for her.

He stood there, staring and staring. "What are you hiding?"

"Nothing. I just hate to keep Lord Urien waiting."

As she spoke, Rhys took two steps toward her and flipped up the hem of her dress.

She jerked it down. "How dare you!" But he had already seen.

He locked his black eyes on her and glared until Bronwen had to turn away. His look told all. He knew exactly who she was. "Bronwen Hardd."

He paced away several strides, dug his heels into the sand, turned, and paced back. With an accusing finger pointed right in her face, he opened his mouth to speak. Then closed it again and paced away.

He returned, stone-faced. "You are a fool."

Bronwen said nothing. What was there to say? With that one glimpse at her withered legs, he understood everything. She was the girl he'd watched become crippled. The girl he'd carried up and down her house stairs. And now she was walking and dancing and embracing the king's son.

He drew his sword, and momentarily, Bronwen thought her punishment had arrived. He strode over to a large clump of marram grass and whacked it off at its base. He slammed his blade back into its sheath. The wind picked up the severed stems and swirled them out to sea.

She brought her hand to her throat. Bronwen had no doubt he wanted to do the same to her neck.

Rhys planted himself in front of her. "I knew it was you. I knew it!" His words barely escaped his clenched teeth. "Show me how this is possible."

Should she show him her magic shoes? In his temper, he might hack at them too. She had to put them on eventually, and he probably wouldn't leave until she had.

"Fine." Bronwen rolled onto her hands and knees and crawled toward the tree.

She'd only gone a few yards when Rhys said, "Stop." His voice was quieter. No longer seething. "You don't have to crawl." He picked her up off the sand; her dress was heavy with water. "Where are we going?"

Bronwen pointed. "Over there by that smaller tree."

He carried her to the wooded border and set her down. She lifted the magic shoes from the tree's hollow. This was the part she'd been dreading. Her moment in the sun had not been worth it. Not anymore. If she'd just kept them on her feet, she would not now be demonstrating to Rhys the horrors of her life.

Rhys. Troublesome man, but she owed him her life. Opposites again. Hot and cold. Love and hate. Not that she hated Rhys, not really. He had saved her again, but now he knew her secret. She did not doubt he would tell Urien. He'd made a point of warning Bronwen that he wouldn't tolerate anything that might threaten the king's son. She couldn't imagine anyone being less of a threat than herself.

"What are those?" he asked, gesturing at the shoes.

She gave them to him. "A fortnight ago, on my sixteenth birthday, my mother and I were visited by a—" Bronwen paused and glanced around. She leaned in and whispered, "Gwyllion." At Rhys's look of disbelief, she quickly added, "I know you think it's nonsense, but I'm telling you the truth." She had practically forgotten what that felt like—truth. "We were scared to death that she meant us harm. Instead, she left me these shoes. When they are on, my legs are healed."

Rhys handed her the shoes. Even though he'd seen her walking around for several days now, it seemed he still wanted proof.

She took a few deep breaths, preparing herself for what she knew would come. She latched one shoe on and then the other. It took only a moment before she rolled on the ground in agony, purging her stomach into the weeds. She cried out, her legs burning as though buried in white-hot coals. Her vision turned black.

"Bronwen?" Rhys shook her. "Bron!"

She opened her eyes and wiped the sheen of sweat from her brow.

"You fainted." He was kneeling on the sand, holding her head and breathing hard again. "For a moment there, I thought you were gone."

Her legs were straight now, strong and true. She must have been out longer than last time for Rhys to think her dead. The pain had been worse. Much worse. At this rate, she might not survive putting on the enchanted shoes many more times.

She stood up and made a vigorous attempt at removing the sand that now completely covered her damp clothing. The wind blew hard, whisking the grains up into her face. "Sorry to disappoint you, but I'm still here."

He shook his head. "Oh, I'm not disappointed. Saves me the trouble of riding out to tell your mother."

There was no reason to linger here; she wanted away. It was done. Rhys knew it all. "I thank you again for the rescue," she said. "Shall we go?"

"No. No, we shall not go."

Bronwen sensed he was working himself up again.

"Don't you think you owe me an explanation?"

She lifted her skirt and displayed her shoes, then pointed to the splash of sick slowly melting into the sand. "You have already seen. There is nothing more to say."

"Where did you get these?" He squatted down and ran a finger along the worn leather.

"I told you, a Grey Maiden."

He gave her a skeptical look. "And you just put them on and your legs are fixed?"

"As you see."

"Is it always like this?" he asked, flicking his eyes to where she had recently been writhing on the ground.

Bronwen nodded. "If you mean the unimaginable pain, the vomiting, and the fainting, then yes. Always."

"Who knows about this?"

"Only my mother. And now you."

"Lord Urien doesn't know." It wasn't a question; it was a statement, and Rhys didn't sound happy about it.

"'Course not. He would hate me." She looked down at the sandy tree roots. She could never tell Urien.

Rhys was angry again. He ran his hands through his black hair. "You are a fool, Bronwen. A fool. I recognized you from the start—you look exactly the same." He waved at her lower half. "Except for the walking bit. That was the part that made me question."

"Rhys, I'm sorry I didn't tell you. I couldn't let the king find out."

"So you lied to the king and Lord Urien?" he yelled. "Why, Bron? Why would you do that? What are you up to?"

"Nothing, I swear," she shouted back. "Do you think I planned this? Do you think I got a second chance at a normal life and thought, well then, I'm going to see if I can deceive the king's son?"

Rhys kicked up a cloud of sand before bending over and snatching up his tunic.

Bronwen let out a long breath of air. "After I showed her the shoes, Mother suggested I come to the city for Calan Mai and to present. It was my only chance to see something of the world. I didn't know Urien would be there; I expected the king and queen. I thought I would do my presentation and never see either of them again."

That had been her plan. Quick as a fox and then on with the rest of her life. But Lord Urien had smiled at her and held her hand. He had made Gwil a King's Man—for her. He had shown her the ocean. Kissed her in the moonlight. "I didn't know it would go so far. I never imagined he would even notice me. Please don't tell him. Promise me you won't tell him."

Rhys hadn't stood still since he first glimpsed her legs. He turned on her and shook his wadded, sandy tunic in her face. "And why would I make such a promise? I am the captain of the guard. I have a sworn duty to the king's son, and you want me to lie to him?"

"I'm begging you. Don't tell." If she could stall Rhys long enough, things might still work out. How, though, she had no idea. "I'll tell him, I promise. Just give me some time. It's my deformity; I will tell him."

"Bronwen, you're not . . . deformed."

She looked at him, into his dark eyes.

"Do you understand what you are asking of me? If Urien finds out that I know, I will lose my position, my men, everything I have worked for. Everything."

She took his hand. "Please. If you won't do it for me, do it for my father."

He took up his pacing again. The wind howled off the sea and through the trees. The waves crashed into the rocks, spraying salty mist into the air. Rhys rubbed his hands over his face.

"I'll keep your secret," he said at last. "For one week. And not a moment longer. If you haven't told him by then, you must promise me you will go home."

"Home? But what if—"

"Those are my terms. Take it or leave it."

One week? That wasn't much time. "Fine. I suppose." It was better than nothing. And by nothing, she meant Rhys running to the king's son and revealing everything this very moment. Which she had no guarantee that he wouldn't still do.

"Do you swear by Saint Cadoc?" she asked, counting on the saint of wisdom to keep Rhys at his promise.

Rhys smiled for the first time since he'd entered the cove. "You're just like your mother, with all her saints and faeries. I said I wouldn't. My word is my word."

She would hold Rhys to his promise. And no doubt he would hold Bronwen to hers. All in all, this wasn't such a bad arrangement. She had one week to prepare Urien for the truth. And if that didn't work out, well, worse things could happen than going home. "Thank you," she said.

Rhys just shook his head. He did not seem happy with this plan, even though he was the one who had come up with it. "Let's go before they send out a search party to find the search party." He shook out his tunic and slipped it on, adjusting his sword belt accordingly. "This will not end well," he muttered.

They started up the path that climbed out of the inlet. The hunting trip was coming up. Perhaps that would be a good time to speak to Lord Urien. Except the outing included many people, giving her and Urien little chance for privacy. Not during the hunting party, then, but soon. Very soon.

And what would happen after he knew? It wasn't hard to guess. The beautiful king's son would likely dismiss her. Send her away like he had the crippled beggar. What had he called him? Unsightly? Or was it unbearable? Either way, her future was doomed. She should never have let this go for so long.

The wind whipped her dress and pulled her hair from its braid. She could not have kept her skirts down to hide her shoes for anything. She shivered from the cold. When they approached the city walls, Bronwen tried to cut north through the woods to enter by way of the east gate.

"Oh, no," Rhys said, pulling her back onto the castle path. "Lord Urien is waiting for you."

She couldn't see Urien now. She was a mess. Wet, tangled hair, gritty with sand and sticky with sea. "I can't. Look at me. I cannot meet him when I look like this."

"Look like what?"

It wasn't Rhys who spoke.

Bronwen spun around. Urien walked toward them, his red cloak flapping out behind him in the heavy breeze.

Chapter Eleven

You'll never plow a field by turning it over in your mind.

"My lord." Bronwen curtsied low, pulling her dress down, though the effort was futile with the wind. "I beg your pardon."

"Pardon for what?" Lord Urien took her hand and lifted her from her bow. He spoke with his usual, pleasant tone, only half serious. "What unspeakable thing have you done now?"

Rhys glanced at her. He knew exactly the unspeakable thing she had done. By the look in his eye, he wanted her to spout it right then and there.

She couldn't. She needed time to think, to prepare. She couldn't just blurt out to the king's son that she was secretly a cripple who could only walk because of faerie shoes. She must choose her moment with care.

Urien turned to Rhys. "What has happened? What took you so long?"

Rhys cleared his throat as though to speak, but Bronwen answered first—cutting him off in case he changed his mind about keeping quiet. "Sir, I thought you were gone for the day. I got lost in the woods."

Rhys cleared his throat again, harder this time.

He was right. Why would she say woods when she was still damp and covered with sand? Her confrontation with Rhys had thrown her off.

"That is to say, I walked through the woods until I found the path you showed me last night." Bronwen kept her head down in an attempt to conceal her disheveled condition, though nothing could stop the wind's twisting her hair into a crow's nest. "I'm very sorry. I know that land belongs to the king, but I wanted to see the ocean again. I fell asleep, and the tide came in."

At least that much of the story was true, but that was as far as she would tell. What happened now was up to Rhys.

He might tell Urien everything. *Please, Saint Cadoc*, she pleaded, *let him keep his promise*. She looked at Rhys, begging him to be true to his word.

Rhys stared at Bronwen for a long time. Finally, he shook his head and said, "It took me some time to find her."

Rhys was getting angry again. Or still was. He hadn't really calmed down since he towed her in from the sea and saw her legs. His hand gripped his sword hilt, and Bronwen feared for the shrubbery.

Urien reached out to Bronwen. With his soft and gentle hands, he lifted her face and brushed the sand from her cheeks, forehead, and lips. She closed her eyes. He smelled of cloves again, sweet and peppery. The wind wrapped his warmth around her, encasing her in his heady and enticing scent.

"You are welcome to our shores anytime. You must have been frightened to death after your brother's drowning."

She didn't look at Rhys, but she heard him groan.

"Yes. I was terrified."

Urien took off his cloak and draped it across Bronwen's shoulders. "Now, let's get you warmed. Your teeth are chattering."

"Sir, I must get home. I'm a dreadful sight."

He tsked her. "Do not call me sir. And you look . . . quite bewitching all windblown and wild. That must have been some tide. I find myself wishing we were back at the shore, alone under the moonlight."

Bronwen was beginning to wish the same thing. How was it that this man could turn her heart into mush? He had some secret ability to send her flying. The hard part was coming down.

He placed his arm across her shoulders and pulled her close, leading her toward the familiar gate in the bailey wall.

She glanced over her shoulder to see if Rhys followed. He was nowhere to be seen.

* * *

Urien dragged a chair closer to the fire for Bronwen. She had protested the whole way into the castle, but Urien would not be denied. Now they were alone in the solar. She'd never dreamed she'd be here, in the royal family's private sitting chamber on the top floor of the keep.

When they'd first entered the castle, Lord Urien had called for a warm bath. Thank Saint Cenydd she'd managed to talk him out of it. She'd said it would be highly inappropriate for her to bathe in the house of the king's son. Urien had relented and, in the end, commended her on her propriety. Narrow escape.

Bronwen did submit to letting a housemaid take her dirty clothes away and comb through her hair. Whipped dry by the wind and pebbled with sand, her hair submitted only mildly to the combing. The maid had produced a gown from somewhere, and Bronwen had slipped it over her head, cinching the large waist tight with a woolen sash. It was not ideal, but it was an improvement.

Urien seated himself on a chair he'd placed beside her. He made a point of looking at her feet. "When are your new shoes ready?"

The shoes! She'd forgotten. She tucked her feet up under the mound of extra fabric that pooled on the floor. "I didn't see the cordwainer."

"He didn't come? I gave specific instructions that he was to be at the inn first thing in the morning." Urien seemed perplexed.

"I did not see him," she repeated.

The thought crossed her mind that they were alone together and this might be an opportune moment to tell him of her hideous secret. Other than the evening on the beach, this was only their second time without an audience. The first, actually, if she included spying Rhys. All she had to do was tell him; she need not remove the shoes to demonstrate. He wouldn't ask for that, would he?

If she made it sound less repugnant than it was . . . My lord, you should know I have a bit of a limp. That's why I wear these shoes; they seem to help it go away. Wouldn't that be enough? She might not need to explain more. Except that she had lied about her name. And her village. And she really couldn't remember what else.

The door to the solar opened, and a tall, graceful woman entered.

Urien jumped up. "Mother?"

Bronwen leapt from her chair, sinking nearly to the floor in a curtsy. The queen! Should she say something? Dare she even look up? She kept her head lowered, barely raising her eyes enough to check Urien's reaction.

He took his mother by the hand and turned her back toward the door. "You look . . . Are you sure you want to be here?"

She pulled her hand away. "Nonsense. It's fine. I wanted to meet this girl you've been talking about."

Urien had told his mother about her? And now the queen had come in specifically to meet Bronwen. Bronwen slowly straightened. When she looked the queen full in the face, she faltered, praying the queen had not heard her little gasp. A small red burn marked the left side of the queen's face, wrinkling her cheek and tugging that side of her mouth into a small but permanent grin. Other than that, the queen's beauty was beyond compare, with her translucent skin, stunning blue eyes, and soft features. She looked like a dream in her flowing silver robes and deep sapphire mantle.

"You must be Bronwen," the queen said.

Bronwen quickly dipped her head, pulling her eyes away. "Your Majesty." She was not prepared for a meeting with the queen. What was she supposed to do? Would now be the time to kiss her ring? Or should she leave? After all, she was not part of the royal family, and she'd been caught conversing with the queen's son in their private room.

Behind the queen's back, Urien mouthed the words "I'm sorry" to Bronwen.

The queen lowered herself into a chair. "My son speaks very highly of your beauty." She tugged her wimple forward, concealing part of the scar.

Bronwen turned again to Urien, shocked that he would mention her existence at all to his mother. There was nothing for Urien to be sorry about. It was the queen's house. She had every right to be there. Bronwen was the one who didn't belong. She fanned out her dress to keep her shoes covered. Thankfully, she had managed a respectable braid in her gritty hair.

"You are very kind," Bronwen said. It would be harder now than ever to tell Urien the truth. Her lie had already spread from him to his mother.

The queen had the same summer-blue eyes as her son. A soft white veil covered her head, concealing her hair. Judging by what Bronwen could see of her light eyebrows and lashes, she guessed the queen was responsible for Urien's fair coloring as well.

Urien and Bronwen sat on the cushioned bench.

Bronwen had no idea what to say, but no one else picked up the conversation. If only Gwenna were here. She could talk to anyone about any subject without pausing for breath. Remembering that the queen had been ill last night and hadn't attended the feast, Bronwen said, "I hope you are feeling better."

"Better?" The queen looked at Urien.

Urien nodded. "We missed you at Calan Mai," he offered for explanation.

"Ah," the queen said. "I'm not unwell. I had an accident some weeks ago with an incompetent serving girl and the curling tongs. I think it best I not appear in public while so disfigured."

Disfigured? Even with the burn, the queen was the most beautiful woman Bronwen had ever seen. Such a small thing mattered not. She was the queen. Some women would burn themselves on purpose simply for the honor of looking like her. Bronwen would have traded disfigurements any day.

"Tell me about your family," the queen said. "Urien tells me your father is dead."

Bronwen recounted her situation. "Yes, he died many years ago. My mother and I live alone. We have a small manor, but we manage all right." These seemed like tiresome questions. Bronwen didn't want to bore the queen. Or make her think Bronwen was destitute.

"Do you have brothers or sisters?"

"I did. My brother and sister both died of the same illness as my father. I nearly died as well, but thank Saint Calon, I survived."

The queen nodded. "And what illness was that?"

Well, Bronwen could slip off her shoes and show her. Or lie. "It was the fever, my lady."

Urien gave her hand a gentle squeeze. "I thought your brother drowned."

Curse that stupid brother. She always forgot about him. "Yes, before the illness. I meant only the brother that died when my father did. I had two. Brothers." She smiled at the queen and hoped her face was a nice mix of sadness and regret.

"That must have been a very difficult childhood. I hope your mother is well?"

"She is, thank you."

The queen asked a few more questions, and Bronwen did her best to answer them truthfully. Eventually, the queen rose and excused herself, slipping out a rear door.

Urien squeezed her hand again. "I'm so sorry about that. She should not have come in here and made you so uncomfortable."

Truth be told, the queen had been kind. But still, she was the queen. To be at ease around her was something Bronwen thought very few could manage.

Urien leaned close and whispered, "I told her she should keep herself away until she didn't look so . . . marked."

Was that why Urien felt bad, because his mother had a burn? "My lord, your mother is exquisite. No one could rival her beauty."

"Except perhaps you."

Bronwen lowered her eyes. If Urien thought his mother unsuitably marred, he would consider Bronwen an aberration. Now was not the time to tell him. Perhaps after the hunt. If she had a whole week, she might as well wait until the end.

She changed the subject. "I never thanked you properly for helping my friend Gwil."

"Gwil?"

"Yes, the, uh, swordsman the other day?"

Urien laughed. "He seems very determined. I believe it will be some time before Rhys forgives me. But your friend is young. There is time for improvement."

Bronwen laughed. "A lot of improvement. Let's just hope the other King's Men survive his training."

She talked for a long time about her friends and her journey here. Urien listened and nodded and asked questions and was generally perfect in every way. She found herself grinning like Cupid's fool.

He walked her to the chamber door. "I'll see you again day after tomorrow for the hunting trip. Rhys will come fetch you and your two friends at first light. Dress warmly."

She nodded and curtsied. "Thank you, sir."

He shook his head. "How often must I ask you to call me Urien?"

He didn't give her a chance to answer. Instead, he kissed her.

Was it normal for her heart to float like this every time he touched her? She didn't know. Nothing like this had ever happened to her before. All she knew was that Lord Urien's touch warmed her like nothing before.

When Lord Urien opened the door, Bronwen expected to see Rhys waiting to walk her home. He wasn't. Another man stood at attention.

"Where's Rhys?" Urien asked. He didn't seem pleased with the change of guard.

The young soldier quickly bowed before Urien. "He had other business that needed seeing to."

Urien considered for a moment. "Very well, Dai. See to it that Bronwen gets home."

Dai? The boy Gwenna had fallen all over herself about? This would be an interesting walk home. Maybe if Bronwen asked the right questions, she could get something sweet out of him to tell Gwenna.

Unfortunately for Bronwen, Dai turned out to be a man of very few words. Her walk home was awkwardly silent. On the other hand, that might make him the perfect match for Gwenna, who had opinions and conversation to spare.

The evening was dark, and Bronwen was happy to have an escort, especially when they passed the alley Rowli and Clovis haunted. When they reached the Fib and Flounder, Dai waited only long enough to see Bronwen through the front door.

She climbed the stairs and found Gwenna waiting for her in her room.

"Where have you been? We waited for you to go to market, but you never came back. You missed the musicians in the square. They had the most wonderful juggler. We thought you were dead. We looked and looked until my feet ached. Even Rhys came searching for you. Gwil's been all over the city until he happened upon Rhys outside the castle gate and he said you were with Urien. Again. What in heaven's name are you wearing? You look terrible. Your hair! Have you been rolling in the sand?"

Bronwen did not look forward to giving Gwenna a full explanation of how her day had passed. She skipped over the water and Rhys and even meeting the queen. She went instead to the part that would take Gwenna's mind far away from Bronwen and Lord Urien.

"You'll never guess who walked me home," Bronwen said.

"It wasn't Urien, was it? He must love you very much indeed to bring you home himself. He must—"

"Gwenna. It was Dai."

It worked. "Why didn't you invite him in? He could have come in for a drink. He might have been hungry. Did he say anything about me? Did you talk about me at all?"

Bronwen answered most of Gwenna's questions—when she was able to get a word in. Then she shooed her out of her room and called for a bath. It took some time to remove all the sand, especially because she kept her faerie-shod feet carefully out of the water.

* * *

Gwil knocked on her door while it was still dark. "Bronwen, time to get up."

She rolled out of bed, stumbled to the water basin, and tried to wash the sleep from her face. It was the day of the hunt.

Yesterday had been slow. She'd waited at the inn, hoping a soldier would fetch her and take her to the castle. None had come. The only visitor who did come was the shoemaker. Bronwen had convinced Gwenna to send him away again but only after promising to speak very highly of her to Dai. Dai was to be part of the hunting group, and Gwenna had spent three quarters of yesterday afternoon fussing with her hair and wardrobe.

Hopefully the cordwainer had gotten the hint and would never return. And even more hopefully, he wouldn't complain to Lord Urien about her. If the cordwainer showed up day after day, Bronwen would have to find a new inn.

The morning was crisp and chilly. She dressed in a warm, woolen kirtle and a green overdress for the hunt. Her mother had always been fond of this garment because it brought out the green in her eyes. She lifted a cloak out of her trunk and clasped it under her chin with a silver brooch.

Gwil knocked again. "Lord Urien's man is here. Are you ready?"

She opened the door. "Yes."

Bronwen had never been hunting before. Last night, when Bronwen expressed concern that she might have to kill something, Gwil explained that the women came only for entertainment and the men did the hunting and killing. Gwil was excited beyond expression.

Gwenna waited outside Bronwen's room. They went downstairs together. Bronwen expected to see Rhys waiting by the inn's front door. Thankfully, it was a different man, one she had never seen before. The last thing she needed so early in the morning was Rhys glaring at her, wondering if she'd told Lord Urien yet. With Gwil there, they didn't need an escort anyway. Unless it was to protect them from Gwil, should he try to use his sword.

They hurried to the castle and were ushered into the courtyard. A group of men busied themselves checking saddles on various horses and inspecting the weapons. Hunting hounds pranced about, sniffing the ground and air with their ears perked forward, keen to every sound. She saw Rhys working on his horse, a giant black beast with a tail that hung to the ground.

Lord Urien stepped out from behind a white stallion. He came over and kissed her hand. "You look lovely as ever."

"As do you." It was the first time she dared compliment him. He smiled and seemed pleased.

"We have a horse for you, here." He led Bronwen to a dappled grey palfrey. "His name is Cythraul. But don't let that worry you; he is gentle and well trained."

Her horse's name meant demon. She trusted that Urien would not put her on too dangerous an animal. She offered up a quick prayer to Saint Seiriol, saint of journeys.

Bronwen hadn't ridden a horse for many years. Her father had taken her riding sometimes, when he'd had errands in the village or when the weather had been particularly fine. After her illness, it was Rhys who had saddled Ferlen and lifted her onto his back, letting her ride for a while around the manor. He had never let go of the reins though. Ferlen was too old for riding now, even if she would have been able.

Lord Urien helped her mount, then climbed up on his own magnificent animal.

Gwenna straddled a grey horse that looked like he could be the brother of Cythraul. Dai was giving Gwenna lessons on using the reins, even though Bronwen knew perfectly well Gwenna was an excellent rider. She'd bragged about it all night.

One of the other men helped Gwil secure his weapons to the horse's saddle. He handed Gwil a bow and some arrows, which Gwil slung crossways over his body. Bronwen made a silent vow to stay behind Gwil when the time to shoot arrows arrived.

Besides Urien, Rhys, Gwil, and Dai, there were two men she didn't recognize. One was wearing the livery of the King's Men, and the other was a young lad wearing a jerkin.

Lord Urien brought his horse up beside Bronwen. "Are you ready?"

She nodded.

"We're off," he called to the group.

Rhys took the lead, with Urien and Bronwen right behind. They walked their mounts through the quiet streets of the city and out the east gate into the woods and the king's land. The sun was not quite up, but its glow ignited the countryside, drawing a slow and steady mist from the ground.

"What are we hunting?" she asked Urien.

"Boar," he said. "So be careful. If we find one, stay back and let us do the chasing."

"Yes, sir." She smiled at him, and he edged his horse closer so their legs almost touched.

"Why am I so fond of you? Can you answer me that?" he asked, his eyes bright in the early rays.

"I assure you, I have no idea."

They rode deeper into the woods. After a time, Urien urged his horse forward to ride beside Rhys. They seemed to be discussing the hunt, pointing in different directions and talking eagerly. Bronwen reined in until she was beside Gwenna and Gwil.

"Morning, my lady," Gwil said.

"Stop. It's just me." Ever since the listing yards, Gwil had been teasing her, calling her my lady and always bowing till he touched the floor.

"Don't mind me," Gwil said. "Because of you, I'm a King's Man. Where is your falcon?" he asked.

"What falcon?" Near as Bronwen could tell, no one had brought a falcon.

"From your lesson the other day with the falconer. I thought you were training for the hunt."

Gwil was talking nonsense. No, wait. She had mentioned something like that as an excuse to avoid the shoemaker. "Oh, yes. Uh. In the end . . . I didn't meet with him. It turned out not to be a good day." Mainly because she'd waded into the water and Rhys had found out the truth. "I see you have a bow. Exactly how much training have you had shooting an arrow?"

He grinned a little sheepishly but didn't blush. "Exactly none."

She was definitely staying out of his range when the arrows came out.

Bronwen looked at Gwenna, surprised that she didn't have a barb concerning Gwil and his hunting skills. Instead, she was hunched over in her saddle, her face the perfect picture of woe.

"Gwenna?"

"I don't want to talk about it." She sounded as though she was wading through the very depths of despair. "My wretched heart is broken and shall never be whole again. My life is worthless, and I am the loneliest person to walk the earth."

"Whatever happened?"

"He already has a girl." Gwenna sighed so heavily her horse's ears flicked round to hear it.

Bronwen hadn't seen Gwenna talk to Dai since the riding lesson hours ago. This was bad news if Bronwen wanted to keep Gwenna's sights off Rhys. Now that he knew who she really was, Bronwen couldn't let them be together. It was too big of a risk. Would Rhys even be interested in a girl like Gwenna? He was so serious. Gloomy. Gwenna was a lively person.

That's what Bronwen loved about her. Gwenna's moods were never halfhearted. When she felt something, she felt it all the way.

"How do you know? Did he say something?" Bronwen asked.

"I saw him. Right before we left the courtyard, I saw him embracing a beautiful, dark-haired girl."

"Well," Bronwen said, mustering an impressive amount of enthusiasm, "we shall just have to show him that you are a better catch."

Leaving Gwenna with a look of absolute horror, Bronwen reined her horse again until she was even with Dai.

He greeted her with a nod. "My lady."

My lady again? She was the same as Gwenna; no one called her my lady. But she hadn't come back to discuss proper names of gentry.

"I enjoyed our walk the other day," Bronwen said, trying to start a conversation that would undoubtedly be one-sided.

"Thank you, my lady." He refused to look her in the eye. Was he really so terribly shy?

"I was sorry you didn't come in for a hot mug of mulled cider. It was a cold night."

He nodded again but didn't speak.

"Gwil was disappointed not to talk with you."

Dai sat quietly, swaying with the rhythm of his horse. Bronwen waited for him to speak, but in the end, nothing came.

"As was Gwenna."

At this, he looked up. Not at Bronwen but at the back of Gwenna. Gwenna kept her head forward, but Bronwen could feel concentration seeping from her as she strained to hear their conversation.

"She told me she very much enjoyed your company at the feast of Calan Mai."

Dai's focus fell to his tan horse's head. Now that she thought about it, the color of Dai's horse matched almost exactly the color of Gwenna's hair.

"Thank you," he said again.

How had Gwenna managed to spend an entire evening conversing with this man?

One of the dogs barked, and the rest of the pack halted, pointing their heads, ears perked forward. Every hound was trained with tense muscles on something invisible through the trees.

"They've found one," Rhys said, pulling a long spear out of his saddle.

Lord Urien did the same while spinning his horse around and coming up near Bronwen. "Stay back. Stronger men than you have been gored by a boar." A grin flashed across his face. "If you follow, follow at a distance, and if you hear the hounds turn and come toward you, get well out of their way." He smiled at her long enough for her insides to melt, then he yelled at the young lad in the back. "Tyrnen, stay with the ladies."

Tyrnen was thin and lean, too young even for goose down on his soft, rosy cheeks. Bronwen assumed he was brought along as a squire for Urien or, if they were successful, to aid in the unpleasant task of eviscerating the spoils of the hunt. Now he was the ladies' chaperone. He did not looked at all pleased.

The hounds tore off, bounding through the tangled underbrush, with horses and riders in pursuit. It unnerved Bronwen how quickly the baying of the dogs faded into the distance.

Chapter Twelve

A well-beaten path does not always make the right road.

"Do we follow?" Bronwen asked Gwenna.

Both ladies stared at the spot where the men had disappeared into the forest.

"Perhaps it's better if we wait?" Gwenna suggested.

It would be safer. And certainly easier than riding through the web of bracken and trees. But Bronwen didn't want to sit here forever. If they followed the men, they might catch up in time to see the kill.

Tyrnen rode up beside her. "Will they be gone long?" she asked him.

A glimmer of hope crossed the boy's face. "They could be gone for a very long time. The boar might outwit them for hours before the dogs corner it. Then Urien will slay it. Then we must wait while they prepare the carcass for transport . . ." The way his voice trailed off suggested that that was only the beginning of the waiting they would be forced to endure if they stayed put.

Bronwen made a decision. "Let's follow. We don't have to rush, but it will be better than sitting here doing nothing."

"This way," Tyrnen called as he swung his horse onto the path through the brambles. Not a path, really, but a sort of trampled gap the rush of dogs and horses had made.

Bronwen followed Tyrnen, keeping her head low and letting Cythraul do the work of picking their way through the branches. She could hear Gwenna behind her complaining about the forest messing up her hair.

In a short distance, the undergrowth cleared and opened into a woodland of older trees—beech, oak, and hawthorn—spaced farther apart. The going was much easier.

Tyrnen clucked his horse into a trot, and Bronwen and Gwenna did the same. It was a beautiful forest, and with the hawthorn in bloom, the air smelled sweet. A thrush called out. When another answered him, he broke into a warbling song. Bronwen caught sight of his brown, spotted body as she passed under a hawthorn. Such a plain-looking bird, but what a beautiful song. Why would he choose to sing in a tree thick with thorns when there were more hospitable branches all around? Perhaps the bird was fond of the scented flowers and was willing to put up with a few pokes.

When they reached a clearing, Bronwen heard the dogs baying in the distance. "They must have it cornered. We're catching up." She urged Cythraul faster.

"My lady," Tyrnen called. "I think we should turn back."

As he spoke, a huge black creature with long yellow tusks charged at them, swerving out of the way at the last moment. Tyrnen's horse reared and stumbled backward, colliding with Bronwen's and knocking her and her horse to the earth. Bronwen managed to free herself, rolling away just as Tyrnen's mount landed hard on her horse.

The pack of baying dogs ran through the clearing, ignoring the mayhem of horses, bent on following the boar.

Gwenna screamed.

Bronwen tried to stand, but when she pushed off the ground, a stabbing pain shot through her arm.

Tyrnen's horse scrambled up, its nostrils flared and chest heaving. Tyrnen lay on top of Cythraul, unmoving. He had been crushed in between the two beasts.

Cythraul neighed and groaned and tried to get up, his legs flailing wildly. If Tyrnen wasn't already dead, he would be killed for sure by the flying hooves.

Bronwen pulled herself up, rubbing her arm. It didn't seem to be broken, but her sleeve was wet with blood. "Gwenna, help me move the boy."

Gwenna dismounted and ran over, her face pale. Careful to avoid the horse's pawing feet, they grabbed Tyrnen and pulled him away from the panicked animal.

"Is he dead?" Gwenna shrieked, wringing her hands.

Bronwen put her head close to Tyrnen's mouth. "I think he's breathing."

The sound of horses thudding through the underbrush brought them up. A moment later, Urien and Rhys burst into the clearing. Urien pulled on his horse's reins, and the animal's hooves dug into the ground. He was off his mount and beside Bronwen instantly.

"What happened? Are you hurt?"

"No. I'm fine." She motioned at Tyrnen's still form. "But . . ." She couldn't finish.

Urien turned his attention to Tyrnen, feeling the boy's body for damage and putting his ear to the boy's chest. "He's alive."

Bronwen crossed herself, thanking every saint she could think of that Tyrnen had survived.

Rhys had also dismounted and knelt at the head of Bronwen's horse. He stroked Cythraul's neck and spoke with a steady, even voice. "Easy there. Calm down. Easy, boy." His slow, rhythmic words somehow managed to still the poor animal.

"Where is Gwil?" Gwenna suddenly asked. If she'd been pale before, she now looked the color of death.

"He and the others rode around to cut him off," Urien said.

It took Bronwen a moment to understand—he meant cut off the path of the boar. She hoped they never found it. This morning, the hunting trip had seemed like great fun. How quickly things had changed.

Tyrnen gasped and rolled onto his side, spitting blood. When he turned onto his back again and saw Urien bending over him, he said in a choked voice, "I beg your pardon, my lord."

Urien grinned. "Are you all right?"

"I think so. Just got the wind knocked out, is all." He coughed and then winced. "That's what happens when two horses make mince pie out of you."

Urien chuckled. "Let me guess: the horses were the crust and you were the mince?"

Tyrnen nodded.

Urien stood up. "He'll be fine."

"Sir, if you don't mind, I'm just going to lie here for a bit," Tyrnen said.

"I don't mind at all."

Bronwen fetched her water bladder from the ground, where it had flown from her horse's saddle. She knelt beside Tyrnen and lifted his head, gently tipping the liquid into his mouth.

He swallowed several gulps, then nodded. "Thanks," he said.

Urien put his arm around Bronwen and pulled her close. "I thought I told you to be careful."

"I was careful. We thought you were miles away when the boar came charging at us. Tyrnen's horse spooked and landed on mine." She rubbed her injured arm.

"You're hurt," he said, looking at the blood on her sleeve.

It must have happened when she dove off the falling animal. The cut wasn't deep, but the blood seeped down her arm. She bent down to tear a piece of cloth from her underskirt, but Urien stopped her.

"No. Allow me." He glanced around the clearing, his eyes landing on Tyrnen. Urien tore a strip of linen from Tyrnen's tunic.

"Please, help yourself," Tyrnen said with a wave of his hand.

Urien tied the cloth around Bronwen's gash. "There you are. Good as new."

"Urien," Rhys said, rising from his post by Cythraul's head. "His leg."

The two men bent down, examining one of the horse's hind legs. Rhys ran his hands along the animal's limb, and the horse whimpered.

"Are they going to kill it?" Gwenna whispered to Bronwen.

"I don't know." Bronwen hoped not. Couldn't they let the leg heal? Broken bones healed all the time. Perhaps the horse would be fine.

Urien gave Rhys some kind of official nod. Rhys walked over to his saddle and pulled his sword from its sheath. In what seemed like an afterthought, he grabbed the boar-spear as well. It was a fearsome tool with a long, thick head and iron cross wings to prevent an enraged animal from working its way up the shaft and goring the hunter.

Bronwen clapped her hand over her mouth. They couldn't kill him. What if the horse's leg was only strained? Bruised? Maybe in an hour or two he would be up and walking. They should give him a chance.

Rhys stabbed the spear into the ground and straddled the horse's neck.

"No!" Bronwen cried. "No. It can heal. He'll be all right if you just let it heal. He only needs a little time."

Urien shook his head. "Even if it does mend, which I doubt, he will be useless. Lame forever."

Rhys's head snapped up.

Bronwen gulped. "Just because he is lame doesn't mean he can't be happy." The horse should be given a chance.

She tried to get her voice under control. *Be sensible*, she told herself. But something rose in her chest, building and growing until it burst out. A monster that couldn't be controlled.

She turned to Urien, yelling at him, screaming into his face. "He deserves to live. Lots of people are lame, and they do fine. They still have worth. You don't kill someone simply because they can't walk. They're not useless. People can do things, good things, even if they are lame. You can't just hate someone because they are lame. You can't turn them away and kill them."

Urien stared at her, his mouth cracked open. They all stared. Even Tyrnen, still lying on the ground, gaped at her with bulging eyes.

"Bronwen?" Gwenna whispered.

But it wasn't Gwenna she turned to. It was Rhys.

His black eyes flashed through her. She hadn't meant to say all that. She hadn't meant to say anything. But the plight of the poor animal seemed so akin to her own she'd lost control. If the horse died, she felt part of her would too.

"Bronwen," Rhys said softly and with more kindness than he'd ever used before. "You are not a horse."

"Of course she's not," Urien said. "Why would you say such a thing?" He led Bronwen away a few paces and placed his hands on her shoulders. "I'm sorry. But this is the way it must be. Even if we try to save him, how would we bring him home? We can't leave him here. The wolves will get him. When a horse is injured, this is the best option. What use do I have for a lame animal?"

None. There was no use for a lame animal. No use at all. "You're right. I know it. I was just upset because of . . . all of this." She waved her hand over the scene of the wounded horse and Tyrnen breathing painfully on the ground. "I'm sorry."

Urien nodded again at Rhys, giving him the command to proceed with Cythraul's execution.

Gwenna's face turned green, and Tyrnen scooted away. Bronwen covered her eyes.

"Urien, perhaps it would be better if I wait until the ladies are gone."

Lord Urien didn't get a chance to respond.

A few grunts and the sound of a large animal crashing through the brambles was the only warning they had before a boar the size of a bear charged at them. With astonishing reflexes, Rhys grabbed the spear and stabbed it into the beast.

The boar fell onto its side, squealing and pawing at the air but not for long. The animal scrambled to its feet and lunged again. Rhys thrust the spear at its chest, leaning into it, using his weight to sink the spearhead deeper and deeper into the flesh.

A second tusked creature burst into the clearing from another direction, heading straight for Bronwen and Gwenna. This boar was even bigger than the first and faster. Urien dove for Rhys's sword that lay on the ground by the horse.

Even Bronwen could see that the weapon was no match for the huge animal. Urien would be gored before the blade could stop it. Rhys was still busy fighting the first boar.

Urien yelled and waved the sword as he ran to cut off the beast's rush at Bronwen. The boar slowed for the briefest moment, then altered course and charged at Urien. He lifted his weapon and braced himself for the blow.

An arrow flew from the forest and pierced the creature's skull. The boar wobbled off balance and stumbled to the ground. That was all the opportunity Urien needed to finish him off. He sank Rhys's blade into the exposed underside of the huge animal.

Rhys rushed to Urien's side, holding the spear high, but the boar was already dead. Urien staggered a little, then searched the direction from which the arrow had come.

Gwil stepped into the clearing, holding a bow in his hand with an arrow notched and ready.

Gwenna's jaw dropped so far Bronwen worried it would never close again. "Gwil?" She blinked her eyes. "I can't believe it. Gwil?"

Gwil was grinning ear to ear.

Lord Urien and Rhys appeared no less shocked than Gwenna, staring in wonder at Gwil.

"Wa—" Urien's voice was weak. He cleared his throat and started over. "Was that your arrow?"

"Yes."

Urien looked confused. "I did not know you were an archer."

Gwil glanced down at the beast. "Me neither."

Bronwen didn't think Urien had blinked since Gwil had stepped out of the woods.

"You"—Urien said—"you shot that arrow and struck a charging boar, and you've never used the weapon before?"

Gwil shrugged. "I speared a fish once. Does that count?"

Urien nodded. "I suppose it does. Lucky you didn't kill me." A smile broke out on his face, and then he laughed.

Gwenna screamed. "Gwil, you're my hero!" She ran straight into her brother's arms.

"No one can deny that he is the hero," Urien said. He shook Gwil's hand, then pulled him into a quick hug, pounding him on the back.

Bronwen couldn't believe it. If this was any indication of where his real talent lay, she hoped Gwil never picked up a sword again.

Tyrnen stood up and leaned over, his hands on his knees.

With her toe, Bronwen prodded the boar Gwil and Urien had killed. It was the biggest animal she'd ever seen, other than a horse. Black, bristly hair covered its body, and it stank like fetid water. Its glassy brown eye stared at her, and its yellow tusks curved out from under a long, filthy snout. Even in death, it sneered at her.

"How are you?" Rhys had come up beside her.

"My heart's still pounding, but I'm fine. I've never seen one up close before," she said.

"I don't mean about the boars."

"Oh." She cast a quick glance at her horse. The poor animal had been lying on its side moaning for a while now. The charging boars had put her mind on other things.

She had behaved horribly toward Urien. If he hadn't suspected anything before, he would now. No one yelled at the king's son. Especially not over a horse.

This was not a question she wanted to discuss right now, especially with Rhys. "I don't know what came over me," she said. "I'm perfectly well, thanks."

Bronwen left Rhys alone with the carcass and joined the others, who were still trying to believe Gwil could have performed such a miracle.

Gwil was recounting his moment of glory, how he'd debated—just for half an instant—whether shooting an arrow in the direction of the king's son was a good idea. In the end, Gwil had concluded if his arrow didn't kill Urien, the boar definitely would.

Urien listened and laughed, then moved back a pace when Gwil, in his enthusiasm, stepped on his royal foot.

Bronwen shook Gwil's hand. "Well played," she said to Gwil.

He laughed and bowed. "You are too kind."

Urien laid a hand on her back.

"Can we leave this place now?" she whispered to him. She didn't want to be here any longer. Dai and the other man had arrived in the small clearing and were disemboweling the boars, preparing the meat to be transported back to the castle. The smell sickened her. Cythraul lay whimpering on the forest floor, waiting for his mercy killing. The trees closed in around her; she could take no more of it.

"Certainly," Urien said. "Rhys, finish the animal and help me take the ladies home. The others can manage the rest."

Rhys picked up his sword again and positioned himself at Cythraul's neck.

Urien pulled Bronwen to the edge of the clearing and held her close, blocking her view. "Don't watch."

As if she needed reminding. Already, she squeezed her eyes tight and covered her ears in case the horse screamed.

In only a few seconds, Urien released her. "It's over."

Whatever Rhys had done—and she was determined not to look—he had done it quickly.

A quiet settled over the clearing. Cythraul's huffing moans had ceased, and even the birds gave up their song—some kind of elemental moment of silence for the end of the animal's life.

But Urien was a man of action. He called out orders again, requesting that the boar meat be properly handled, that Gwil's boar head be brought back to the castle, and on and on. Bronwen stopped listening. She strained to hear the thrush singing in the trees or a wren calling, anything that would be a sign of life in this place of death.

Gwenna came over and took Bronwen's hands. "What a horrible thing. I'm so glad it's over. I've never seen so much blood in all my life."

Tyrnen approached with Gwenna's horse. The boy walked stiff and bent, but considering what had happened to him, it was a miracle he could move at all. Gwenna mounted and swung her animal in the direction of Dai, but it looked as though he would be staying behind to tidy things up.

"You are short a horse," Urien said to Bronwen. "We'll have to double up for the ride home, all right?"

"Yes." Bronwen pictured herself sitting behind Urien on his fine white stallion, her arms wrapped tightly around his chest. Perhaps a stolen kiss. Then at least this wretched outing would end with something good.

"My horse is worth half my kingdom. I can't risk overburdening him." Urien called Rhys over. "She rides with you."

Her dream poofed into thin air. It had been a long ride out, and now she faced a much longer ride home. No doubt Rhys would spend the entire trip lecturing her about the wrongness of keeping secrets. If only Rhys would go off to battle. There must be a rebellion somewhere that needed quelling.

Rhys climbed into his saddle, then Urien hoisted Bronwen up behind him. She scooted as far back as possible without sliding off the horse's hind quarters.

Rhys shook his head. "If you fall, I'm not stopping to pick you up."

"Fine by me," Bronwen said.

Urien led the way, with Rhys, Bronwen, and Gwenna following. The rest stayed to work. When they reached the main path, Urien kicked his horse into a canter. Rhys's horse lunged to catch up, and Bronwen had to cling to Rhys. She could feel Rhys's body shake with laughter. It was indeed going to be a long ride home.

Chapter Thirteen

You must crack the nut before you can eat the kernel.

Two days had passed since the boar hunt, and Bronwen had seen nothing of Lord Urien. No one came from the castle to collect her. Nor did she have any indication of when—if ever—she might see him again. A large shank of boar meat arrived for the Fib and Flounder's cook, and the innkeeper raised his prices again. That was the closest she came to anything associated with Urien.

"Maybe something happened to him," Gwenna suggested. "He could be sick."

Bronwen had wondered this too. But why would no one tell her?

Gwenna and Bronwen had pelted Gwil with questions about Urien's whereabouts. Gwil spent most of his time training with the King's Men now that he'd proved himself a capable archer. Gwil told them Urien had been to the archery range the day after the hunt, but he hadn't seen or heard anything from him since.

Rhys had given her a week to tell Urien, but how could she tell him if she never saw him? Perhaps Urien's feelings for her had changed after she'd yelled at him on the hunt. If so, she might never need to tell him. Rhys may have worked himself up for nothing.

Bronwen and Gwenna went to watch Gwil practice, but there was no sign of Urien or Rhys. When Dai showed up, Gwenna lost interest in watching for Urien and ended up chatting nose to nose with Dai. If he had his eye on another girl, Bronwen saw no hint of it in the way he leaned in close to Gwenna. Bronwen left and walked home.

The moment she entered the inn, the innkeeper seized her and steered her into the common room. There sat a man wearing a thick canvas apron and holding a heavy bag of tools.

"The king's shoemaker," the innkeeper said. "Says he won't leave till he sees you."

A pox on that determined cordwainer! He was very diligent about his work. Bronwen couldn't avoid him now. This whole thing with the shoemaker was pointless. Even if he made her the finest shoes in the kingdom, she could never wear them.

Perhaps if she removed only one shoe he could take his measurements. But she'd never worn only one for more than a few moments. She dared not risk it.

Bronwen curtsied to the tradesman. "How kind you are to wait for me." And by kind, she meant stubborn.

The cordwainer plunked Bronwen down in a chair, then reached for her feet. She jerked them away, tucking them under her seat.

Her fingers rubbed at her throat. "I'm sorry to tell you that . . . I have been out walking. In the dirt. And mud. My feet are a mess. I couldn't possibly show you such filthy feet. It wouldn't be proper." At the man's scowl, she quickly added, "It might sicken you."

The cordwainer grunted, his face hard and surly. It was a toss-up as to who took the least pleasure in this between him and Bronwen. He reached again for her feet, and she swung them away.

"There's no mud on your shoes, so what are you about, girl?"

It seemed this man was past pleasantries. Who knew how long he'd been waiting here to fulfill Lord Urien's orders? Bronwen had already avoided his first two visits; his patience must have run dry. She had to tell him the truth. Not, obviously, the whole truth, but enough. And she had to sound like she meant it.

"I really am sorry. But I never remove my shoes in public. Not for anyone," she said, trying to sound final. "You can take the measurements with my shoes on or not at all." Hopefully he wouldn't hold her down and rip them off.

The man glowered at her. He took out a piece of cloth and traced the outline of her feet with her faerie shoes on. His fingertips were russet-tinted from leather working, and his apron was smeared with tallow, giving him a slightly rancid odor. With a flaxen cord, he measured various places around her foot, tying a knot in the string to mark the lengths.

She asked him if he had spoken to Lord Urien that day. The shoemaker grunted again and mumbled words Bronwen had trouble deciphering. Something perhaps ending with, "Never see him again."

The shoemaker finished his work, packed up his tools, and left, but not without bestowing on Bronwen one last look of abhorrence.

That night, Bronwen lay in bed, staring at the rafters. She must have angered Urien. What other explanation could there be? When she yelled at him in the woods and told him not to kill her horse, she had insulted him. No one yelled at the king's son. He was used to respect. He demanded it.

Besides, what reason would Urien have for wanting her when there were so many girls he could choose from? Girls far better than Bronwen. Girls who were perfect and whole. In all likelihood, he had already found one. A beautiful lady who never got caught in the tide, who kept herself neat and proper, and who never raised her voice at her future king.

She rolled over to face the wall. At least this way he need never know about her legs. She could leave quietly and live her life. No more hiding. No more lies.

* * *

The next morning, the cordwainer showed up with the most beautiful pair of shoes Bronwen had ever seen. Made of a smooth, heavy silk on top, they matched her dove-grey gown perfectly. The toes ended in an elegant point, and intricate patterns in dark blue covered the entire surface. The soles were cordovan leather. He must have worked through the night.

"Has Lord Urien seen these?" Bronwen wanted any indication that he thought about her at all.

The cordwainer gave her the same glowering look he had yesterday. "No, my lady."

"Did he know you were coming here today?"

He shook his head. The way he scowled at her, shifting and rubbing his scruffy beard, seemed beyond mere annoyance. There was something else going on, something else he wanted to say.

"What is it?" she asked.

His gaze wandered out the inn's front window, and his jaw muscles bulged. "I am no longer in the king's employ. I leave the city today to find work elsewhere."

"Why? What happened?"

He looked her full in her face. "Lord Urien was not pleased that I failed to come here earlier, on the day he first appointed."

"But—" Holy saints! What had she done? Bronwen tried to remember what she had told Urien—that she hadn't seen the cordwainer. Urien must have taken that to mean the cordwainer had not come at all.

The cordwainer's face told her everything. This man blamed her, and for good reason. Because of her, he'd lost his livelihood, was forced to leave his home, disgraced. This was what her lies had led to.

With a voice like a dried-up well, she asked, "Did he speak to you?"

"I received a message several days ago commanding me to complete this order and then I was dismissed." The cordwainer gave Bronwen a stiff bow, then turned and walked out the door of the inn.

No wonder he was so harsh yesterday; he'd already been discharged. Maybe Bronwen could talk to Urien to try to clear it up—if he was willing to grant her an audience. Then he might let the shoemaker stay. But then Urien would know she had lied to him. That one little lie might not matter so much. The problem was, it would lead to more difficult questions.

She fingered the beautiful shoes. What a waste. She had no use for such fine things now that Urien no longer cared for her. She groaned at her own stupidity. She couldn't have worn the shoes even if she was marrying the high king.

Bronwen tucked the new shoes into the depths of her trunk. Tomorrow marked the end of her week, and she had still heard nothing from the castle. It was over. She had offended Lord Urien, and he had moved on. Now she must do the same. She had no doubt Rhys would follow through on his threat and expose her to the king's son.

Gwenna came into Bronwen's room with a pile of mending. She sat on the bed beside Bronwen and started work on a loose hem.

Bronwen picked up one of Gwil's shirts with a tear in the shoulder seam. She threaded a needle with a linen strand. "I can't stay here," she said to Gwenna. "I have to leave this city."

"Where will you go? Home? By yourself?"

Bronwen had promised her mother she would go to the shrine of Saint Cynedd and give thanks for her miracle. She must do at least one thing right. She would keep that promise.

After all, this had been the plan from the beginning. Do her presentation, then get on with her life. Her time with Lord Urien had been wonderful and exciting, and she would always love him, but it was an illusion. Who would want a crippled wife?

"I'm going to Ynys Môn, to the shrine of Saint Cenydd."

"The saint for the crippled? Why? Are you still upset about the horse?"

Gwenna had handed her the perfect excuse. "Yes, I am. It's my fault he broke his leg, and I feel I should make penance."

"Bronwen, a wild boar charged right in front of us. How is that your fault?"

"Urien told me if I heard the dogs coming in our direction, we should turn away. Even Tyrnen warned me to head back. I heard the dogs and went on anyway. I wanted to catch up with Urien."

Gwenna set her sewing down. "It happened too fast. We could not have prevented any of it. And look at Gwil. He's one of the best archers the King's Men have ever seen. If it weren't for the boars, he would still be swinging a sword while brave men dive for cover. How long would they have tolerated him with such pitiful skills? Maybe fate set all of that in motion for him. Did you ever think of that?"

The discovery of Gwil's archery talent was the one good thing to come from the disastrous hunt. It had been a terrible day, first with the horse, then with her insolence to the king's son. No wonder Urien had made her ride home with Rhys. Urien's horse was strong enough to carry three Bronwens. The prince had sent her with Rhys because he'd already made his decision.

She needed to leave, and she would start with the pilgrimage she promised her mother.

"Either way, I've made up my mind. I'm going to the island of Ynys Môn."

"But Urien could still call for you. You can't give up so easily."

"Gwen, if he wanted me, he would have called for me long before now."

Gwenna shrugged. "You can't know that for sure."

Bronwen stood and laid her mending aside. "At least come with me to the church to see the priest."

The priest would help Bronwen find other pilgrims heading to Holy Island. It was his job to arrange traveling companions for pilgrimages such as hers.

Then, after she visited the shrine of Saint Cynedd, she would go home—where she belonged, at the base of the mountain with her mother calling, telling her to put the geese in. The greatest blessing of leaving Sedd Brenhinol would be seeing her mother again.

Gwenna jumped up. "Yes. And we can visit the market on our way. You never know who might be out and about on market days."

Gwenna had been patient with Bronwen during the past few days, but she was not the kind of girl who thrived on sitting home with a moping friend. She preferred action, activity, and essentially anything that might involve meeting young men, especially if one of them was Dai. The castle posted guards in the market square, so Gwenna's chances of seeing him were better than fair.

They walked through the streets toward the center of town, the trickle of tents and vendors thickening until they reached the market. Booths and carts crowded the outer cobblestone ring of the square while sheep and geese grazed in the grassy center.

Gwenna stopped at a cart with bolts of cloth. She picked up a silk the color of the sun's morning rays and held it to her face. "Don't you think this becomes me?"

Bronwen didn't have the heart to tell her that gold—Gwenna's favorite color—did not suit her at all.

Bronwen lifted a rich, dark-blue linen up to Gwenna. Her hair glowed a soft flaxen color and her two-toned eyes, with the outer rim of blue and the inner ring of brown, lit up as though a candle burned behind them. "Gwenna, I know you love the gold, but this color makes you stunning."

Gwenna stayed at the cloth cart, stroking the woolens and caressing the brocades, while Bronwen wandered on, past the vegetables and fruits, past nuts and eggs. A ragged lady with blue woad painted in swirls and knots all over her face sat on a tower of fur pelts. She held out a hand filled with small animal bones.

"Come here, girl. The bones will tell your future," she called in a raspy voice.

Bronwen already knew her future: *you will spend the rest of your life alone*. Why waste good money to hear it spoken out loud? "No, thanks."

She wandered on until she came to a cart filled with spices. She closed her eyes and breathed in the mix of flavors. She recognized some items— cardamom, lavender, rose hips, sandalwood.

"How much for some cloves?" Bronwen asked, pointing at the small, dried, brown buds that looked like miniature maces.

"Karanfil. Come from far away," the vendor said in a heavy accent. "Very expensive." He had a shimmery red cloth wrapped around his dark hair, and his skin was the color of cinnamon. A gold ring glinted in the side of his nose.

"How much?" she asked again.

He took out a small muslin pouch and poured a handful of cloves into it. "Three penny."

That was an exorbitant price. A whole day's wage for a tradesman. "How much can I get for one penny?"

He emptied the pouch and, with his fingertips, pinched a smaller bunch of cloves into the bag.

She handed him a tiny silver coin. "You're a thief."

The exotic man grinned and tied the bag with a woolen string. "Thank you. Come back soon."

She snatched the pouch. "How can I? I have no money left."

She took a deep whiff of the bag. Urien. These cloves were not for cooking or flavoring stale cider. They were her memory of the king's son. For the rest of her life, this peppery-sweet scent would be her portrait of Urien.

"Bronwen!" Gwenna called through the crowd. "Look at this."

Bronwen turned to find Gwenna beaming, accompanied by Gwil and Dai. At least Gwenna's luck had not run out.

"Good morning." Bronwen curtsied.

Gwil gave her a huge smile. "My lady." He had his bow and quiver strapped to his back.

"I see you are off to shoot things," Bronwen said to him.

"Yes, well, they wisely gave up trying to teach me the sword."

Bronwen laughed. "Very wisely."

"Gwil and Dai are heading to the training yards. We can go watch," Gwenna said, bouncing on her toes. "It will be great fun. Do you want to come? Please say you'll come."

Watching Gwil shoot did sound like fun, but Bronwen had her errand. "You go on. I'll catch up. I have to stop at the church."

"The church?" Gwil asked.

Before Bronwen could come up with a tactful way to beat around the bush, Gwenna answered. "Bronwen has it in her head that she should go to the shrine of Saint Cenydd to pray for the lame horse. I mean, the dead one. Gwil, tell her not to go. It's too dangerous. Some knave will rob her and leave her for dead on the side of the road." Gwenna turned to Bronwen. "Or worse," she whispered with horror. Bronwen could only guess at the gruesome images that flashed through Gwenna's mind.

Gwil nodded. "I've never said this before, but I have to agree with Gwenna. It is dangerous to travel alone."

"I'll be fine. I'm going now to talk to the priest. He'll join me with a trustworthy group." Bronwen shooed them off to the archery range. "I'll catch up later."

She crossed the cobblestone path and pushed open the heavy oak door of the church. It took a moment for her eyes to adjust to the dark despite the sconces laden with burning candles. Tallow. Bronwen hated the smell—like meat left out in the sun for too many days. It got into her hair and clothes and lingered for days. Her father had always splurged on beeswax because tallow gave her mother a headache.

The church appeared empty, but the priest—or someone—had to be close by. It was unlikely they would leave candles burning unattended.

Bronwen walked up the nave and knelt down in one of the pews. She crossed herself. *Saint Cenydd, forgive me for looking beyond my worth. A king's son is not for me. I will not forget again that I am crippled.*

She lifted the little pack of cloves from her belt and smelled it—to relieve the stench of smoking tallow. The spices immediately filled her with memories of Urien's kiss by the water in the moonlight.

She heard footsteps behind her on the stone floor. The priest. She tied the pouch to her belt and rose.

It wasn't the priest. It was Rhys. She hoped he wasn't here to gloat. He had warned her she was a fool. He'd been right. The last thing she wanted was to listen to him crow about it.

"Rhys." That was all the welcome she could muster.

"You're going alone to Ynys Môn?" He skipped a greeting altogether.

"How do you know?"

"Gwenna told me."

She meant well, trying to keep Bronwen safe, but sometimes Bronwen wished Gwenna didn't like to talk quite so much. Already, Gwil thought Bronwen was daft for wanting to pilgrimage for a horse.

Rhys would see right through that excuse. "I have to. I made a promise to my mother. Besides, it seems I've run out of time."

"Oh, yes," Rhys said. "Tomorrow marks one week since we made our deal. I'd almost forgotten."

Which, of course, was a lie. Rhys had probably been pacing day and night, counting down the moments until he could expose Bronwen's secret.

Bronwen curtsied and headed toward the side door. She thought the cleric might be working in the garden. "I have to find the priest, Rhys. Good-bye."

"Wait."

Bronwen stopped, her back still to him.

"Do you need anything? To help you on your way?"

She turned. "What?"

"Money. Supplies." His eyes fell on her legs. "A horse. It is three days' walk. A horse can get you there in one."

She hadn't expected this from Rhys. She took it as proof that he wanted her to leave quickly. Maybe he had broken his word and told Urien the truth already. That would explain why Urien had forsaken her. And why Rhys was so willing to help her get out of the city. Only, it wasn't Rhys's nature to make a promise and then go back on it.

"I see what you're thinking," he said. "But you're wrong. I gave you my word."

She had no way of knowing what Rhys had told Urien. Nor did she understand why Rhys, who was so opposed to deceptions of any kind, would have made such a promise in the first place. Rhys was closer to Urien than anyone. If she found out something horrible about Dai, wouldn't she run to Gwenna and tell her? Yet, if Rhys was telling the truth, he had kept her secret all this time. "I don't understand why. Why haven't you told Urien anything?"

Rhys shrugged. "In honor of your father, I suppose. He was good to me. He gave me work when no one else would. If it weren't for him, I'd be a beggar in the streets. Then . . . well, you've been through some hard times, you and your mother." He spoke as though far away, his eyes staring blankly at the colored-glass window above the altar. "Perhaps I can repay him by helping you." He looked at her and grinned. "Heaven knows you don't deserve it."

Bronwen did not answer.

"What's the matter? Don't you trust me?"

Whether she wanted it or not, her trust had fallen into his lap. It was too late to take it back. Not that she would because somewhere deep inside, she did trust Rhys. Though she'd never admit that to him.

"Do I have a choice?" she asked.

"No." Rhys pointed Bronwen toward the main door. "Let's go. I don't like churches."

"You're a heathen," Bronwen said.

She'd meant it as a joke, but Rhys stopped and considered. "I suppose I am. Isn't that what they call you if you've never been baptized?"

Bronwen gasped. "You've never been baptized?" This explained a lot. No wonder none of the villagers would give him work. And worse, the infants who missed out on baptism were the ones stolen away by the faerie folk and replaced with a creature of their own. Bronwen took a step away from him. "You could be a changeling."

Rhys laughed out loud. "What if I am a changeling?"

She reached out one finger and poked Rhys's shoulder as though he might be made of spirit and air. "It would explain your poor manners."

"Bronwen," he said, shaking his head. "You are a fool." He herded her across the threshold and out into the sunlight.

"Can you be ready to leave tomorrow at daybreak?" Rhys said once outside in the noise of the market.

She nodded.

"I'll come for you at the Fib and Flounder with a horse and escort."

She couldn't imagine a journey with Rhys. Alone. She shuddered. "By escort, you mean . . . ?"

He read her thoughts again. "It won't be me, so you can calm down."

She owed him dearly for his help. To make arrangements for her pilgrimage was a great service. If Rhys really did intend to repay her father, this would do it.

She wanted him to know. "Thank you. I mean it."

He stared at her for a moment, then turned and walked away. "See you tomorrow," he said over his shoulder. "Dawn."

Chapter Fourteen

Never give cherries to pigs or advice to fools.

The next morning as the mist was lifting from the streets, Bronwen waited in front of the Fib and Flounder with Gwenna, who had not stopped weeping since the previous evening when Bronwen had told her she would be leaving so soon.

"You are my dearest friend. How shall I live without you? I feel sick. Am I hot? Feel my forehead. I'm sure I have a fever. Why must you go? There are other men here besides Urien."

That was true. There were other men in the city, handsome and strong. Gwenna had no idea how completely unsuitable Bronwen was for any of them. Nor would any of them ever consider her. Her place was with her mother. Alone with her mother, then, eventually, just alone.

The clopping of horse hooves echoed down the cobblestones, and Gwenna's sobbing increased. It had to be Rhys approaching.

Bronwen clung to her self-control, not wanting a scene in the middle of the street, even though at this hour, it was empty. If she didn't calm Gwenna, Bronwen would end up crying too.

"Gwenna, I'll see you again." Bronwen groped through her mind for a way to steady Gwenna. "I know! We can meet just like we did the first time, at the Inn of the Silver Knife. It's a good halfway point between our two homes."

Gwenna wiped her swollen eyes. "Yes . . . yes, we can do that. We can meet. On Michaelmas. And then you can come stay with me. I'll be all alone, and the house will feel deserted without Gwil." Apparently, Gwenna had forgotten the gaggle of siblings still at home with her father.

"I'll plan on it," Bronwen said.

Rhys rounded the corner with a horse in tow. Three other horses followed, along with two men, only the tops of their heads visible behind the cluster of animals. Rhys nodded at Bronwen. "You ready?"

"Yes."

A large man stepped out from behind the herd, and a stick man stepped out from behind him.

"No." She recognized the men, and now she knew for certain that Rhys was planning something awful. "I'm not going to Ynys Môn with them."

Rhys had a smug grin. "Rowli and Clovis? I already told you they're harmless."

"They weren't harmless the other night. Or don't you remember. Maybe you were the one befuddled by too much ale."

"You really don't trust me, do you?" He didn't wait for an answer. "You will be perfectly safe."

"But—"

"Perfectly safe. I promise." Rhys held out the reins of a chestnut horse with a black mane, tail, and feet.

Bronwen loved her instantly. "She's beautiful."

"She is," Rhys agreed. "And she's trustworthy." He added extra emphasis on the word trust. "Rowli and Clovis will take you to Ynys Môn and then on to Glyn—" He paused and looked around. "To your home."

Gwenna's sobs increased.

"Then they will bring the horse back to me here."

It was a long time to be in the care of the two men who had tried to murder her on Calan Mai. Perhaps being a changeling meant Rhys was unstable in his mind. Not that she had proof that he was a changeling. Yet.

She had packed her few belongings, and Clovis was loading them onto Ferlen, Bronwen's old packhorse.

"I have one more thing I need to get," she said to Rhys.

Rhys nodded while adjusting the girth on Bronwen's saddle.

Bronwen ran up to her room. She had two items left there, her crutch and the shoes from Lord Urien. She wanted Gwenna to have the beautiful shoes, but she couldn't simply hand them over. Gwenna would never accept them without a lot of questions. Bronwen wrapped them in a linen cloth and snuck down the hall. Elen was still asleep in the room she and Gwenna shared. Bronwen dared not risk waking her.

She opened the door to Gwil's room and tiptoed in. Gwil didn't stir as she tucked the fine shoes into the back corner of his trunk. He would find them soon enough, and Gwenna would get them in the end.

She ran back to her room and pulled out a long, thin object. Her crutch. Though it was still wrapped in sackcloth, anyone with half a brain would know what it was. Once she got home, she would need it. She hadn't wanted to bring it down earlier in case it became a topic of discussion with Gwenna while they waited.

She carried the wrapped crutch down the stairs and out to the waiting group. Rhys recognized it instantly. "You brought this?" he whispered, leaning down and putting his mouth close to her ear.

"I had to," she whispered back. "I didn't know if . . . How can I wear them forever?"

He took it from her and handed it to Clovis. "Put this on the horse too. And don't lose it."

Clovis ran his broomstick fingers along it. "What's this?"

"It belongs to her mother," Rhys said.

Clovis stowed the crutch on the side of the pack animal.

Bronwen couldn't believe it. Rhys had lied for her again. He was the one constantly reminding her she was a fool for not telling the truth. That lie plus the horse almost made up for subjecting her to Rowli and Clovis for who knew how many days.

Rowli licked his thick finger and stuck it in the air. "Good day for travel."

"A good day, indeed," Clovis said. He hopped onto his horse, a lean creature with ribs fluting its sides.

If those two gave her any grief, she would never forgive Rhys. Not that she would ever see Rhys again, so her refusal of forgiveness would go unappreciated, but what did that matter? The slow burn of anger would get her through many a long winter night.

The front door swung open, slamming into Bronwen and knocking her off the stoop and into the arms of Rowli.

"Get off me." She pushed away and brushed her clothing, careful to remove any bits of Rowli that tried to cling.

Gwil rushed out. "Oh, sorry about that." His hair was mussed, and his eyes were still swollen with sleep. He had no shirt on, and Bronwen was surprised by the strength in his lean frame. "Why didn't you wake me?" he asked. "I thought I missed you."

"I would not have left without a good-bye." Against all decorum, Bronwen slipped her arms around Gwil's bare chest and squeezed. "You saved Lord Urien's life in the forest when you shot that boar. And probably mine too. I shall always remember you as my champion."

Gwil pulled her in close. "And I shall always remember you as mine."

She let go and stepped back. "At least we are even."

She turned to Rhys. "It was the hunt, wasn't it?" she quietly asked.

"The hunt?"

"Yes. And the lame horse. He seemed fine before that, but after my fit . . . it changed his mind. That's why he's no longer fond of me, isn't it?"

Rhys took his time to answer. "I'm his captain, not his confessor. He does not share with me the feelings of his heart."

In many ways, this wasn't the worst ending she could imagine. At least Urien didn't know about her legs. If her greatest fault was losing her temper instead of being a cripple, perhaps that wasn't so bad.

She shook Rhys's hand. "Thank you." She owed him quite a lot. More than she gave him credit for. Keeping her secret. Saving her life—twice, if she included the incident with Rowli and Clovis, an event she believed more and more Rhys had arranged from the beginning. And now he was helping her on her way. "I believe my father would be pleased."

Rhys held her hand for a moment, then grinned. "Have fun with the boys."

"Disgusting."

Bronwen saved her last good-bye for Gwenna. Bronwen put her arms around her while tears steadily trickled down Gwenna's face. "Gwenna, I shall miss you the most. I've never had a friend until I met you. I'll see you in four months' time, on Michaelmas. At the crossroads."

Gwenna just nodded and sniffed, wiping her face with a handkerchief.

Gwil helped Bronwen onto her horse, and Clovis led the way. Somehow, miraculously, Rowli had managed to hoist his bulk onto his animal, and he fell in step behind her. She wished she could have seen the feat of strength that must have been exerted to get such a substantial man onto such a wide horse.

"What is the mare's name?" she asked Rhys as she passed him.

Rhys's smile was devilish. "Gwyllion."

Bronwen crossed herself and prayed, *Saint Morwyn, save me.*

* * *

Faerie name or not, the animal was pleasant enough to ride. They made good time, and by midday, Bronwen and her companions reached the Afon Menai—the narrow stretch of seawater that separated the island of Ynys Môn from the mainland.

The tide was low, and water swirled and churned around the exposed sandbars. She had heard many times of the dangers of crossing the Afon Menai. As the tide rose, the water flowed in from both the north and south, creating violent currents. It was not uncommon to hear of a boat that had been capsized, and crossing at low tide exposed the traveler to dangerous quicksand.

Clovis rode up to a ratty-looking man with grey hair and a beard that looked as soft as iron shavings.

"Who's that?" Bronwen asked Rowli.

He did not answer. His head hung forward, and he let out a soft snort.

"Rowli," she said louder.

He jerked his head up. "Mutton, indeed." He smacked his lips, and his head drooped again, supported by the thick ring of flesh around his neck. Back to sleep.

"Never mind."

Clovis returned and explained that the grey-bearded man would guide them safely across the sandbars.

Bronwen muttered a last prayer to Saint Seiriol to keep them safe on their journey and then tacked on a quick one to Saint Afon of the waters for protection from the swirling tides. The sand was not exposed for the entire crossing, so the horses had to wade some of the way. They were putting their lives in the hands of the guide.

The bearded man set off on foot into the muddy strait, followed closely by Clovis. Bronwen urged her horse on, but at the edge of dry ground, her animal balked. She kicked and prodded, but the creature wouldn't budge.

"Come on. Let's go." The horse laid its ears back flat. "Come on, Gwyllion." She hated using that name. It was never a good idea to speak the names of the faerie folk. She still wasn't convinced it was the horse's real name. Rhys had seemed very pleased with himself when he'd said it and then downright euphoric when it turned Bronwen white.

As luck would have it, when she said the horse's name out loud, the animal's ears perked up, and it set off, following the squelching trail through the mud behind Clovis. Perhaps Rhys had told the truth about the horse, though only a halfwit would pick such a name.

Bronwen had been staring at the back of Clovis—the horse's bony haunches and Clovis's bony backside—all morning. It made the sudden appearance of Rowli's roundness right beside her even more disturbing.

He held out a strip of dried meat. It looked like he had been carrying it clenched in his fist for weeks.

Although her stomach rumbled with hunger, she declined. "That's very kind, but I'll have to pass. You have it."

He crammed the entire clump in his mouth. "Mutton," he mumbled.

Bronwen followed the exact path of the guide across the muddy seabed until they came to a larger stream. The guide waded through, and the water came up to his waist.

Clovis told her to go next.

She urged her horse into the water, holding her feet up higher and higher so they wouldn't get wet. The salty water would ruin her shoes, and she didn't want them to fall apart before she got home.

Finally, her horse climbed the bank on the opposite side, and Clovis dropped some coins into the bearded man's hand.

The island was a beautiful place. The waving hillocks of green grass looked as soft as a downy pillow. A few clusters of trees sprang up along the way, and a steady wind blew from the west, bringing the sweet fragrance of meadow grass.

When darkness fell, they stopped and set up a little camp. Tomorrow, Bronwen would cross another much smaller channel to reach the rocky cliffs where the shrine of Saint Cenydd was built.

The whole island was a holy place for those mysterious folk who lived there before the word of God. She'd heard rumors of burial mounds and stone circles, rocks etched with ethereal designs in patterns of knots and swirls. A full moon rose from the east and cast an eerie glow on the landscape. With the wind blowing the grass and the moonshine rippling across it, everything looked alive.

"A good night for the Pooka," Rowli said, throwing some branches onto the fire.

Leave it to Rowli to speak out loud the name of the woodland faerie folk. Though smaller than the mountain Gwyllion, Pooka were capable of great mischief. They loved to dance around a fire with light shining from their fingertips. Harmless enough until their fondness for snatching human babies drew them to the nearest cradle.

"Pooka, indeed," Clovis said. "The island is wild with them. Did I ever tell you the time I saw a faerie elf? Little black thing ran right 'cross my path. Lucky I had my brother with me—he's a changeling, you know. Ugliest boy I ever seen."

"Ugly, indeed. D'you know, I think I've seen uglier." Rowli grinned a greasy grin. "I believe it was your mother."

Clovis stared at him. Bronwen thought there would be a fight for sure. Then Clovis burst out laughing. "D'you know, I believe you're right."

They laughed as though offending Clovis's mother and the faerie folk meant nothing. If a Pooka heard them, there would be trouble tonight.

Maybe she should move closer to the men, just in case. Bronwen looked at Rowli. He licked the fingertips of one hand while the other dug deep into his food bag. He swallowed whatever he'd stuffed into his mouth and then belched. Thankfully, the fire didn't go out.

"Bless you," Clovis said. He cracked his bony knuckles and then his chicken neck, jerking his head this way, then that. He cleared his throat and spat a greenish clump into the grass.

On second thought, perhaps the Pooka weren't so bad. She pulled her bedroll away from the fire.

"Not still 'fraid of us, are you?" Clovis said, wiping his chin.

"You mean because you tried to kill me on Calan Mai?" Despite Rhys's promise of safety, a night alone with these two did not sound harmless.

"Scared indeed," Rowli said. "D'you know, perhaps we went too far."

"Too far?" Bronwen asked.

"Indeed," Rowli said. "We was supposed to scare you, is all. You know. Knock some sense into you, he told us."

"He?" Although she had a good idea of who *he* was.

"Rhys, of course," Clovis said.

"Rhys, indeed," Rowli added.

How dare he. He'd let them frighten her near to death just so he could prove his point. It had worked. Even if it was contrived, she'd never brave the city alone after dark again.

Clovis wadded up his cloak to use as a pillow. "Hope you're not mad. Rhys pays us well, and we do what he asks."

"Don't you worry," Bronwen said. "Next time I see Rhys"—which would probably be never—"I'll tell him exactly what I think."

Rowli and Clovis found that enormously funny. They laughed and laughed. She pulled her thin blanket up over her ears.

Cold from the earth crept into her body. The chuckles and snorts from the other side of the fire eventually died, replaced by steady snores from Rowli and occasional whimpers from Clovis.

When her vision became no more than half moons, a cry rose from a grove of trees in the distance—a cry she'd heard before, the stormy night of her sixteenth birthday. And again at the beach with Urien.

There were not supposed to be Gwyllions here on the island. The crooked face of the faerie witch from home filled her mind. It was a face she would never forget. Could it be the same one?

In a puff of smoke, the fire went out. Rowli and Clovis slept on, undisturbed by the shriek from the woods. Even if it was a Gwyllion, it would stay in the trees, concealed. Bronwen hoped.

Clouds moved in, covering the moon. The world went black. A light flickered in the trees. One lantern blinking through the darkness.

Maybe Bronwen's time was up and the hag wanted the shoes back. Perhaps because Bronwen had not fulfilled her destiny with them, she would be forced to return them. She had failed with Lord Urien.

The light in the trees moved away, beckoning her to follow. She was a fool if she did. But hadn't she been a fool all along? She had fooled herself into thinking she was something special, someone a king's son might love. Lord Urien had not been fooled.

The light summoned her again, urging her to come. She tossed off her blanket and followed. She could not hide from the faerie folk, especially not from a witch. If the Gwyllion had come for her, the Gwyllion would have her. That was simply the way it was.

When Bronwen reached the grove of trees, the light moved on, bobbing across the grassy plain toward a towering mound of earth that jutted its rounded top into the blackened sky.

An ancient barrow. A hill made by men of old to house the bones of their dead.

Bronwen would not follow. Not in there.

She turned back toward camp, but the moment she spun around, she came face-to-face with the Gwyllion.

Chapter Fifteen

You can keep away from the rogue, but you cannot keep yourself safe from the liar.

MORE THAN ANYTHING, BRONWEN WANTED to scream. But that would offend the Gwyllion. She dipped into a tiny curtsy and said in a stilted whisper, "May God prosper you."

The Gwyllion said nothing. Her ragged grey robes hung loose from her skeletal frame. Her ashen skin flickered a sickly grey in the lamplight, and inside her lopsided eyes churned a grey mist.

It was the same faerie witch who had come down from Mynydd Moel, the one who had visited her mother and her on that night weeks ago. The one who had given her the shoes. She'd never heard of a Grey Maiden so far from the mountains before. For some reason, she had followed Bronwen to the city of the king and then to this island.

The Gwyllion lifted the lamp to Bronwen's face and stared without blinking. Bronwen looked away, then looked back, but the misty eyes did not waver.

The Gwyllion spoke in her gravelly voice. "Lift up your skirts."

Bronwen did. It seemed the Gwyllion wanted her footwear back. Bronwen held up her dress so the light from the lamp fell on the plain brown shoes. At least Urien wasn't here to see this. Not that he cared anymore.

"There is still time," the Gwyllion rasped. "You must not look with your eyes if you wish to find what you are searching for."

More riddles. Impossible to understand. Did the Gwyllion mean finding the shrine of Saint Cenydd? Or maybe finding her way back home? But then how would she get home without her eyes?

"I have no idea what you mean." Bronwen immediately regretted her words. She sounded insolent. Somehow, being around the king's son had made her bold. She should not question the witch.

"There is still time," the Gwyllion repeated.

Time for what? Bronwen tried to remember what the hag had said on the night she had given her the shoes. *Stars do not shine on dreamers. They shine on those who see the truth.* Bronwen saw the truth. It was hiding under her skirts, concealed by the enchanted shoes. Urien, Gwenna, Gwil—they were the ones in the dark.

The Gwyllion reached out and laid her bony hand on Bronwen's arm, turning her halfway around.

Bronwen stood at the entrance to the barrow mound, staring into its dark cavern. Without taking a step, the Gwyllion had transported her across the field to the threshold of the ancient tomb. The piled earth created a huge circle. Around the base lay a rock wall that had long since tumbled down. Two stone pillars with a third across the top formed the low opening to the barrow.

The Gwyllion vanished, the lamp gone. Bronwen was alone.

Perhaps the Gwyllion meant that there was still time for her friends to see the truth. For Urien to see the truth. But if he saw her crippled legs, he would banish her from the city. If that's what the hag wanted, she could simply take the shoes now.

A soft gust of air from the tunnel rustled her skirts. Perhaps what Bronwen was searching for was in there. Why else would the Gwyllion have set her here? It would be impossible to find, not knowing what it was. And she was meant to find it without using her eyes? Was there something she wasn't supposed to see? None of this made sense.

The clouds that came in with the Grey Maiden drifted away. In the moonlight, the worn carvings on the posts and lintel looked like coils of rope. She traced over them, her fingers dipping in and out of the grooves as she ran them along the cold and weathered stone.

Who had made such beautiful designs? They must have labored for years to work these labyrinthine patterns into solid stone. It would have taken dozens of men even more years to pile the earth into such a mound. Who was so important that they deserved this much fuss about their burial?

Bronwen lowered herself to her hands and knees and crawled in.

The cold air hit her hard, and she shuddered. By some miraculous feat of construction, the moon was at the perfect angle to the entrance of the mound, and it shone in, illuminating the path. After a short distance, the tunnel opened, and she could stand. The passage grew taller the farther in she went until the ceiling was beyond her reach.

The walls were covered with more carvings—circles that wound around and around, swirls and knots looping and twining.

She reached the end of the passageway, half expecting to find a pile of bones and a skull wearing a crown of pure gold. There was none. Anything valuable would have been plundered long ago.

The only monument inside the mound was a stone altar at the end of the pathway. As she came upon it, she heard a rustle behind her. She spun around, but the tunnel was empty. She shuddered again. What if the noise had come from something unseen? Something unseeable.

A different type of carving, this one grand and striking, covered the wall above the altar. It depicted a woman with long, flowing hair. To her left stood a regal man reaching out to her. This couple must be buried here—a king and his beloved queen.

A piece of the carving was missing. Whether by time or a grave robber, Bronwen didn't know, but a shard of stone had fallen, leaving a patch of rough, broken rock below the woman's knees, where her legs should be.

The moon continued on its course. Bronwen scrambled to find the missing piece, but the light was gone. She swept her hands across the ground, feeling for anything that might have fallen from the carving. Never before had she seen darkness like this—so entirely void. She had to find that piece to make the lady whole. The queen had to be whole.

Bronwen's hands fumbled in the dark, clawing through the rubble for the missing piece. It had to be here. Maybe she could come back in the morning and reattach it. How? Tree sap, perhaps. Or mud. A mixture of both?

Another noise. In the passageway this time . . . and a light coming toward her. It had to be the Gwyllion. Or the ghosts of the dead. Without the glow from the moon, the barrow no longer seemed like a good idea. The moonlight could have driven the spirits away, and now, in the dark, they were returning.

She stood, pressing herself against the back wall as the light approached. If it was the Gwyllion, she might be all right. If a demon of the barrow, she didn't have a hope.

She whispered a prayer. "Protect me, Saint Morwyn, from the evil that approaches."

"Bron," a deep voice called. "Are you in here?"

Rhys.

The darkness in the passageway was so complete the light from his torch barely illuminated what was within a handspan of the flames. He reached the altar and moved the light back and forth until he found her.

In the faint light of the torch, Bronwen could just make out his black eyes. They didn't look happy. Still, Bronwen took a step closer. She'd been expecting something much worse.

"What in the name of heaven are you doing here in the middle of the night?" His voice echoed off the walls, sounding even more rough than usual.

"I thought you didn't believe in heaven," she said.

"I believe you believe in heaven. I'm telling you now that you will not be going there."

Rhys could be right about her slim prospects of the afterlife. She had lied to the king and his son. And to pretty much everyone else. But Rhys was not one to talk of reaching celestial heights.

"I shall get much closer than you ever will." She went back to running her hands along the ground. The missing stone had to be there somewhere.

Rhys stepped around to Bronwen's side of the altar. "What are you doing?"

"Looking for the queen's legs."

There was silence. Then Rhys asked quietly, "Did something happen to the shoes?"

"Ouch!" Bronwen sucked her finger. "I cut myself on something."

Rhys lowered the torch, and Bronwen lifted a jagged rock with a polished surface on one side.

"Look! I found it! Her legs." She touched the carved feet. "They're perfect. I knew they would be. And I found it without using my eyes, just like the Gwyllion said!"

"What are you talking about?"

She put her hand over Rhys's and lifted the torch. "See the image above the altar? A piece of it broke off. I found it."

He studied it for a bit, then lowered the burning light.

This had to mean something. First the carving of the man and his lady and then finding the missing legs. Bronwen examined the stone. Maybe it held magic, like the shoes. Except it felt no different from any other rock, not alive and intense as the shoes had the first time she had held them.

"Urien was not happy when he found out you left," Rhys said.

She went perfectly still. Did that mean he still cared for her? He'd left her alone for so long, with no word at all. She'd had no chance to tell him the truth, and her one week ended today. Or was it yesterday? She couldn't tell if she was at the end of this day or at the beginning of tomorrow.

According to Rhys's terms, if she didn't tell Urien within the week, she had to leave. And that's what she had done. Maybe she'd gone too soon. There was still time, the Gwyllion had said. Just because she'd run out of time with Rhys didn't mean she was out of time with Urien.

Unless Rhys had revealed her secret anyway.

"You told him? He must hate me now."

"Bronwen." Rhys took a few breaths, as though he were about to speak, but each inhale only resulted in an empty exhale. At last, he managed to say, "He doesn't hate you. I wish he did. He doesn't know. You were on your way home, so I let it go."

So that's why Rhys had been so eager to plop her on a horse and shoo her off with Rowli and Clovis. He probably locked the city gates and swallowed the key after she left. That way Urien need never know that his captain of the guard and Bronwen were in collusion. Smooth water made for easier sailing.

An icy breeze whiffed across her neck. She glanced over her shoulder into the nothing, then slipped nearer to Rhys and his needlepoint of light.

"He insisted we come after you."

Bronwen almost dropped the stone. "He's here?" This was terrible. And wonderful. "Why is he here?"

"I think you know," Rhys said. "But your time is up."

Naturally he would remind her of that. But there was hope. If Urien had followed her all the way to Ynys Môn, perhaps he might be more forgiving than she thought. Even then, telling him was a huge risk.

She studied the queen's legs in the stone remnant. What if it was a sign from the Gwyllion? A promise. Or a picture of the truth. A new kind of truth.

Bronwen had crippled legs, but she wanted a whole life. And the only way to get it was with a whole and perfect body. The Gwyllion had worked great miracles. She must possess the power to heal her legs permanently. If Bronwen found what she was looking for.

This rock, the carving—they could mean only one thing. Bronwen looked up at Rhys and smiled. She'd figured it out. Everything made sense to her now.

If Lord Urien loved her, really loved her, the Gwyllion would make her whole. That was what she truly wanted. And these carvings gave proof that the Gwyllion would help her. Why else would the witch send her into the mound to find the image of the two lovers, of the lady with the perfect legs? The shoes were only a taste of what the Gwyllion could do for her if

Bronwen found what she was looking for. And she had. Urien. He was here; he must feel some affection to come all this way.

She had to keep it all hidden until she was absolutely certain of Urien's feelings. Then she'd find the Gwyllion and be healed. It had worked for Saint Cenydd; it would work for her. She hugged the broken stone to her chest.

"What are you all worked up about?" Rhys asked. "It's just a bit of rock."

She had to hold him off for a little longer. "Please," she said to Rhys. "I need a few more days." She showed him the perfect legs on the shard. It seemed so obvious to her now. This was the Gwyllion's plan all along. How could Rhys not understand?

Rhys pointed to the stone. "This is not you. It has nothing to do with you. It's just a piece of ancient ruin. You've let this Gwyllion nonsense go to your head. You think that if Urien loves you enough, he won't care about your legs."

Bronwen couldn't help glancing down at her magically straightened limbs.

"You're wrong," Rhys said. "How can he love you if everything he knows about you is a lie?"

Bronwen shook her head. "It's not a lie. I mean, yes, I lied about some things, but not everything. Not about the important things."

"Then why won't you tell him?"

"Because . . ."

Rhys folded his arms, waiting for an answer. He would never understand. He had never had to walk through the village while people pointed and stared, while those who should have been her friends turned away.

"Because even though my legs are straight, he would see me differently."

"Hmm," Rhys said. "How is that love?"

Bronwen didn't answer. She didn't need to explain herself to Rhys, especially when he was being purposefully hardheaded. She just needed to get him to leave her alone about it. The Gwyllion had shown her what her future held. All Bronwen had to do was stall for a little more time.

"Just say nothing to Urien. Please. That's all I'm asking."

Rhys's jaw went immediately back into clenched mode. "No. I already gave you a week."

"Last week doesn't count. I didn't see him. I wanted to tell him, but I never got the chance. I'll do it," she lied. She had no intention of telling Urien anything, not with the end so near. "Soon. I just have to wait until the right time."

"The right time passed ages ago. This will not end well, Bronwen. Either you tell him tonight, or I will."

"No!" If Urien found out, he would cast her off, and then she'd never get what she truly wanted. Apparently, Rhys didn't care about that. "If you do, you will be punished for withholding the truth. I'll tell him you knew from the beginning."

In the flickering light of the waning torch, Rhys's face was hard as stone. "Who do you think he will believe? The girl who deceived him or the captain of the guard who has saved his life countless times?"

Rhys! He was like the plague, never going away. Why did he send her off only to follow along behind? Why didn't he cross the Afon Menai at high tide and drown?

How was he the same boy who had mopped her forehead with a damp cloth while she'd cried out all those years ago? What had happened to him to turn him so hard? It seemed all he cared about now was destroying her.

If this was how Rhys wanted to play, she could go along. "Fine. I'll tell him you hurt me."

He reeled back as if she'd slapped him. "What?"

"I'll tell Lord Urien you attacked me. No"—she had a better idea— "I'll tell him you kissed me. Against my will."

"That's ridiculous."

"Is it? A few tears might be very convincing."

"Bronwen, I don't know what is going through that head of yours. I am not the enemy here."

"Then why can't you leave it be? It's my life and my choice. Why can't you let me live it?"

He moved closer until he towered over her, his black eyes glinting. "I . . . I have . . ." He snatched the rock fragment from Bronwen and flung it against the wall. "Bronwen, you are a fool."

She expected to hear this; she just wondered why it had taken so long. She stepped toward him. "And don't think I didn't find out about your schemes with Rowli and Clovis. How could you let them scare me like that?"

"How else was I supposed to coax some sense into you? You wouldn't listen to reason."

She raised her voice. "You could have followed me without the feigned murder plot."

"That would've kept you out of danger one night, but what about the next? Or the next?" He stood so close now they almost touched.

"You are not my father, and you have no right to interfere."

"I don't want to be your father. I just want you safe."

And before she could answer, he pressed his mouth on hers, surprising her with his gentleness. *Push him away*, she thought. *Push away*. But she didn't. Her arms wouldn't move. She just stood there until he released her.

She opened her eyes, not realizing she had closed them. She should be furious. When she had threatened him earlier, about telling Urien he'd kissed her, she had no idea he'd carry it out. She would have slapped him if only she could take her eyes off his lips.

He took a step back.

At the very least, Bronwen had something real to bargain with. Thank the saints she hadn't threatened to accuse him of anything more.

A new light flickered in the entrance to the barrow. "Rhys?" the king's son called.

Chapter Sixteen

He understands badly who listens badly.

RHYS SNATCHED UP HIS TORCH and called to Urien. "In here. I found her."
He moved toward the door, pausing to whisper with Urien as they passed.
Rhys knelt and crawled out through the entrance. A few unsavory words
made their way back to Bronwen when he smacked his head on the low
ceiling.

Bronwen waited in the dark for Urien and his torch to reach her. The
cold from the earth and stone soaked into her bones as though the spirits
of the dead had washed over her. She smoothed her hair back and tugged
her skirts lower.

When Urien stood in front of her, she dared not look up. She curtsied
low. "May God prosper you." The last time she'd used that greeting, It was
to the Gwyllion. How quickly things changed. One moment she was face-
to-face with a faerie witch, and the next, she gazed at the fine boots of the
king's son.

"God's welcome," he said. He took her hand and lifted her from her
curtsy, holding on even after she was standing. "You left. Did I offend you?"

"No, my lord."

"Are you angry with me?"

"Not at all, my lord."

"Then why did you leave without a word?" He lifted her chin, forcing
her to meet his gaze. His light hair and blue eyes glowed eerily in the
torchlight, but it did not diminish his beauty. She hadn't seen him for over
a week; she'd forgotten how handsome he was.

"I thought I was the one who angered you. When I didn't hear from
you after the hunt."

"I had to ride south on the errand I postponed after Calan Mai. I sent my man to you with a message."

"Forgive me, sir; I did not see him."

He put his arms around her, pulling her close. He smelled like heaven. The packet of clove spice hanging at her waist was nothing compared to the scent that filled her now. She leaned in, holding tight.

"Let's get out of this dreadful place," Urien said.

"One moment." She took the torch from Urien's hand and lowered it to the rubble on the floor. She found the fragment of the lady's legs, broken into three jagged parts. The carving had survived from the age before time, and Rhys had destroyed it in the blink of an eye. The poor queen would never be whole again.

"What's the matter?" Urien asked. "Did you lose something?"

"No." She set the broken shards on the stone altar. "I'm ready to go."

Urien led her down the narrow passage, bending lower and lower as they reached the entrance. Bronwen crawled out first, with Urien close behind.

She hadn't realized how old the air in the barrow had tasted until she breathed the fresh summer breeze.

Urien stood up behind her. "I haven't been out to Ynys Môn for years. I forgot how beautiful it is." He cast his torch on the ground and stamped it out. The light of the moon illuminated far more than the flames had.

Lord Urien pulled her close again, his mouth landing softly on hers. Rhys's kiss had been vinegar; Urien's was warm, sugared wine. Yes, she had lost control on the hunt, but under the circumstances, it could have happened to anyone.

Far too soon, Urien pulled away, taking both her hands in his. "Your leaving has done one thing," he said, and in the silver glow, his eyes danced.

"What is that?"

"It has made me realize I cannot live without you, Bronwen. I love you. If it pleases you, you shall be my wife."

Bronwen's hands slipped from Urien's, and she took a step back. Her legs were still crippled. The Gwyllion had barely told her she had more time, and now, here stood Urien, asking her to marry him. Bronwen turned her head, peering over her shoulder. Was the Gwyllion still near?

Urien had just said he loved her. According to Bronwen's reckoning, that should be enough. That had to be what the Gwyllion had given her the shoes for in the first place. She pulled down on her dress again until the hem dragged on the ground. What if the Gwyllion didn't show up in time? What if the Gwyllion didn't heal her soon . . . It was unthinkable. *You are a fool*, Rhys had said, but—

Rhys! If she strolled back into camp on the arm of the king's son, Rhys would summon a council and blurt out everything. Rowli and Clovis would wrestle her to the ground and pry her shoes off, and Urien would watch the whole mess, repulsed.

"Bronwen?" Urien asked.

Her fingers lingered on her lips, where Rhys had kissed her. She would deal with Rhys later. Right now, Urien had asked her a question. She kissed his hand, the very act she was meant to do the first time they had met, but he had kissed hers instead. "My lord, I'm pleased beyond words."

"Urien," he reminded her, embracing her again. He stepped back, holding her hands, watching her. "You are irresistible in the moonlight."

She must look wild after riding all day, then tunneling around under the barrow mound.

"Do you love me, my pretty and perfect Bronwen?"

Rhys's words echoed in her mind. *How is that love?* She pushed them aside. Rhys didn't understand her heart, but that was no reason for her to doubt her own feelings. Of course she loved him. He was handsome and strong. And the king's son. What about him wasn't to love? "My lord—"

He cleared his throat.

"Urien. I love you."

He picked her up and twirled her around once, then set her on the ground. "In the morning, we shall return to the Sedd Brenhinol to tell the world." He took her hand and set off toward the dim glow of the campfire.

"Sir. Urien." She looked over her shoulder but saw no sign of the Gwyllion's bobbing light. "Might I visit the shrine of Saint Cynedd before we leave?"

"Saint Cynedd? He who was crippled? Why on earth would you want to go there?"

Because I am a cripple. Because without my magic shoes, I cannot walk. Because if you saw me as I really am, you would be disgusted. "I promised my mother I would."

"Is that why you came? I wondered what would bring you here."

She coughed to clear the itching in her throat. "Yes. Um. My mother knew a girl who was left lame after an illness. A cousin. She was healed. Later. By a miracle. My mother made me promise to come offer thanks."

"Oh? What was her name?"

"Iola."

"Lucky for her. What a horror to be crippled."

She could never tell him. He must never find out. "Yes, indeed. A horror." Bronwen kept searching the darkness. For a moment, she thought she heard the Gwyllion's cry, but it was only the wind whistling in the trees.

She had no place marrying the king's son. She should have waited until her legs were strong, until after the Gwyllion fixed her.

But how could she say no? Urien loved her. He was the king's son. And he loved her.

She'd been so sure in the barrow, but out here, the difficulties pressed in on her. Bronwen had put her faith in a faerie witch. A risky venture. And yet, it was the Gwyllion who had led her to this point. It had to be for a reason. Bronwen was on the right path; in her heart, she knew it.

He loves me, she repeated. *Everything will work out.*

Gwenna would be beside herself. Bronwen laughed softly as she imagined the shock on Gwenna's face when she returned to Sedd Brenhinol with plans to marry Urien.

"Why do you laugh?" Urien asked.

"I don't know." She should be worried sick, overcome with panic. But walking through the tall grass, holding Lord Urien's hand, made it hard to concentrate on the complications ahead. "I suppose because I'm happy."

He stopped. "There is something I want to tell you." He put his mouth close to her ear and whispered, "I'm happy too." He leaned back. "Now, if we are to cross with low tide, we must leave before first light. There won't be time for the shrine."

This did not seem the best moment to turn her back on the saint of the crippled. She needed all the help she could get. She'd dug herself in deep, and without some intervention by powers beyond the mortal, she couldn't see any way out.

"I understand," she said. *Forgive me, Saint Cenydd. And Mother.*

They arrived back at the fire to find Rowli and Clovis still sound asleep. Rhys was piling wood on the flames—throwing the branches on with more force than necessary. He glanced up at Bronwen and Urien holding hands and slammed a particularly heavy log onto the pyre. A cloud of embers flew into the sky.

The boy Tyrnen was there, pounding the last of a tent stake into the ground. Apparently, when the king's son traveled, he didn't sleep on a bedroll under the stars. He had a small canvas enclosure, big enough for a pallet or two.

Bronwen put a hand on Tyrnen's shoulder. "How are you recovering from your accident on the boar hunt?"

He grinned at her. "Some parts are a little stiff, but I'm fine, my lady. Thanks for asking." He bowed as he backed away.

Urien led her to the tent door and pulled back the flap. "For you. No lady of mine sleeps out in the open like a common peasant." He touched her cheek with the back of his fingers. "Get some sleep. We leave in a few hours."

She smiled up at him. "Good night."

Inside the tent, a bed of furs and linens lined one side, and in the small remaining space, a single candle burned in an iron holder. He'd brought all this comfort for her. She crawled into the soft furs and blew out the flame.

* * *

They woke, as Urien had promised, before the first light of the sun slivered over the mountains to the east. She had half a mind to run back to the barrow mound to see if she could piece together what was left of the broken legs. But for what purpose? Her story was not in the stone but in the representation.

Urien stayed close to her as they broke camp, offering her bread and cheese for breakfast and letting her drink out of his flask. Rowli and Clovis set off on their own, their services no longer needed now that Bronwen had a royal escort. Tyrnen collapsed the tent and rolled it into a ball, securing it to the back of a horse. It took all of his strength to heft the heavy canvas onto the animal, but he managed.

Rhys avoided Bronwen; anytime she glanced up and caught him looking at her, he turned away.

"Rhys," Urien said as he checked his horse's gear. "Why did you not deliver my message to Bronwen?"

He was the man Urien had sent? Rhys? He purposefully didn't tell her Urien had gone away. At the market when she told him she was leaving, he had said nothing. Even when she asked him outright yesterday morning why Urien had not sent for her, he kept silent. If he was not the enemy, he should try to act less like a traitor.

Rhys stared at Bronwen for a moment, then said, "I didn't go myself. I sent a page. He must have gotten distracted."

He was lying. Bronwen saw it in his eyes. But there was nothing she could do; Rhys held her secret, and any accusation on her part would lead to all sorts of unpleasant repercussions, even with the kiss as collateral.

"As soon as we return, dismiss him," Urien said.

"Yes, sire," Rhys said. He dumped a pail of water on the coals, and steam hissed up and surrounded him.

Urien set a fast pace until they came to the Afon Menai. The tide was out, and the same man with the wiry grey beard guided them across the muddy flats. When they came to a freshwater stream that fed into the sea, they stopped to rest and let their horses drink.

Urien wouldn't hear of Bronwen going back to the Fib and Flounder. He insisted she have a room in the castle.

As they rode into the courtyard, several young stable boys ran out to tend to the horses. Urien led Bronwen inside and ordered a servant to fetch Luned.

A large, round woman dressed in brown hurried down the corridor. It was the potato woman from the day of the presentations.

Urien told her to prepare Bronwen a room of her own.

Luned stared at him for a moment, then bowed. "Yes, my lord." She waddled away.

A short time later, Bronwen found herself set up in a small chamber with a soft bed, a window overlooking the water, a wash basin on a table, and a huge trunk for her belongings. Someone had brought her things in from the horses, and they lay on her bed, still in bundles. Her crutch was nowhere to be seen.

The potato woman opened the door. "Anything else, my lady?"

Bronwen nearly asked about her crutch but then decided against it. She didn't need it anymore. She ran a hand through her tangled hair. "Would it be possible to have a bath?"

Luned nodded. "I'll have the water brought up. Shall I send one of the queen's ladies to assist you?"

Heavens, no. What a mess that would make. "No, I'll bathe myself."

Luned walked to the door, then paused as though she had more she wanted to say.

"Is there something else?" Bronwen asked.

"Well, I was just wondering."

"Yes?"

"Supper will be served soon. I'll send someone to fetch you." And she hurried out the door.

Bronwen unpacked her few belongings, then sat near the small blaze in the fireplace. Tomorrow, she would begin her search for the Gwyllion. The hag had been following her since she left home. She couldn't be that hard to find. It could take a few days, but there was nothing else for it. This was the only way her plan would work. And she would make it work. The more Bronwen thought about it, the more confident she became.

With a quick knock on the door, a scullery maid backed in carrying a tub. Other servants came along behind her with pitchers and buckets of steaming water. They emptied their containers into the bathing tub, then quickly left.

Once Bronwen was alone, she lowered the door latch, locking anyone else out. She hadn't removed her shoes for some time. Not since she waded in the sea. What a featherhead idea that had been, to take her shoes off in such a place. Perhaps that's why Rhys's words never failed to sting. They were true—she was a fool.

Better to not take them off again until her business with the Gwyllion was complete. She knew not how many more times she could survive the pain of healing. Each time she put the shoes on, she wandered closer to death.

She slipped into the warm water, keeping her feet dangling over the side. She was becoming very proficient at washing herself in this position. She rubbed lavender oil over her skin, then dressed in her dove-grey gown. She was just twisting her hair up into a simple coil on her head when there came a knock at her door. The servant to call her to supper. She unhooked the latch and opened the door.

Rhys. He wasn't under the command of Luned, so he had no business here. Except to ask forgiveness for not passing on Urien's message. And to apologize for his kiss. Her eyes settled on his lips for a moment.

She took a deep breath and stepped away. "What now?"

"What else? Urien sent me to fetch you for supper." He smiled as though nothing untoward had ever passed between them.

"Fine," she said. "And I believe you owe me an apology."

Rhys slipped into her room and closed the door. His smile dropped like a rock hurled from the parapet. "What are you thinking?"

Bronwen sighed. "Please, can we not have this conversation again? I know what you think of me. You've told me plenty of times." Bronwen turned back to her burnished mirror and wedged a comb in her hair to keep it up. "I'm not as witless as you assume. I have a plan that is going to work. Everything will turn out. You'll see. Lord Urien will not be hurt."

He wiped his hand across his face and groaned. "Has it never occurred to you that it is not for Urien that I worry?"

She hesitated a moment. Since the very beginning, Rhys had been obsessed with protecting Lord Urien. Doing everything Urien asked of him—from fighting his fights to running his errands. Lately, most of those errands seemed to involve Bronwen.

The secret truth about her crippled legs hung from her neck like a millstone. She was weary to the bone from dragging it around. Rhys was the only one among all these people who knew her for what she really was. With him, she didn't need to hide.

She couldn't deny that at times, there was peace in his presence. But it seemed unlikely he'd worry more about her than the king's son.

"Bronwen," he said. "When you were sick, who made you a doll to help you deal with the pain?"

"You did."

"Who carried you outside in the middle of the night to use the privy?"

Bronwen's cheeks flushed, and she looked away. "You did." He'd carried her more times than just in the middle of the night.

"And who made you the crutch you no longer believe you need?"

She'd never wondered where the crutch had come from. Her mother had given it to her after her father died, after she knew Bronwen would live but never walk properly again. Bronwen hadn't questioned its origin—until now. "You made it?"

He nodded. "Is it so very hard to believe that I might not want to see you get hurt?"

He'd said something similar in the barrow too, just before he'd kissed her. About keeping her safe.

They had been close while he had lived at their home. Even though he was a paid worker, Rhys had always felt more like a friend. Perhaps the only one she'd ever had, at least until she'd met Gwenna. She supposed it possible that, for old time's sake, there was a chance he didn't want her hurt.

Bronwen rubbed her temples. She'd barely gotten any sleep last night, wandering around Ynys Môn, cavorting with Gwyllions, rogues, and future kings. Her head ached. Rhys still had not offered one word of regret for his lack of decency. Urien loved her. They were to be married. She had complete faith that the Gwyllion would heal her. What was left that might hurt her?

"Rhys, I appreciate you saving me that day in the cove. And all your kindness when I was young. But I think it's best if we don't talk about this anymore." She reached around him to open the door.

He put his hand on the latch to stop her. When she looked at him, he said, "I'm sorry about the barrow. Really, I am." He seemed uncomfortably sincere. "I don't know what came over me, and I apologize."

She couldn't stop her eyes from roaming one more time to his lips. She shook her head. "I suppose it wasn't so very bad." She remembered only too clearly her own loss of judgment on the day of the hunt. When tempers flared, it seemed reason went up in smoke. "I'm more angry that you didn't tell me Urien had ridden south. How could you keep that from me?"

"Ah," he said. "For that, I am not sorry. I know you think me a tyrant, but believe me when I tell you, it was for your own good. You do not know him like I do."

And now they were back where they had started. This argument was futile. Things had worked out in the end with Urien, even with Rhys's lack of cooperation. She opened the door. "Come, let's not be late for supper."

"Yes, my lady." He led her down to the great hall, where Urien waited.

Chapter Seventeen

Let not your tongue cut your throat.

In the great hall, one table was laid out near the side wall. A few candles stuck into an iron centerpiece cast a meager light on the food. Tyrnen sat at the lower end of the table, away from the dais. His small, wiry frame leaned heavily on the wooden planks. The poor lad looked exhausted.

Rhys slipped onto the bench beside him, slapping his shoulder in greeting.

Urien had already started eating, but he rose as Bronwen approached. His eyes roamed over her. "Perfect. I never knew such beauty existed."

Bronwen flushed again. If she must blush, she preferred it to be because of Urien's compliments rather than Rhys's talk of midnight privy runs. "Thank you."

"You must be starving."

Bronwen hadn't eaten much since she left the previous morning for the shrine of Saint Cenydd. Somehow, she'd lost her appetite while traveling with Rowli and Clovis.

"I regret that my father and the rest of the house have already dined," Urien said. "We are quite late, so it's just us tonight."

"All right." She dipped her bread into the trencher of stew.

He leaned in close, taking a deep breath. "You do look lovely tonight. And you smell like a walk in a summer garden."

She smiled up at him. "And you smell like a Christmas pudding."

He laughed softly. "But I wonder. Why do you not wear the new shoes I had made for you? I've been wanting for some time to see you in shoes befitting a lady."

Rhys had been deliberately ignoring them, but at this, he looked up.

Forget about him, she thought. This was between Urien and her.

"I thought," Bronwen said, "since it's so late and everyone has eaten, I might just wear my plain shoes. The others are so beautiful I'm afraid I'll ruin them."

"Nonsense. Soon you'll have many shoes. I'll wait here. Go put them on."

Lord Urien mentioned nothing about his cordwainer or having to find a new one. Perhaps in a city like this, there were many to choose from. He picked a terrible time to take such interest in her shoes.

Unless he suspected something. She stole a quick glance at Rhys, who seemed to be waiting for her new shoes with even more interest than Urien.

She pulled her skirts lower, even though she was sitting at the table and Urien had already seen. "I . . ."

"Go on," Urien said, urging her toward the door. He spoke as though teasing, but underneath his smile lay something more. An intensity as though this mattered greatly to him. It could be suspicion. Or he was simply tired of her wearing such unbecoming shoes, especially when he had gone to the trouble of putting a perfectly fine pair in her possession.

The problem was, they were not in her possession anymore.

No. The problem was, she couldn't wear them even if they were sitting on the table in front of her.

She rubbed the back of her neck. "Sir, I didn't want to tell you this, but . . ."

Urien stared at her, his eyes open wide, interested in what she didn't want to say. Rhys sat motionless, waiting. Even Tyrnen was watching her now.

Bronwen cleared her throat. "I believe there is a thief at the Fib and Flounder."

"What?" Urien said, slamming his mug on the table, while at the same time Rhys muttered, "Here we go again."

"I put them away in my room, but when I packed my belongings yesterday morning, they were gone." She showed him her empty hands as if that proved her story. "I looked and looked."

Urien scowled. "Isn't that the second pair you've had stolen since you've been here?"

Was it? Bronwen thought back. What had she said about her shoes? That they'd fallen off the cart on the way to the city. No, wait. That's

what she had said to Gwenna. She'd been with Urien on Calan Mai—
she remembered now—walking along the shore. She had told him her
shoes had been stolen. How genius of her to corroborate her own story.

"Yes, the second pair." She tucked a loose lock of hair behind her ear.
"I wonder if the other guests have had any problems."

"We have penalties here for thieves," Urien said. "Rhys, first thing
tomorrow, go to the inn and look into it."

The annoyance on Rhys's face was impressive. He knew the shoes
were not stolen. "Sire, I have work to do tomorrow with the King's Men.
I haven't been there to train them for some time." Another irritated glance
at Bronwen. "Perhaps I could send someone else instead? I have two men
who are masters at finding what's gone missing. Remember a few months
ago when your falcon was stolen? They are the ones who found her and the
man responsible. And two weeks ago, when the baker's cart was taken from
the market and no one saw anything? My men found it near Serenbach,
along with the young scoundrels who stole it. And don't forget the—"

"Yes, yes. Enough. Just see to it that the thief is found. And I want to
see him personally."

With Rhys in charge of finding the shoe thief, she had nothing to fear.
He wouldn't waste his time on what he knew did not exist. His feigned
investigation could drag on for days, giving Bronwen time to find the
Gwyllion.

Urien went back to his meal. When he had sopped his plate clean, he
walked Bronwen back to her chamber.

"Are you finding your rooms adequate?" he asked.

"Yes. More than adequate. They're lovely."

"And you have everything you need?"

"Yes, everything."

"Are you sure? Because I can have my mother arrange for anything
that might be lacking. Wardrobe, candles, um . . . parchment. A lady."

"A lady," Bronwen said. "Sir. Urien. Might I bring my friend Gwenna
as my lady?" Gwenna would die of joy to live in the castle.

"If that is your wish, then so be it." He ran the back of his fingers along
her cheek and chin. "So beautiful."

She looked up into his soft blue eyes. She'd never seen a man so
handsome in her entire life. He drew her in and kissed her with a fire that
made Bronwen's hands reach of their own accord for his golden hair. She
twined her fingers through it.

Urien released her and stepped back. He was breathing heavily, and his eyes burned bright. He opened the door to her chamber and motioned for her to go in. "I think it would be wise for you to leave me now."

"Yes." She was a little breathless herself.

He snatched her back for one more quick kiss, then she stepped into her bedchamber and closed the door.

She crossed to the window. In the last of the fading light, silhouettes of the evening swifts soared through the air. For the first time in her life, she understood how they felt. If she spread her arms, she could lift into the sky. All that was left was to locate the Gwyllion. She was so close to putting all her worries behind her. So close she could almost taste it— like warm honeyed milk on a cold, wintry night. Almost there.

* * *

Bronwen jumped out of bed the next morning. She had a full list of things she needed to accomplish. Well, only two things, but they were important. First, visit Gwenna and tell her the good news. Second, wander the woods until she found the Gwyllion.

She had been thinking about what Rhys had said on the day she got caught in the tide about the old hag he had met in the streets. The hag had told him where to find Bronwen.

Rhys had denied it, but it had to have been the Gwyllion. Who else would have known Bronwen's whereabouts? She had told no one where she was going. And no other stranger would have taken notice.

In the great hall, food lay on the table, and people milled around, eating and talking. She didn't see Urien anywhere, nor Rhys, thank Saint Cadoc. She took the bowl of porridge a servant girl offered her and ate.

Tyrnen tapped her on the shoulder. "My lady, Urien asked me to give you a message. He didn't want to wake you. He went to the listing yards with the men and says he'll see you for the meal at midday."

"Thank you, Tyrnen."

Dai sat on one of the long benches, talking to a fine young woman while he ate his breakfast. She had long dark hair, and according to Gwenna, so did the girl who had dashed her hopes.

Bronwen wanted to find out more. She finished her porridge and went to him. "Hello, Dai."

He nodded, glancing only momentarily up at Bronwen. "My lady."

Bronwen turned to face the girl, waiting to be introduced. For being such a reserved man, he had been conversing easily with this person.

Dai tipped his head toward the lady. "This is my sister."

Sister! That explained a lot. Gwenna would be elated to learn this, although Dai had forgotten to mention his sister's name.

"Mared." The girl said, introducing herself and sliding off of the bench to curtsy. "May God prosper you."

No one had given Bronwen the formal greeting before. "God's welcome." She didn't deserve such preferential treatment, but a small part of her swelled, grateful for the honor. It was certainly a far cry from the pitiful looks she was accustomed to back home. *If the village could see me now.*

What a horrible thought. She could never go home. At least, not with Urien. The entire village would demand an explanation. Even if she was no longer crippled, he would know she used to be. That would lead to confessions about Gwyllions and faerie shoes and so much more.

She had not thought of this. Marriage to Urien would mean giving up her mountain home forever. Her mother would come here, of course, but Bronwen could never go home.

Her family name! How would she explain that to Lord Urien?

"My lady?" Mared said. "Is something wrong?"

"No," she said, pulling her mind back to the great hall. "I just . . . I was thinking. It's nothing." Bronwen smiled.

Mared took her seat beside her brother and went back to her porridge.

"Dai," Bronwen said, returning to her original purpose. "I'm wondering if I might ask a favor?"

He nodded again.

"I wish to visit Gwenna at the Fib and Flounder this morning. Would you take me there?"

* * *

Bronwen and Dai set off into the crowded streets. Dai kept quiet as they walked along. Occasionally, Bronwen attempted conversation, but she couldn't draw him out. Gwenna really was the perfect match for him. Bronwen could see it now: Gwenna and Dai sitting around the hearth, Gwenna talking his ears off, Dai listening quietly, grinning. A picture of marital bliss.

When they reached the inn, Dai bowed to her before turning to leave.

"Wait," Bronwen said. She had not asked for Dai's company without reason. "Come in with me. Until I know she is here. Otherwise, I have no one to take me home."

He nodded. His usual response to anything that didn't require actual words.

She entered the inn at the same moment a kitchen boy was coming down the main stairs. "Is Gwenna in?"

"Yes," the boy said.

"Go fetch her, please."

The boy turned and trotted back up. Bronwen gestured for Dai to go into the common room.

A scream of delight burst from the top of the stairs. Gwenna ran down and fell into Bronwen's arms, hugging and screaming and bouncing until Bronwen nearly toppled over.

"I thought I'd never see you again. And here you are. Whatever happened?"

Bronwen pried herself from Gwenna's embrace. "Well, it turns out Lord Urien is not angry at me. There was a misunderstanding, but it is all cleared up. And we are to be married."

"Married?" Gwenna reached out a hand, steadying herself on the stair rail. "You . . . marrying . . . the king's son?"

"Yes."

"I . . . Well, I thought maybe . . . And I teased you. But I didn't actually believe . . . We were just having fun. Daydreaming. But now . . . In truth?"

"Yes. He followed me to Ynys Môn and asked me to come back. He said he wanted to make me his wife." It was every girl's dream. And it was happening to her. "He moved me into the castle. And now I am in need of a lady in waiting."

Gwenna squealed again and pulled Bronwen in for another suffocating embrace.

"Bronwen Hardd, you are the best friend a girl could ever have."

She pried herself from Gwenna's grip. Gwenna still had no idea Bronwen had told Urien her family name was Mawr. Nor that she'd lied about her village. She would have to explain a few things to Gwenna before letting her loose amongst the inhabitants of the castle.

Bronwen rubbed her temples to ease the sudden headache.

Gwenna grabbed Bronwen's hands. "Shall I get my things now? Or do I wait for an invitation from the castle? Heavens! I will need some new clothes. And I need to tell Mother. At the end of the week, Gwil moves into the barracks, and Mother said we must leave then too. Poor thing, she'll be heading back to Father alone now. But she'll be so happy for me. And for you too, I'm sure. I can't believe it."

"I have one more surprise for you," Bronwen whispered.

"What? What is it?"

Bronwen tipped her head in the direction of Dai, who sat at a table in the common room, looking uncomfortable. He had been watching the reunion play out in the entryway, no doubt overhearing most of their conversation. Gwenna was not an especially quiet person.

When Gwenna glanced over at him, he gave her a small nod.

Gwenna leaned in close and asked, "What is he doing here? What about his lover?"

Bronwen snorted. "Gwenna, he doesn't have a lover, for heaven's sake. She is his sister. She attends the queen."

Gwenna combed her fingers through her hair. "I should have dressed better. I'm wearing wool. Do you think I should go change? Or is silk too fine for—" She thought for a moment. "What are we doing today?"

"We are going to the market. And wouldn't it be nice to have a handsome soldier with us? I'm sure Urien wouldn't want me wandering the city unaccompanied."

Gwenna's smile was all Bronwen had hoped for. "Excellent plan."

Bronwen motioned for Dai to join them. He did, avoiding looking directly at either of them.

"Dai," Bronwen said. "We would like to go to the market. Can you take us?"

"I should be training." He glanced up at Gwenna. She nodded some encouragement. "But Urien wouldn't want you out alone."

"Thank you," Bronwen said. "I'm sure you're right. I won't forget to tell him of your diligence."

They left the Fib and Flounder, weaving their way through the cobblestone streets toward the center of town. Bronwen studied the crowds, searching for the Gwyllion. She had a hard time imagining the Gwyllion within the city walls, but that's where Rhys had met her.

Gwenna talked a river to Dai, who listened and nodded and smiled the whole time. Just like Bronwen had pictured.

They passed Rowli and Clovis heading the opposite direction. Bronwen looked away in hopes that they wouldn't spot her.

"Good day, my lady," Rowli said.

"Good day, indeed," Clovis echoed.

"Yes. Hello," Bronwen said. Her one day spent with those two had been more than enough.

When they reached the market, Gwenna tugged Dai to her favorite spot, the cloth venders. She held up different fabrics, asking for Dai's opinion. "Very nice," he said about each one.

"Gwenna," Bronwen said. "I'm going to the church. I'll catch up with you in a bit."

Gwenna nodded, barely taking her eyes off the many fabrics. Or Dai.

Bronwen used her chance to steal away. With Dai and silks to occupy her mind, Gwenna wouldn't notice her absence for some time. She kept her head down and made her way toward the east gate, slipping past the guards and heading out into the same forest where she had heard the Gwyllion's shriek on Calan Mai.

How did one find a Gwyllion? Most people did everything possible to avoid the faerie folk, especially the witches.

Bronwen walked and walked, peering into the woodlands. If she didn't find the Gwyllion today, she'd have to come searching again tomorrow. Maybe she could sneak out after nightfall. The Grey Maiden was more likely to be out in the dark.

A twig snapped behind her, and she whirled around. "Hello? Are you there?" She didn't know what name to use. Did Gwyllions have names? They must, or how would they get along with other Gwyllions? This was absurd, wandering through the king's forest, debating with herself about the private life of a Gwyllion.

She had no way of knowing exactly how long she'd been searching, but judging by the distance the sun had traveled across the sky, it had been the better part of the day. Gwenna would have missed her by now. More than likely, they would have assumed Bronwen had returned to the castle.

Saint Morwyn, help me find the faerie witch.

Bronwen turned south, toward the sea.

"Gwyllion? Are you there?" she called, feeling like the biggest fool. Then she told herself not to think such things; it would only justify all of Rhys's claims. "I need your help."

"My lady?"

Bronwen spun around. "Dai, I thought you were with Gwenna."

He dismounted and approached her, keeping one hand on his horse's reins. "Are you hurt?"

"No. I was just . . . What are you doing here?"

Dai examined his boots before answering. "Looking for you. You're needed at the castle."

"Where's Rhys?" It had always been Rhys who appeared out of nowhere, plucking her from the wilderness and bringing her home.

Dai shrugged. "Looking."

"How did you find me?"

He adjusted his sword belt and cleared his throat. "An old woman near the eastern gate. She told me."

The Gwyllion! That conniving faerie witch knew the whole time that Bronwen was out looking for her. Did that mean Bronwen had been wrong about the Gwyllion healing her? Oh, merciful saints! What if the Gwyllion had changed her mind? It couldn't be. The signs had been clear. Bronwen just needed to try harder, after dark. She had only ever seen the Gwyllion at night.

"My lady?"

Bronwen looked up at Dai.

"Lord Urien wants you back."

Bronwen nodded, and Dai boosted her up onto his horse. She had missed the midday meal. She hoped Dai wasn't in trouble for escorting her from the castle. It wasn't his fault she'd slipped away under his watch. "Is everything all right?" she asked as he swung up into the saddle in front of her.

"It's not my place to say." Dai kicked his horse hard, and the beast lunged into a gallop. Bronwen clung to Dai's waist as the trees whirled by.

The closer they got to the city, the faster he urged his horse. They raced in through the gate and charged their way through the streets. The sound of the animal's hooves clattering on the cobblestones was the only warning people had to dive out of the way.

This was more than missing a meal with Urien. Something was wrong. Had he been hurt?

By the time Dai plunged his horse into the courtyard, Bronwen half expected to see the entire royal family laid out in shrouds, ready for burial. But there were no corpses. Just Rhys waiting for them, his hands balled into fists. Dai reined his animal to a stop in front of him, and Rhys reached up and pulled Bronwen off.

"What is it? What's wrong?" she asked.

Rhys shook his head. Bronwen thought she had seen the whole gamut of glowering looks Rhys had to offer, but this was a new one. His jaw muscles bulged, and his eyes glinted with something more than anger. Usually, his brows were a straight line of fury; today, a knot had grown in the center. Rhys was worried.

Gwenna came running out of the castle, her face wet with tears. She flung her arms around Bronwen and sobbed. "Thank the saints you're back. You can't believe what has happened."

Bronwen's worst fears were confirmed. Someone must have died. Maybe word had arrived from Glynbach that her mother had passed away. Alone. Bronwen should have never left her.

"It's Gwil." Gwenna wiped her eyes in vain; they immediately filled again. "He's been arrested. But now that you're here, everything will be fine."

Rhys pulled on Bronwen. "You need to come."

"Gwil? What happened? What did he do?"

Rhys swallowed hard. "You should have told me you hid the shoes in his chamber."

Chapter Eighteen

There are many a ship lost within sight of the harbor.

RHYS USHERED BRONWEN INTO THE castle, to the great hall, where Urien sat on the dais in his gilded chair. He rose when she entered and took her hand, leading her to the seat beside him.

She didn't belong on the throne; they weren't even married yet. But Urien waited for her to be seated. She slid into the chair, trying hard to ignore the tiny thrill that shot through her. Someday, this would be hers—a golden seat beside her golden-haired king.

"I have good news," Urien said. "We have found the shoe thief."

His words snatched Bronwen down from the clouds.

Gwil. What had happened to Gwil?

The side door opened, and a large soldier led Gwil into the hall. He stood in front of the dais with his hands bound. At a nod from Lord Urien, the soldier forced Gwil to his knees in the middle of the stone floor. Rowli and Clovis—

Oh no. Rowli and Clovis.

"What is this?" Bronwen asked Urien. Although the moment she saw Rowli and Clovis, she pieced it together. Rhys, being the thorough man he was, had told his two best men to go to the inn to search for the shoes. He must have assumed Bronwen had thrown them out. But the shoes had been found. Right where she'd left them.

Bronwen gripped the arms of her chair to keep her head from spinning.

Urien stood. He wore his crown, displaying to the entire hall his authority. "Rhys has uncovered the truth." Urien nodded his approval at Rhys. He spoke loudly so the whole room could hear. "He sent his men to the inn to investigate who has been stealing shoes. When they searched the building, they found Bronwen's shoes in this man's chamber." Urien pointed at Gwil. "This is how you repay me for making you a King's Man? You are clearly not worthy to bear my name."

Rowli and Clovis stood behind Gwil, grinning and holding the beautiful shoes, still halfway bundled in the scrap of linen.

Gwil had done nothing wrong. Bronwen could easily explain this as a simple misunderstanding, if it weren't for the fact that telling the truth about the shoes might mean telling the truth about everything.

What was the worst that would happen to Gwil? She looked at Rhys questioningly. He shook his head. Something bad.

Saint Cadoc, saint of wisdom, forgive me. How had she let it come to this?

Perhaps all was not lost. Bronwen forced herself to give a lighthearted laugh. "What a fool I am. I must have misplaced them. I've been so preoccupied lately." She gave Lord Urien what she hoped was a charming smile while beads of sweat trickled down her back.

Gwenna smiled too, relieved. It was only natural she would believe Bronwen. Her brother was not a thief. This was the simple explanation Gwenna had been waiting for. Now that Bronwen had cleared it up, Gwil would be released.

Rowli bowed as best he could considering his bulk. "Sire, we found the shoes concealed in this cloth and hidden away in the far corner of his trunk."

Clovis also bent, following the example of his larger partner. "Hidden, indeed. Who misplaces shoes in such a careful way?"

Rowli turned to Clovis and spoke to him as though there were no other people in the room. "D'you know? The innkeeper's wife told me the boy's family is without income. His mother said Gwil would do whatever it took to save his family's land."

"Hmm," Clovis said. "No income, indeed. These shoes would pay a cottager's rent for a year."

"D'you know? I believe you're right."

Urien interrupted their conversation. "Is this true?" he asked Gwil. "That your family is in debt?"

Gwil lowered his eyes, staring at the floor. "It is." He lifted his gaze to look directly at Urien. "But that doesn't make me a thief." He glanced at Bronwen.

Was he accusing her of something? How could he believe she had done this on purpose?

"I am not a thief," Gwil repeated.

"Of course he's not," Bronwen said, still trying to sound pleasant, as though all of this was just a little furrow in an otherwise fine day. The room swirled around her, and her blood turned cold. She had to remain calm if she was to convince Urien that this was a big fuss over nothing. "It's my fault. Sometimes I'm such a straw head."

Urien patted Bronwen's hand as it clenched the throne. His voice was soft and sweet. "I understand it is difficult for you to accept the guilt of this man. You trusted him. But he has been caught red-handed." He turned to Rhys. "You know the punishment."

Rhys nodded. He glared at Bronwen, waiting for her to do something. But what could she do? If she let her secret out now, Urien would know everything. Gwil could survive a few days in prison. Just long enough to find the Gwyllion.

She dropped her head into her hands. How could she think that? Was she really willing to let Gwil go to jail? How could she even consider something so low?

Bronwen rubbed her eyes hard with the palms of her hands. It did nothing to clear her vision. Cold sweat dampened her brow. She had to say something. End this. *Tell him now*, she told herself. The words refused to leave her mouth.

The soldier holding Gwil left the room, returning shortly with a large block of wood.

"The penalty for thieving is the loss of a hand," Urien announced.

Bronwen's stomach lurched.

Gwenna screamed and sobbed. Dai put his arm across her shoulder, and she buried her head in his chest, her whole body shaking.

Rhys spoke up. "Sire, he is your best archer. He saved your life in the forest. Perhaps some mercy would be in order. Some time in the dungeons might teach him a lesson."

"I already show mercy," Urien said. "Two pairs of shoes have been stolen. I show great leniency by requiring only one hand. By law, he should forfeit both."

The soldier removed a dagger from his belt and sliced the ropes that bound Gwil's wrists. Seizing the dangling cord, he stretched Gwil's arm across the wooden block.

"Bronwen, do something!" Gwenna screamed.

Bronwen wanted to. More than anything. She wanted to stop it all. Her body wouldn't move.

Rhys's sword rang out as he pulled it from his side.

Gwil's face was the color of snow. Of the tiny white lilies that grew only on the peaks of Bronwen's mountain home. She missed those beautiful flowers, strong and delicate, blossoming where other plants could not find root.

Gwil's breathing came hard, but somehow, he managed to keep his voice steady. "I did not steal anything. I swear it."

Urien sat down in the chair beside Bronwen, pleased with the outcome of the events.

Rhys stepped up to Gwil, and the soldier pulled Gwil's sleeve up, exposing his skin. Rhys didn't take his eyes off Bronwen. *Say something*, he yelled with his dark stare. *Are you really going to sit there while an innocent man loses his hand?*

Bronwen clawed at her neck. How had this become such a tangled mess? She had to speak up. But what could she say to change Urien's mind? Her world spun faster and faster until all she could see was the small white snow lilies clinging to life along the jagged cliffs.

"My lord," Rhys said to Urien. "Are you sure about this? He saved your life."

Urien's look would have wilted weaker men. "His hand or your head."

Rhys clenched his jaw and raised his sword. The blade glinted in the sunlight streaming in through the upper windows.

"Wait!" Bronwen cried. "Stop. It's not Gwil's fault. I put the shoes in his room."

The hall fell quiet, except for the swish as Rhys slid his sword back into its sheath.

"My lord, I am the one who put the shoes in his room," Bronwen whispered. Her voice sounded like thunder in the silent room.

Urien smiled at Bronwen. "I know this is hard. Perhaps you would like to wait outside. You don't need to watch."

"Sir, what I say is true. I couldn't wear them, so I hid the shoes in his chamber."

Gwil stared at Bronwen, a baffled look on his face, but at least some color had returned to his cheeks. Gwenna ran to her brother and hugged him.

Urien's attention was only on Bronwen. "Why? Why wouldn't you wear them? You told me you loved them. Did you lie?"

Did I lie? She had told so many lies they could not be counted. She had woven a perfect tapestry of lies, each one looping and twisting around the other until the individual strands could no longer be distinguished. They all combined to form one image—Bronwen, strong and whole, loved, respected.

If she tugged on this one strand, the whole tapestry would unravel.

What would be more painful? Watching her world fall apart thread by thread or burning up quickly in one giant blaze? Both options led to the same result. Lord Urien would know he had been deceived. He would know she was a cripple.

He had told her he loved her. Would that be enough to save her? Love might help him see past her lameness. He would be shocked, maybe even hurt that she hadn't told him the truth, but given time, he might see she was still the same girl he had fallen in love with. And she still had the enchanted shoes.

Bronwen stood and left the dais. She cast one last glance at Rhys.

He shook his head. He didn't mean, *No, don't do it*. By that small gesture, Bronwen knew she was on her own. Rhys had not had the power to save Gwil when all he was accused of was stealing a pair of shoes. Rhys pitied her, but he could not help her.

It had been years since she'd seen a snow lily. After the sickness destroyed her legs, she could no longer climb to the mountain peaks. They would be blooming now, just in time for summer.

She knelt in front of the king's son, searching his eyes for a flicker of hope. Of love. Of forgiveness. "I'm so sorry, my lord. I didn't mean for it to go so far. Each moment I spent with you, I swore would be my last. But each moment only made me want one more. I am not what I appear to be."

"Bronwen," Rhys said.

She waved her hand to stop him from speaking. Wasn't this what he'd been urging her to do all along? She had to do it now, while the sight of Gwil with his arm stretched across the chopping block still burned in her mind.

She sat back on the floor. With shaking hands, she unhooked each of her magical shoes. She slipped them from her feet, hiding her head in her hands. She dared not look up at Urien. She would rather die than see the revulsion on his face.

Chapter Nineteen

An angel on the road, a devil at the fireplace.

URIEN LEAPT FROM HIS THRONE as her legs withered.

Murmurs of disbelief sifted through the room.

"All of you, leave us!" Urien roared.

The crowd scuttled for the doors, jostling their way through the narrow passages. Gwil scrambled up, staring at Bronwen's legs. Dai dragged Gwenna from the room, her eyes fastened on Bronwen's twisted feet. Even Rowli and Clovis backed away in astonishment. "Crippled, indeed," one of them whispered.

Only Rhys remained. He hadn't moved since Bronwen had taken off her shoes. She thought Urien would order him away, but he did not.

Urien stared at Bronwen. His warm summer eyes had turned to ice. Never before had she seen such anger—such repulsion—in another's eyes. She thought Rhys had a fearsome scowl, but even his darkest glare was nothing compared to the venom dripping from Urien.

"Why have you done this?" he asked through clenched teeth.

"Sir, I never meant to. I never thought . . ." That was the problem. She hadn't thought. She had received the shoes and seen the hope of a new life unfold before her. She had never considered things through to the final outcome.

"I demand an explanation." Urien spoke in a low voice, hard as the cold stone floor on which Bronwen sat, unable to stand.

She smoothed her skirts down to cover her legs. "When I was young, a sickness came to my family, taking my father, brother, and sister, leaving me like this. A few months ago, on my sixteenth birthday, a faerie witch came to my house. A Gwyllion. For some reason, she gave me those." Bronwen pointed at the shoes she had laid aside. "When I put them on, I am whole. My mother thought I should come to the city to be presented. It was a dream I had given up on. With the shoes, though, I had a chance." She looked pleadingly at Urien. "When you asked me to the feast, how could I say no?"

Urien backed away from her and took up pacing across the dais, his heavy boots smacking the ground. Those smacks were meant for her. She deserved them.

"So you lied to me. Even when I asked you to marry me?" He said the word *marry* as though it made him ill.

"I wanted to tell you, but I couldn't. I thought I could fix it. I was wrong." Even if she ever did find the Gwyllion, it was too late. Urien knew what she was.

He lifted the hem of her dress just enough to expose her legs. He stared at them for a long time. Bronwen wanted to crawl away and die. She wished now that the wild boar had taken her life. Maybe it didn't matter. She would perish from humiliation at any moment anyway. *I am ready, Saint Cenydd. Come take me away.*

"Get up," Urien ordered.

"Sir, I—"

"Get up. Now." He drew his hand back as if to strike her but seemed to restrain himself at the last instant.

Bronwen pulled herself onto her knees, wishing with every moment that the floor would give way so she could disappear into the earth forever. Anything would be better than this. She placed her stronger right foot on the floor and strained to rise up on her twisted feet. She fell hard, crying out as her head struck the ground.

"Get her out of my sight," he yelled. "Lock her up where I can never see her again."

Rhys scooped up Bronwen and carried her quickly from the great hall. Her enchanted shoes lay on the floor, right where she'd set them. She watched them disappear as the door to the castle closed behind her. They crossed the courtyard, past Gwenna and Gwil and everyone else. Bronwen buried her face in Rhys's tunic. She couldn't bear to see the disgust on their faces like she had on Lord Urien's.

If only the Gwyllion had never come. If only she hadn't been so keen to present. If only.

Rhys kicked open a door and descended a dank, narrow staircase. The sickening stench of rotting humanity rose up from the darkness below.

"Open this door," Rhys demanded of the jailer.

The man did as he was ordered, using a large key that jangled on a leather cord full of others just like it.

"I want clean straw in here immediately," Rhys said. "And a blanket and candles. Do you understand?"

The man nodded. He had a circle of baldness on top of his head that made him look more like a monk than a man in charge of torturing prisoners. The jailer left, and Bronwen heard him repeating the orders to others, passing the workload on to the servants lower in the chain of command.

Rhys set Bronwen down on a crate, the only item in her cell other than the rancid straw. She covered her nose with her sleeve to filter the putrid smell. It didn't help.

"Rhys, you were right. I was a fool."

He gave her shoulders a squeeze. "I can't stay. I must return to Urien. I'll try to calm him. Perhaps he will spare your life. I'm so sorry, Bronwen."

He disappeared into the dark.

Spare her life? Bronwen shuddered. Execution. Put to death. Killed.

It was nothing less than she deserved. At least she wouldn't have to see Urien again. He loathed her now. She knew it the moment she looked into his eyes, eyes so full of disgust.

Surely it would be something quick. Hanging. That seemed preferable to beheading. After watching Rhys nearly de-hand Gwil, the thought of an axe coming down on her neck made her cringe. Burning at the stake was out of the question. She would pray for hanging.

A group of men swooped in with pitchforks, scooping away the rank straw. A boy who looked about Tyrnen's age scattered new straw across the packed dirt floor. He must have taken pity on her because he smiled at her and went back for another load. He spread a second layer, then bowed. "There you are, my lady. Nice and soft."

She most definitely wasn't my lady anymore. "Thanks," was all she said.

He left, and the jailer returned with a wool blanket and a small cluster of candles, one of them burning in a rusty chamberstick. "Mind you don't set your floor on fire, my lady."

She was alone. Alone with her shame and her crippled legs. She had been a fool to think a gift from a faerie witch would bring anything but sorrow. She should have burned the grey bundle containing the shoes the morning she found it.

Her poor mother would be alone now while Bronwen rotted away in her cell. No, she reminded herself, rotted in her grave.

Would Urien really have her executed? If he truly loved her, how could he so easily have her killed?

Urien had scorned the beggar in the street, and he had tried to keep Bronwen from seeing his mother's burned cheek. It should have been obvious from the start that he could not abide deformity. She shook her head. It was obvious. If only she'd not been so foolish to ignore it. Had she honestly believed he would overlook her ruined legs when he could not overlook his own mother's blemish?

Then there were the lies. If her lameness was not enough to anger him, her lies surely were. He was the king's son—not used to being lied to. Her lies alone warranted death.

But what about forgiveness? Was that not also part of love? If he ever loved her, how could he not forgive?

Bronwen wrapped the blanket around her, tucking in her bare feet. She lowered herself off the crate and scooted over to the corner, where she could lean against the wall.

She closed her eyes, huddled in the straw, and pictured her mountains— the rocks and stunted trees clinging for life on the windy slopes. The tiny snow lily thriving on barren stone. She could almost smell the holly and pine, hear the honking of her geese as she prodded them in at night.

Maybe the geese had the right idea after all. Why try to be a swift? Why dance and soar in the great wide open where hawks and falcons lurk, where one strong wind could blow her so far off course there was no way back?

Better to be safe on the ground, tucked into the fold, where she belonged.

* * *

She must have fallen asleep because the next thing she heard was the jangle of keys and the door creaking open. Was she to be executed so soon? She wasn't ready. She backed as far into the corner as she could.

Rhys closed the door behind him. He had a plate of food and a mug of water. "How are you?" he asked as he handed her the plate.

She stared vacantly at her food for a moment before looking up. "You have been kind to me."

"You didn't always think so."

How many times had she been angry with him when, all along, he had been trying to save her from this exact situation?

Bronwen took a bite of bread and chewed, trying hard to swallow. Her stomach tightened, and she laid the plate aside. "What's going to happen to me?"

"I tried to convince Urien that you didn't mean to deceive him." His hollow tone told her he had not succeeded. "Tomorrow you will have a trial, and if no one takes up your cause . . ."

"I hope it's hanging," she said, still thinking of Gwil and the chopping block.

"You should be glad to know that I've talked him down from drawn and quartered."

"Is he really that mad?"

Rhys nodded. "He is."

She tried again to eat a few bites of the barley bread. It was tough and dry. "Why?"

"Do you really need to ask?"

No. She knew better than anyone what she had done.

"You pretended to be something you are not. To the future king."

As always, Rhys was right.

"Why did you hide the shoes in Gwil's room?" he asked.

Bronwen shrugged. "I thought I was leaving for home. I wanted Gwenna to have them, but her mother was asleep in her room. I never thought Urien would come after me and ask me to marry him."

"Why didn't you tell me at supper that night?"

"I don't know. I didn't think it mattered. I thought you were just talking. It never occurred to me you would actually send men to investigate."

"I had to. Urien does not always look it, but he is smart. He follows through on his orders. I would be the one in here if I purposefully disobeyed him."

She took a sip of the water. If Urien found out Rhys had kept her secret, Rhys's life would also be in danger. She moaned out loud, thinking of the terrible things she had said to Rhys. Worst of it was, in her heart of hearts, she had never meant any of them. "I'm sorry, Rhys. I'm so ashamed."

He squatted beside her. "I have to go. He doesn't know I'm here. He has decreed no visitors. Bronwen, I want you to understand that he is my ruler. I have to follow his orders. I swore an oath."

"I know. Whatever happens, none of it is your fault."

He left her sitting on the floor. She pecked at her cold pottage and bread, and when she could eat no more, she placed the plate near the door.

Her candle burned low. She lit another and fit it into the holder. With no windows in her prison, she was grateful to Rhys for the bit of light.

She stared at the candle, watching it burn lower and lower, the flame steady and bright as it slowly consumed itself.

The door opened again, and this time, Gwenna slipped through. She leaned her back against the door as it closed and stared down at Bronwen, huddled on the floor.

For once in her life, Gwenna was speechless. She must hate Bronwen now. Bronwen didn't blame her. Because of her lies, Gwenna's brother had almost lost his hand and his livelihood and his place with the King's Men. Or maybe he had anyway.

"Is Gwil all right?" Bronwen asked.

Gwenna swallowed hard. "Yes."

"And is he still with the King's Men?"

"Yes," Gwenna whispered. "I think after you . . . I think Lord Urien forgot about him."

"Good."

Gwenna hadn't moved. People naturally recoiled from cripples. It was always the same—pity or repulsion. Why could there not be anything in between?

"How did you get in here? I thought he said no visitors."

Gwenna finally tore her eyes off Bronwen's legs, even though they were hidden under the blanket, and looked her in the eye. "I gave the jailer my gold brocade. He said it would look fine on his wife."

"Gwenna, no. That was your favorite gown."

Gwenna shrugged and glanced around at Bronwen's new surroundings. Just that morning Gwenna and Bronwen had been jumping with joy to be living in the castle. Now Bronwen would finish her days in this wretched cell—not that there would be very many days.

"What will you do?" Bronwen asked.

"Dai has asked me to marry him." Gwenna smiled, then quickly wiped it away.

"I'm happy for you."

Gwenna shook her head. "What happened to you?"

"Nothing." It seemed Gwenna thought Bronwen had recently turned crippled. Not the other way around. "I have been this way for a long time. Then I received those plain brown shoes . . . Do you remember? The ones I would never take off?"

Gwenna nodded.

Bronwen quickly told her the rest while Gwenna listened, frowning. "Why didn't you tell me?"

"If you saw me like this," Bronwen waved a hand over her decrepit body, "I knew you would despise me."

Gwenna knelt and reached for Bronwen's hand. Her touch was light at first but then tightened. "You underestimate your friends."

Bronwen had not expected those words. "You mean, you don't hate me?"

Gwenna settled herself on the crate. "I'm shocked. And sad that you thought you couldn't trust me. And I admit I was mad that you lied— especially for Gwil's sake. But no, I don't hate you. You're my friend. The dearest friend I've ever had. And if we don't end up in the castle together, then so be it. It's probably for the best." Gwenna smoothed the top of her skirt. "I've decided that Urien is not so pleasing as we first thought. This explains so much about your odd behavior. And why you always wore those stupid shoes. Whatever happened to the new ones from Lord Urien after the great hall? Did he take them away? They might fit me well. I shall have Dai look into it."

Gwenna had found her tongue, and now that she'd started talking, she didn't seem to want to stop. Bronwen never imagined anyone would still like her once they saw her crippled legs, but Gwenna prattled on about Dai and "when you get out of here" as though nothing between them had changed.

Bronwen couldn't help herself. She rose onto her knees and threw her arms around Gwenna. "Thank you. You're the only friend I have."

Gwenna hugged her tightly. "Don't be silly. What about Gwil? And Dai? And Rhys? Even now, Rhys is trying to talk sense into Urien."

The jailer knocked at the door. "Time's up, miss."

Gwenna gave Bronwen one more squeeze. "I have to go."

Bronwen whispered into her ear. "I'm sorry, Gwenna. Please tell Gwil I'm so sorry. I never meant for any of this to happen."

The door creaked, and Gwenna was gone.

Bronwen lay on the straw, stunned. Gwenna had seen her shriveled legs. She knew about her secrets and lies. Yet she had given up her favorite dress just to visit her.

The uneven dirt floor dug into Bronwen. She rolled onto her side, pulling the blanket with her. Gwil seemed unharmed, so that was good. And Gwenna's prospects looked bright. Bronwen worried about Rhys. If he pushed Urien too hard, he would get himself in trouble. She hated not knowing what was going on out there. If only he would come.

How long had she been in here? She had no way to know the time of day. Not that it mattered. Her cell was midnight anyway. It must be dark outside because the world was quiet. She closed her eyes to sleep, but only visions of Urien's horrified face came to her.

Something rattled her plate. A rat, searching for leftovers. Bronwen made sure every part of her body was tucked under the blanket.

Keys clanked in the lock. Rhys. It had to be. She grinned at how lightly he'd taken Urien's orders for no visitors. Her candle had gone out, and all she could see was darkness.

The straw rustled as the door opened, followed by the scent of cloves.

Chapter Twenty

He who deceives shall be deceived.

"Give me your light," Urien ordered the jailer.

The man handed his lantern to Urien and stalked away into the complete darkness.

Bronwen pushed herself up to sitting. She had not expected Urien to come—not after his last words to get her away, where he could never see her again. She brushed the straw from her hair and made certain the blanket covered her lameness.

Urien closed the door with a thud, and the flame in the lamp flickered and nearly went out. He sat on the crate and placed the light beside him, then leaned forward, his elbows on his knees. His beautiful golden hair was perfectly in place, but something brewed behind his eyes.

He didn't speak for a long time. Perhaps he came to deliver her fate. Rhys had mentioned a trial, but she didn't see much point in that. She had shown her twisted legs to the world—what could possibly be said in her defense?

She wanted to reach out and take his hand. If he just looked at her, touched her, held her, he might realize he still loved her. He would know she was the same Bronwen as before.

She could endure the silence no longer. "My lord?" she whispered.

Urien did not look up. "I want to know why you did this to me."

She had no answer.

She could give him Rhys's explanation: *Because I am a fool.* Urien already knew that. *Because my mother sent me* only covered her first lie, not the multitude that came after. *Because Gwenna filled my head with a fairy tale.* Perhaps that might have fueled the flame, but Gwenna was not to blame.

Bronwen had only herself to thank. The path that had led her here—to this prison cell—was full of twists and turns, but she had trodden it willingly. If only she had heeded the warning signs. There had been many.

The brightness of a crown may have blinded Bronwen for a moment, but Urien himself had stolen her heart. Had it not been her love for him that had kept her weaving her tapestry of lies?

He waited for an answer.

Bronwen placed her hand on his. "Because I loved you." Only after she said it did she realize she had spoken as though it was a thing of the past.

Urien huffed softly. A bitter laugh? Or a regretful sigh?

Perhaps Urien was only in shock—as Gwenna had been. Bronwen had revealed herself with no warning, no preparation. No wonder he had taken it so hard. Given time, he might come around. Even the toughest meat softened as it stewed.

Still, that iron in his eyes as he had first looked upon her broken form—she would feel that sting forever. Even if Urien did take her back, her love for him had changed. Perhaps she was not the same Bronwen as before.

"How is that love?" Rhys had asked. She didn't see it then, that night in the barrow, but Rhys knew something about Urien's love that she had not. She had been so desperate for Urien's affection she never stopped to look deeper. She had never paid attention to what lay beyond his flattering words and gentle kisses.

"I wanted to tell you every day," she said at last. "But how could I? I tried to leave, remember? I saw how repulsed you were by the cripple in the street. I didn't want you to feel that way about me."

He pulled his hand away. He still had not looked at her.

"What about Rhys?" he asked.

"Rhys?"

"How long did he know?"

There was a thorny question. Bronwen didn't want Rhys in trouble, but it sounded as though Urien already knew. It's possible he was asking for other reasons—to make sure they both had their stories straight. In any case, Bronwen was done with lies.

"The day I got caught in the tide. That's when Rhys found out for sure. But he may have had suspicions sooner. He used to work on our manor, years ago. I didn't think he recognized me."

Urien nodded. "That explains why he tried to talk me out of going after you when you left for Ynys Môn."

Rhys had done what he could on Urien's end to keep them apart, but still, his words surprised her. "From the moment he found out, he begged me to tell you. He threatened that if I didn't say something to you, he would. I made him swear not to. I made him promise to give me more time. Sir, you cannot blame Rhys."

At last, Urien looked up, right into the depths of her eyes. The candle flickered from his far side, casting his face in shadow. Bronwen could not see his features. Yet she was visible in full light. She offered a tentative smile.

"I don't blame Rhys," he said, his voice barely a whisper.

Urien stroked her face, gently brushing back her hair and lifting her chin. He coaxed her to her knees, bringing her face close to his. Bronwen closed her eyes while his spicy sweet smell drifted through her.

"I'm sorry," he said. His breath tingled her lips. "You have no idea how sorry."

"It is forgotten," she whispered. And with his warmth and beauty so soft and near, she almost believed it herself.

He leaned so close that as he spoke, his mouth brushed hers. "I can never forget. You were so perfect."

Urien stood, leaving Bronwen floundering for balance. "Rhys has always been faithful to me. I wish to heaven I had heeded his advice."

He snatched up the candle and left, slamming the door and making the floor rushes blow up into Bronwen's face.

She collapsed onto the crate, burying her head in her arms. The coldness of his final words revealed exactly how he felt. He hated her. Not because of her lies. He despised her for her repulsive form. In her heart, she had known it from the beginning. Who would want a crippled wife?

Tomorrow she would face her judgment. She knew what the outcome would be. Execution. *Please let it be hanging.*

Chapter Twenty-One

Death considers not the fairest forehead.

BRONWEN AWOKE CONFUSED. THE DARKNESS deceived her, robbing all sense of time. After crying until she had no tears, she'd fallen asleep leaning against the crate. Her neck ached.

She strained to hear the happenings from the outside world. There were shouts from somewhere—probably the courtyard—and the occasional slamming of a door. She reckoned it was morning. The day of her trial. Today she would meet her end.

Her mother would be devastated. If Bronwen got a last request, she would ask Rhys to take her a message. She could ask for parchment and ink and write it herself, but she could not think of a way to tell her mother she died because she had lied to the king's son about her crippled legs. She would leave it to Rhys. He would know what to say.

Urien's visit last night had left her empty and hard. He had never really loved her, not if his affections turned so quickly to hate. Then again, he never really knew her. Urien knew only the Bronwen she had pretended to be. She'd always hoped love could see beyond the imperfections.

Not that her crooked legs could be considered a mere imperfection. She'd been a fool to keep her secret from Urien, but she'd been an even greater fool to think that any man would ever see past her crippled legs.

The tap of boots on stone echoed in the corridor—someone descending the stairs.

They were coming for her.

Her heart clenched in one giant, painful squeeze.

She wasn't ready to die.

She lifted herself onto the crate, straightening her dress and running her trembling fingers through her hair.

Two men whispered outside her door. The jangle of keys on a chain. Who would be sent to bring the traitor to court?

At that moment, there was only one person she wanted to see. But he was not the one standing in the doorway.

The jailor held up a small torch. It wasn't much light, but compared to what she'd had, it blinded her. She blinked and shielded her eyes. "Gwil?"

"My lady." Gwil bowed. "I am sent to bring you to the castle." He wore the King's Men tunic, so at least he had not lost his position because of Bronwen.

"Please, Gwil," she said. "We both know there are no ladies in here." She swept her arms to indicate the stone walls and straw-covered dirt floor, her waste bucket rancid in the corner.

He stepped into her tiny cell and looked her in the face. "You are to me."

He smiled at her with the same smile he always had. He didn't avert his eyes in disgust. She never would have guessed the awkward boy she'd first met at the Inn of the Silver Knife would turn so quickly into such a man.

He held out a hand, ready to help her to her feet and then accompany her across the courtyard to the great hall. Bronwen allowed herself a small grin. Yes, he had grown up, but in many ways, he was still the same old Gwil. "You know I can't walk, yes?" she said.

A long-absent hint of red crept up his neck and flushed his cheeks. "Sorry. Forgot."

Gwil lifted Bronwen into his arms and carried her up the narrow stairs and out into the light. If the brightness of one torch was blinding, it was nothing compared to the morning sunlight. Her eyes burned. She buried her head in Gwil's shoulder.

"How do you plan to defend yourself?" he asked quietly.

"Defend myself?"

"Yes. You must let someone take up your cause. Plead your innocence."

A claim to innocence was beyond her reach. Her guilt was obvious, written on her crooked legs for the world to see. It was not a trial that awaited her in the great hall, only sentencing, a chance for the king's son to tell his kingdom about the deceitful crippled girl and declare her punishment.

"No one will take up my cause. Urien knows what I did, and there is nothing left to plead. I have no defense."

Gwil slowed his pace. His arms had to be aching from carrying her, yet he seemed reluctant to reach the castle. "Bronwen, don't you dare give up. He is being an imbecile about this. Don't give up without a fight."

"Gwil." She gave his cheek a kiss. "You have been so good to me."

He stopped and hitched her up higher in his arms. "Do not speak to me like you are saying good-bye."

The door to the great hall opened, and a guard motioned Gwil to bring her in.

"Listen," Gwil hissed in her ear. "You must tell Urien you were bewitched by the Gwyllion."

"Bewitched? But—"

"Do it." It was all he had time to say before he crossed the threshold into the hall.

The room was filled with people. They parted, opening a pathway to a single stool set directly in front of the dais. Gwil lowered her onto it, then stepped away, positioning himself beside Gwenna and Dai.

Lord Urien sat on a throne. Bronwen was not surprised to find the queen absent, but she thought at least the king would be there. The other throne—the one she had sat on just yesterday—had been removed.

Behind Urien stood Rhys, captain of the guard, one hand resting on the gilded back of Urien's seat and the other on his sword. He looked at her, his eyes dark and shuttered.

Lord Urien did not stand when he addressed the assembly. He raised his hand, and the crowd hushed. "We are here today to pass judgment on this woman, Bronwen Mawr."

She had forgotten to tell Urien her real name was Hardd, not Mawr. Should she do so now? She listed in her mind the falsehoods she had told that still needed clarification. She looked at Rhys, ready to confess the truth, but he shook his head the smallest bit. A signal for her to keep silent.

The door to the great hall opened. The queen entered, followed by two of her attendants, one of them Mared, Dai's sister.

Lord Urien jumped from his seat. "Mother." Clearly, he had not expected her.

The queen's wimple covered most of her face, especially the scarred side. She walked to the center of the dais. Of all people, the queen would be sympathetic to Bronwen's cause. She had been so kind to her in the solar. But when the queen's eyes rested on Bronwen, they held no sign of sympathy.

"My lady," Bronwen said.

The queen lowered her gaze to Bronwen's deformed legs. Her lip curled as though she'd just caught a whiff of stable waste. Without a word, she nodded to her son and left the room.

She had come to see the crippled girl. The girl who had been so unworthy to be in her presence.

Lord Urien waited for the door to close behind his mother. He sat back in the throne and turned his attention to Bronwen. "Bronwen Mawr, you are accused of lying to the king and of gross deceit against the royal family." Though he spoke with authority, Urien's body sagged in his chair and dark circles shadowed his eyes. It seemed he'd had a restless night, though his lack of sleep did not diminish the hatred that flooded his voice. "What do you say?"

Everything Urien claimed was true. She could not deny it. All she could do was plead for mercy. She had to convince Lord Urien that it was never her intent to hurt him. Gwil had told her to blame the Gwyllion. Everyone feared the faerie folk—except Rhys—so perhaps it might help.

Bronwen considered the Gwyllion's part in all of this. Something in the shoes had called to her to put them on, but after that, Bronwen had worn them because she'd wanted to.

Or so she thought. Had the power of the shoes muddled her mind? It seemed not. She felt the same in her head as she always had, but how could she ever be sure?

One thing was for certain; she would not lie about it again.

She looked over at Gwil. He nodded his head and mouthed Gwyllion. She turned to Rhys. He surprised Bronwen by also nodding. Why? What did he know?

"Speak," Urien said.

"Sir, I cannot excuse what I have done."

The crowd shuffled and nodded in agreement. They probably longed for a good execution. Now that the festivities of Calan Mai had died down, they needed a new entertainment.

"I can only say how very sorry I am, and I pray Your Highness will understand I never meant for this to happen."

Another nod from Rhys, not of agreement but of urging. He wanted her to say more.

"I received a pair of enchanted shoes from a faerie witch. A Gwyllion. I could not resist them, my lord." What she said was true. *Let them make of it what they will.*

Urien stood. He looked out over the group that lined the sides and back of the great hall. "She admits she has lied and deceived. But because she claims she herself was bewitched by a faerie, there is only one way to prove her guilt. I call for a wager of battle."

Murmurs swept the room. Trial by combat? It was almost unheard of. Why would Lord Urien offer her that? This news opened a tiny window of hope—a chance to survive, an opportunity for her to leave the city with her life. But at what price?

As a woman, she would have to have someone champion her. She glanced at Gwil. He looked just as shocked as everyone. A wager of battle called for swords, not bow and arrow.

Hopefully Gwil recognized he could not win such a wager. But if not Gwil, then who? Dai? Rowli or Clovis? Those were all the men she knew. As far as she could tell, Gwil was the only one who even liked her. None of them deserved to come to harm on her behalf.

Urien would not fight for himself and risk mortal injury. The ruling men never did. He would choose his best man—Rhys. If Gwil went against Rhys, Gwil would certainly be killed. What purpose would that serve? Two deaths instead of one.

Lord Urien raised his hand again, calling for silence. He motioned for Rhys to come forward. "I call Rhys ap Morgan to fight in my stead."

As she knew he would. This whole scenario was ridiculous. No one could beat Rhys, so why did Urien even bother with the wager? She had lied. She was crippled. It had nothing to do with combat or winning a fight. No man in his right mind would choose to go up against Rhys and defy the king's son.

Rhys stood before Lord Urien. "I will not fight for you."

Urien stared at him. "What?"

Rhys took a step back. "I take up my sword for Bronwen."

Bronwen's heart stopped. Had she heard right? Urien would never stand for this. He put all of his trust in Rhys. This would be nothing short of treason.

Bronwen tried to catch Rhys's attention, but he kept his eyes on Urien. She glanced at Gwil. He had a knowing smile on his face.

This must have been Rhys's plan from the beginning. No other explanation made sense. How long had it taken Rhys to convince Urien to call for a wager of battle? No wonder Urien looked so tired. Rhys had likely spent most of the night persuading him that the Gwyllion had bewitched her, that the only way to prove her guilt would be some sort of trial. No doubt he had tutored Gwil too, instructing him to make Bronwen blame the faerie witch. Rhys would never have mentioned to Urien that he would not fight for him, so now his treachery was double.

It was an enormous risk on Rhys's part. His debt to her father surely didn't run that deep.

Urien cast Bronwen a vicious look. If he hated her before, he must despise her now—betrayed as he was by his friend and captain. Urien had undoubtedly come to the same conclusion as Bronwen, that Rhys had contrived this whole wager of battle. Rhys should not throw away everything in an attempt to disprove what everyone already knew to be true.

"No," Bronwen said. "I refuse—"

"Quiet." Rhys cut her off. "Do not speak, Bronwen." He glared at her until she lowered her eyes.

Lord Urien's words to Rhys were tight and strained. "You have one chance to withdraw. If you lose, the girl forfeits her head."

Bronwen put a hand to her throat. So much for a hanging.

Rhys nodded. He'd known how it would be before he put his plan in motion.

Lord Urien turned to the crowd. He needed to claim a champion to fight in his stead. The King's Men all looked away, choosing instead to examine the floor, the rafters, the windows over the dais. None wanted to go up against Rhys.

No one could beat him. Would that be enough to spare Bronwen's life? It seemed ridiculous to be fighting for something so plainly obvious. But if a victory for Rhys meant she was innocent—at least in the eyes of the law—she might live to see another day.

"I fight for myself," Urien announced.

The hall erupted in gasps.

By the look on Rhys's face, he had not expected this.

"Now. At the listing yard." Urien turned his back on Rhys and left the room.

"Rhys," Bronwen called.

He did not respond. He and Gwil were conversing quietly with their heads together.

She needed her crutch. She could not end this mess confined to a chair.

Gwenna appeared beside her and knelt on the ground.

"Help me, Gwenna. We have to stop this."

Gwenna shook her head. "It won't do any good. This was Rhys's plan. It's what he wants." She put her arm around Bronwen. "It's the only way to save you. Don't you see?"

Bronwen gripped Gwenna's arm. "What if he gets hurt?"

"Don't tell me you're still worried about Urien?"

"No. I meant Rhys."

Gwenna leaned back, sitting on her heels, studying Bronwen. "I thought you hated him."

For a while, she'd thought she did. Or at least his meddling ways. But that felt like ages ago. Now, it seemed, she couldn't get him out of her mind. "That doesn't mean I want to see him killed. Or Urien. Neither of them should be in danger. I have to end this."

She slid off the chair and began crawling across the stone floor to Rhys.

Rhys glanced over Gwil's shoulder at her, then said something under his breath to Gwil and left the hall.

Gwil stepped down from the dais and lifted Bronwen. She stood with Gwenna and his support. "Come on," Gwil said. "We've got a battle to watch."

Two guards appeared in front of them, blocking their path.

"What's this?" Gwil asked.

"Lord Urien's orders. He wants her under guard so she don't run away."

"Idiots," Gwenna said. "She can't even walk."

"Lord Urien's orders," the guard repeated.

"Fine," Gwil said. He lifted Bronwen into his arms. "You can follow behind," he told the guards.

This really was a different Gwil than she'd ever seen before. What had happened to the shy boy who couldn't even sit at the table without spilling his drink? The guards obeyed, walking behind as they crossed the courtyard and made their way toward the lists.

"Gwil, you have to talk some sense into Rhys." Bronwen couldn't imagine what would possess Rhys to fight the king's son. "We can't let him ruin his life."

"Would you rather see your head roll?"

Gwil's words brought forth the image of his hand stretched out, Rhys's gleaming sword poised, glinting in the sun. If Rhys lost the wager, Urien would probably force him to chop off Bronwen's head.

"Gwil, I never got the chance to tell you I'm sorry about putting the shoes in your room. I thought I would never be back. I only wanted Gwenna to have them after I was gone. I never dreamed it would come to all this."

He glanced down at her with a serious smile. "I know, my lady. And don't worry about Rhys. He made his choice."

Gwenna walked beside them, occasionally patting Bronwen's shoulder for good measure. Gwenna had been right. Bronwen had greatly underestimated her friends.

From the moment Urien lifted her hand during her presentation, she had been blinded. His shiny crown and golden hair now seemed like tarnished brass compared to the real gold of Gwenna and Gwil.

And Rhys.

A large crowd had gathered around the fence of the listing yard—far more people than those present in the great hall. Word had spread quickly.

Gwil set Bronwen on a center bench, then disappeared. There were only a few seats on the raised platform for viewing the yard. The bulk of the spectators crowded against the rail. Gwenna sat beside Bronwen. The two guards took up post at the entrance to the arena. Either they didn't reconsider Bronwen much of a threat, or they wanted a closer view of the action.

The two ornate chairs reserved for the king and queen were empty. Did they not know their son was competing personally in a wager of battle?

The queen had seemed attentive, verging on doting over her son. Was her burn so humiliating that she couldn't even come to watch him fight? What about the king? What excuse did he have? An improperly fitted tunic?

Bronwen did not lament their absence. She would have hated sitting there under their very noses while their son fought because of her.

"Here he comes," Gwenna said.

The crowd hushed as Urien entered the arena dressed for battle. He wore a shirt of mail over a thick, padded gambeson. A helmet covered his head and neck but left his face open. His sword swung from the belt around his waist, and in his left hand he carried a circular shield.

Bronwen wanted to melt away like a candle burned too long. The Gwyllion's diabolical plan to ruin her life had worked. Or perhaps this was her punishment for not making her pilgrimage to the Shrine of St. Cenydd. More than anything, she wanted to be reduced to a pile of wax.

Rhys hopped over the fence into the yard, dressed like Urien, except he did not wear a helmet. His thick black hair shone almost blue in the morning sun. His shield was smaller, and he already had his sword drawn.

Chapter Twenty-Two

A woman can beat the devil.

RHYS AND URIEN FACED EACH other in the center of the yard. By the scowl on Rhys's face and the fact that Urien had not yet pulled his sword from his side, it seemed neither was pleased with the way things were turning out. Friend against friend. And Bronwen the cause of their division.

Quick as lightning, Urien pulled out his sword and swung at Rhys. Rhys blocked him with a loud clang that echoed in the stillness. Urien swung again. And again. Rhys blocked every stroke but did not strike back.

"Fight me," Urien yelled. He came at Rhys over and over.

Rhys deflected all of Urien's advances. No one moved in the crowd. Bronwen had to shield her eyes from the brilliant sun to watch the battle.

"Come on, then," Urien yelled again. "This was your idea. Fight me." He smashed his shield into Rhys's chest.

Rhys staggered back a few steps. When he recovered his balance, he lunged at Urien.

To Bronwen, it looked like some kind of barbaric dance—the two men circling, striking, and blocking, spinning and dodging in a perfect rhythm. The clash and ringing of metal on metal, the scuffle of boots in the dirt, the grunts of fighting men the only sounds to fill the air.

Rhys struck out at Urien with his shield, catching him across the side of his head. Urien's helmet flew off, and blood dripped from his lip.

Sweat matted Urien's hair. It must have been an oven inside the metal helmet with the sun beating down. Both men stepped apart for a moment, bent and breathing hard. A fire burned in Urien's eyes. It frightened Bronwen. He had always been so easy before, constantly teasing and quick to laugh. Now he looked like the wild boar that had nearly killed him.

Urien charged at Rhys with a savage yell. They pounded at each other, on and on, swinging their swords and battering with their shields.

Urien's skill surprised Bronwen. He'd always made Rhys do his fighting for him, so she'd assumed Rhys would quickly beat him. But Urien returned all of Rhys's strikes with powerful moves of his own.

Urien swung his sword hard into Rhys's shield, knocking him off balance, but Rhys used the momentum to spin full circle and land a blow on Urien's arm.

Urien stepped back, pressing his hand on the injury. When he took it away, his fingers were red.

Bronwen covered her eyes. How could she watch either one of these men die? One was the king's son and the other the captain of the guard. Both of their lives were worth ten times her own.

"Help me, Gwenna," Bronwen said. "Help me stand. I need to stop the fight."

Bronwen clung to Gwenna's arm, putting most of her weight on her friend.

"Stop!" Bronwen called. She tugged on Gwenna's arm, and they limped forward, ducking under the rail of the listing yard. "Stop!" she called again.

Rhys backed away from Urien, holding up his hands. His face glistened with sweat, and his breath came hard. He had a cut above his left eye, and a thin line of blood trickled down his cheek.

Leaning on Gwenna, Bronwen hobbled forward, then fell to her knees. "Lord Urien," she said. "I yield. I am guilty of all you have said. Take my life and end this."

Urien scowled at her with a look of ultimate contempt. "Guards," he called. "Get her out of here."

The two men who had been guarding the entrance rushed forward and grabbed Bronwen by her arms. They dragged her toward the platform. Each of them had a sword hanging from his belt. But also a dagger. She snatched one of the knives from its sheath and sliced at the man, grazing his forearm. They dropped her.

Bronwen scrambled to her knees and held the dagger's point to her heart.

"What are you doing?" Rhys asked. "I can beat him."

Bronwen looked at Urien. He was watching her, finally looking at her as he hadn't since she removed the shoes. His eyes were softer—still full of anger but not crazed.

"I don't want him beaten," Bronwen said. "I couldn't bear it if anything happened to him."

Rhys shook his head and turned away.

Urien stared at her.

"I couldn't bear it if anything happened to either of you. Not because of me."

Rhys spun around. "So what? You're going to cut your heart out?"

"If it will stop the fighting." She spoke softly. Urien and Rhys moved closer to hear. "It's not right that either of you get hurt when I am the one to blame."

Rhys stabbed his sword into the packed dirt. "Just when I thought you were done being a fool." With one step, he swiped the dagger from Bronwen's hands. He flipped it so he gripped the blade and then tossed it to the guard.

Bronwen kept her eyes on Urien. He moved closer and bent down, wiping his brow with his gloved hand.

"You lied to me," Urien said, his voice slow and deliberate. Yet there was something in it, something beyond the threatening words.

Over Urien's shoulder, Bronwen saw Rhys take up his sword.

"I did lie about the shoes and my legs," she said. "And I am more sorry about it than you will ever know. But I did not lie about this." She gestured at some invisible bond between the two of them. "I loved you."

Urien stared at her, seemingly oblivious to the crowd that strained to catch their words. Rhys inched closer.

Bronwen spoke quickly. "I am the one who must be punished. Not you or Rhys. Please. Take my life, and justice will be served." She lowered her gaze. "I would ask for a hanging though."

Urien didn't move. His sword thudded as it slipped out of his hands and hit the earth. He backed away a step. Then two. "Take her," he said, his eyes still on Bronwen.

"Sire?" Rhys asked.

Urien turned his head toward Rhys, though it seemed difficult for him to take his eyes off Bronwen. "I said take her. You have won. I yield my claim."

No one moved for a long moment.

"Do it," Urien said. "Before I change my mind."

Rhys cast his shield aside and pushed his sword into its scabbard. He plucked Bronwen from the dirt and carried her from the yard. With giant strides, he hurried toward the stables.

Her trial was over. Urien must have found some kind of mercy deep inside because now, it seemed, she was free to go. Maybe, in some small part of his soul, he still loved her.

She was surprised to find she didn't care. What she'd said was true—at least partially true. She thought what she'd felt for him was love. But when the man who asked her to marry him, who said he wanted to spend the rest of his life with her, threw her into prison and suddenly could not bear the sight of her, well, her feelings had changed. What she'd thought was love was something else.

Rhys's huge black horse waited for him, hitched to the stable fence, saddled and ready to go.

"What are you doing?" she asked.

"Getting you out of here, like Urien said." He set Bronwen on the horse behind the saddle. She leaned out of the way as he swung his leg up and sat in front of her. With a quick jab to its side, the horse bolted out of the paddock.

Bronwen threw her arms around Rhys and clung with all her strength as the beast charged past the spectators. Bronwen caught a glimpse of the golden-haired Urien treading his way to the castle. He did not look up as they flew past.

For the second time in as many days, Bronwen sat astride a horse as it plunged through the city streets.

"Where are we going?" Bronwen called to Rhys.

"I'm taking you home."

Chapter Twenty-Three

In every pardon, there is love.

RHYS KEPT HIS HORSE AT a run until they cleared the east gate. As they moved into the trees, he slowed to a walk.

Bronwen could hardly believe what had happened. "Am I really free?"

"Yes," Rhys said. "But if I were you, I wouldn't think about going back anytime soon."

"Never," she told him.

"Not even to see the handsome Lord Urien?"

She shook her head. He was a bad dream—the kind that started off wonderful but ended with screaming.

"I think I'll be fine if I never have to see Lord Urien again," Bronwen said.

Rhys twisted around in his saddle and looked at her. "Do you mean that?"

"Yes." She relaxed her grip on Rhys's waist but kept her arms around him even though the horse walked at an easy pace. "I may have been overwhelmed by his good looks and his royal charms at first, but now that it's over, I don't feel sad to leave him." She shrugged. "Not like I thought I would."

Urien was disgusted because of her deformed legs. He hated her for being crippled and keeping it secret. But as she thought about it, Urien had something of his own he tried to keep hidden, something deeper than twisted limbs. Something broken at his core.

They rounded a turn in the forest path. Up ahead, someone waited for them. It was Tyrnen. He sat astride a horse and held the reins of two others—one of them being her own horse, Ferlen.

"What's Tyrnen doing here?" Bronwen asked.

"He's coming with us," Rhys said.

"Us?"

"I told you. I'm taking you home."

Yes, he had said that. But was he really going to take her all the way to Glynbach? More likely, Rowli and Clovis lurked somewhere nearby, waiting to escort Bronwen back to her mountain village. Then Rhys would be free to return to Sedd Brenhinol to resume his status as the best warrior the King's Men had. Surely when tempers died down Urien would want Rhys back in his service.

"What about my things?" Bronwen asked. All her clothes were still at the castle, and her crutch was who knew where. Without her faerie shoes, she needed that crutch.

"And what about the shoes. Where are my enchanted shoes?"

"Urien has them, I think. I haven't seen them since you took them off."

She'd wondered if she might not get them back. But if Urien had them, she'd never see them again.

Rhys reined in his horse as they reached Tyrnen, then slid off. "Your belongings are all here." He motioned at the bundles strapped to Ferlen. A long, thin object covered in sackcloth hung at the horse's side. Rhys took it from the animal and unwrapped it.

It was her crutch. He leaned it against a tree, then reached up to lift Bronwen off the stallion.

She stared at him. "You did this."

Rhys lowered his arms. "Huh?"

"You worked this all out, didn't you? Convincing Urien to call for a wager, prompting Gwil to tell me to blame the faerie witch, having everything ready to go, Tyrnen waiting in the forest."

"Yes," he said, reaching up again to help her down. "And I would like to get moving as soon as possible in case Urien changes his mind, so let's go."

She leaned down, and Rhys caught her as she slid off the giant animal. He carried her toward the tree and her crutch.

"Rhys?"

"Hmm?" He grunted as he set her down and handed her the crutch. He turned and unbuckled his belt. He seemed preoccupied, his mind working on other things.

In light of Rhys's gallant rescue and the trouble he'd gone to to carry it out, Bronwen had some preoccupations of her own. All this time, she had assumed Rhys was protecting Urien, keeping Urien from getting hurt. That was Rhys's job, after all.

He'd tried to tell her the night she moved into the castle. But like so many other times, she'd refused to hear. He hadn't been protecting Urien. He'd been protecting her. Rhys knew Urien better than anyone. He knew what would happen when Urien found out about Bronwen's legs. He understood the truth about Urien's crooked soul.

The only reason for Rhys to insist so vehemently that she tell Urien her secret was to keep her from getting hurt. To prevent the ordeal she'd just gone through from happening.

While Bronwen stood contemplating, leaning on her crutch, Rhys and Tyrnen switched into some kind of practiced routine. Rhys took off bits of clothing and weaponry, passing them to Tyrnen, who tucked them safely onto the extra horse. Tyrnen pulled off Rhys's outer tunic—the one with the ensign of the king—and worked on stowing it in a small saddle pouch.

Rhys struggled to remove his mail. Bronwen hurried over to him. She hadn't used her crutch in weeks. She'd forgotten how proficiently she could get around.

"Let me help you with that," she said.

Rhys didn't question her ability to be useful. He didn't comment on how a crippled girl wasn't strong enough to assist. He didn't object, saying her frail frame might get hurt. He simply bent forward, arms up, and Bronwen tugged, pulling the heavy metal garment over his head. When it was free, the weight of it knocked her to the ground.

"You all right?" Rhys asked, picking up the mail and handing it to Tyrnen. Rhys lifted Bronwen and tucked her crutch back under her arm. "Can you loosen the laces?" he asked, turning his back to her.

Bronwen untied and eased the cords that secured his gambeson. He wiggled out of it until all he wore was a linen undershirt that clung to his sweaty chest.

He tossed the gambeson to Tyrnen, who in return handed Rhys a water bladder. Rhys took a long drink. It struck Bronwen again that it was as though they'd done this same thing many times before.

Bronwen couldn't take her eyes off Rhys. He had saved her. Again. Risking his own life, his position at court—everything—to help her. She didn't understand this man at all.

"What?" he asked, finally noticing her staring.

"Rhys, I'm sorry. You tried to warn me. I didn't listen. I didn't understand what you were telling me."

"Well, you were—"

"A fool. I know."

Rhys grinned. "That's not exactly what I was going to say."

"What?" She wanted to know. "What were you going to say?"

He thought for a moment. "Besotted."

That did sum up her stupidity quite well. "What will you do now? I mean, after I get home? Go back to Urien?"

Rhys shook his head. "He'll never take me back. Not after this."

She was a destroying angel. No, more like some kind of wingless dragon, a pathetic, feeble, limping beast scorching as she went, leaving a wide path of destruction behind her.

"You shouldn't have done this. You should have let me die. I deserved it."

"Maybe," Rhys said. Tyrnen handed him a new tunic, dark blue and made of wool—something fit for traveling. Rhys slipped it on over his shirt. He chuckled. "You certainly did get yourself into a mess."

"And you should not have given up your position with Urien to get me out of it."

Rhys finished fastening his sword belt around his waist. He tugged and straightened his clothes, then looked at Bronwen. His black eyes gleamed as he appraised her long and hard. "Bron, do you know what your problem is?"

A list of problems ten miles long flitted through her mind. Rhys had a point to make, so nothing she could say would matter anyway. Better to let him get on with it. "No."

"You think your problem is this." He pointed to her crippled legs. "When really, it's this." He touched his fingers to her heart. "You think that because you are lame no one will love you. You think your limp is all they can see. You are wrong."

She shook her head. Rhys was the one who was wrong. Who in her village cared at all for her? Wherever she went, people stared or turned away. In the end, her deformity was all Urien saw. Even after asking her to be his wife, as soon as she showed him her legs, he tried to have her executed.

"But—"

Rhys waved his hand, cutting her off. "What did Gwil see?" he asked. "After he learned the truth?"

Bronwen shrugged. When Gwil came for her to take her to trial, he said she would always be a lady to him.

"Well?" Rhys asked, pressing her to answer.

"He called me 'my lady.'"

Rhys nodded. "And Gwenna?"

"She said I was her friend. A good friend."

Rhys nodded again. "I've known you for a long time now. I saw how hard it was for you to lose so many of your family. I saw you suffer beyond what I thought you could endure. I saw you struggle to overcome the greatest hardships life has to offer. When I look at you now, I see a woman who is both beautiful and strong."

Bronwen lowered her head. It wasn't like Rhys to speak to her thus, so gently and kindly. Since she met up with him in the city, he'd kept things more on the vexed and annoyed side. She glanced up at Tyrnen. He quickly turned away and fussed with his horse's bridle.

"That is not what Urien saw," she said.

"Then it is Urien who is the fool for not seeing what he had."

She couldn't help smiling. Clear back when she was a girl, Rhys had known what to say. And he'd done it again just now. He'd teased and joked and then spoken the exact words she'd needed to hear.

"But what will you do? Where will you go?" she asked. He would never find a position as good as captain of the guard.

"I've been thinking," he said. "Maybe I'm ready to settle down. I'll take you home, then find myself a nice girl to marry." He looked thoughtful as he considered his future. "Maybe there is a family somewhere who needs a good, strong man. A family with an available daughter. But she must also be a lady. And someone who will be a good friend." He brushed a leftover straw from her hair, never taking his eyes off hers. "Someone who is both beautiful and strong."

Did he mean her? She glanced over her shoulder as if some exquisite maiden might emerge from the trees. That seemed more likely than Rhys meaning her. He knew she was lame.

The Gwyllion's words came to her mind. *Stars do not shine on dreamers but only on those who see the truth.*

What was the truth?

She had been a dreamer; that was truth. To think she had honestly believed she would marry the king's son. No girl had dreamed bigger. She'd thought Urien's love for her was truth. She had been altogether wrong. Urien had not loved her; that was Urien's truth.

What was Rhys's truth?

A dozen scenes played through her mind. Rhys, sitting at her bedside through the night, trying to bring down her fever. Rhys, rubbing her feet with salve, working to get some strength back into them. Rhys, carrying her up the mountain to see the snow lilies in bloom. Rhys, facing Urien in the wager of battle, giving up everything—to save her.

He'd done more for her than any other man alive. That had to count for something.

That had to count for everything.

The truth hit her softly yet utterly and completely. She cared for Rhys more than she'd ever cared for anyone.

She lowered her eyes and stared at her ruined legs.

But no.

It couldn't be.

She was mistaken.

With barely a whisper, she repeated the question she had asked herself for eight long years. "Who would want a crippled wife?"

Rhys took a step toward her. With a rough and calloused finger, he wiped a tear from her eye, then reached out, pulling her close. "I think I might know someone."

She closed her eyes and breathed in. Rhys did not smell like costly scented oils. He smelled like strength and safety. He smelled like hard work during the day and warm, quiet evenings by the fire. Soft whispers in the bed at night. No spice from anywhere in the world could smell better.

She lifted her head so she could see his face. "Do you mean Gwil?"

Rhys grinned. "Well, look at you making jests. I learn something new about you every day."

But, of course, that wasn't true. He knew her better than anyone.

Rhys leaned down and kissed her, one hand pressed on her back and the other laced in her hair. She took hold of his shirt with both hands, pulling until the space between them disappeared.

It left her breathless.

Not breathless because of fear, worrying in the back of her mind about hiding her secret. Rhys kissed her for herself, knowing full well the lies she had told and the truth about her legs. That Rhys would love her—and she knew beyond doubt that he did—that was what took her breath away.

Tyrnen had apparently had enough of standing awkwardly by. He cleared his throat. "Rhys, should we move on?"

Rhys pulled away and nodded. He placed one more kiss on Bronwen's head. Then he and Tyrnen turned their attention to securing the gear, organizing it on the animals, and shifting the loads to keep them balanced.

Bronwen's gaze wandered out into the forest. A light flickered through the trees. A lantern, barely visible in the daylight.

The Gwyllion.

Bronwen glanced at Rhys and Tyrnen. Tyrnen had his horse's foreleg curled onto his knee, and Rhys was bent over it, running his hand along the hoof. Bronwen slipped away into the woods, following the light. The Gwyllion might have the shoes. Maybe Bronwen could get them back.

The Gwyllion waited for her in a clearing. She clutched a grey bundle in her skeletal arms. Her lopsided face contorted into swells of wrinkles and sags—a smile of some sort, Bronwen supposed. Or maybe a grimace. She couldn't tell.

Coils of grey mist swirled in her eyes and seeped out from under her robes. She stared at Bronwen without speaking.

Bronwen's eyes fell to the bundle in her arms. Was it the shoes? It looked like the shoes. How did she get them from Urien?

The Gwyllion squeaked and rattled, her shoulders jerking up and down. She was laughing.

"Why are you here?" Bronwen asked, no longer caring about offending the faerie witch. "Haven't you done enough?" Bronwen took another step toward the bundle.

"I am but a weary old woman. What could I have done?"

"You gave me the shoes and made me believe myself in love with a man who tried to kill me."

The Gwyllion shrugged. "I gave you the shoes. What you did with them was entirely up to you."

Bronwen said nothing, her thoughts absorbed by the bundle. Was it them, wrapped in that mound of cloth?

"And?" the Gwyllion prodded, glancing over Bronwen's shoulder. "Did you find what you were looking for?"

Bronwen's mind flashed to Rhys. "Yes. Yes, I did. But as you see, I am still lame."

The Gwyllion nodded, regarding Bronwen with her misty grey eyes. "You want the shoes back." The Gwyllion slowly held out the bundle, offering it to Bronwen.

Several paces separated her from the Gwyllion. Bronwen took a step forward. It would be better for Rhys if she could walk. A long and tedious life waited for him if he was married to a crippled girl. The shoes would make it so much easier.

She leaned on her crutch and took another step. Rhys said he loved her for who she was. And wearing the shoes was not easy. The pain when putting them on was nearly unbearable. But what was a moment of pain if it would make Rhys happy?

She took another step. If she stretched out her hand, she could take them. They would be hers forever. She need not wear them every day, only on special occasions. Or when life called for a strong set of legs.

She reached out.

Rhys hated the shoes. It had taken all his self-restraint to keep from hacking them to pieces that day on the beach—and probably every day since. Only a moment ago, with her warped legs and her crutch under her arm, he'd told her she was beautiful and strong.

If she took the shoes now, it would not be for Rhys but for herself. To appease her own misgivings. To make her into someone else.

What was Bronwen's truth?

She'd thought the shoes would make her into something better, but they hadn't. They'd led her down a murky path of suffering and sorrow.

Who was she really? Bronwen perfect and whole, hiding behind lies and deceit? Or Bronwen the crippled girl, broken but strong, out there for all to see?

She had Rhys now. And her mother. And Gwenna and Gwil. And Tyrnen. They all loved her for herself.

She didn't need shoes or faeries to be whole. She was whole already. She had always been whole.

That was her truth.

Legs twisted or straight did not change who she was in her heart. But Urien had not looked at her heart. He, like so many others, judged only the vessel, not knowing what was inside.

"No," she said, though her voice shook. "No. This is who I am. I will be loved or hated for myself."

She took a step away from the Gwyllion, her eyes still on the bundle. Another step back. And another. Until she bumped into someone. She spun around.

"I turn my back for one moment . . ." Rhys said.

Bronwen flung her arms around him, letting out a quick, choking gasp. "I didn't take them."

"I know," Rhys said. "I saw. Did you think I'd let you wander into the forest alone? It's dangerous out here."

Bronwen turned back to the Gwyllion. She was gone. Just a tendril of grey mist lingered, quickly swept away by the breeze.

"You made the right choice," he said.

It had nearly torn her in two, but yes. *Thank you, Saint Cadoc, giver of wisdom.* She had made the right choice.

"And you!" Bronwen jabbed her finger at Rhys's chest. "You have to acknowledge that the Gwyllion is real."

He laughed. "Very well. I admit I saw something that looked like it may have been similar to what people describe as one of the faerie folk." Rhys lifted her up and headed back toward the horses.

"You don't have to carry me. I can walk." She held up her crutch to prove her point.

He pulled her closer, tighter in his arms. "I know."

Rhys hoisted Bronwen onto the back of his horse. "Let's get you home." He handed the crutch to Tyrnen, who stowed it on the palfrey.

Rhys mounted, and Bronwen slipped her arms around his waist. Maybe she didn't need to be a swift after all. Perhaps there was something between swift and goose. She thought of the thrush in the hawthorn grove on the day of the boar hunt.

He did not soar through the skies or waddle on the ground. He was content to sit among the thorns, wearing his brown mottled plumage, singing his beautiful song.

Over Bronwen's shoulder, Sedd Brenhinol disappeared forever. She turned her face forward. Whatever the Gwyllion had intended by giving her the shoes, Bronwen's contentment was complete. She'd found her truth; it had been in her heart all along.

About the Author

JULIE DAINES WAS BORN IN Concord, Massachusetts, and was raised in Utah. She spent eighteen months living in London, where she studied and fell in love with English literature, sticky toffee pudding, and the mysterious guy who ran the kebab store around the corner.

She loves reading, writing, and watching movies—anything that transports her to another world. She picks Captain Wentworth over Mr. Darcy, firmly believes in second breakfast, and never leaves home without her verveine.

To learn more about Julie Daines or to contact her, visit www.juliedaines. com.